To Josh, for being my exception.

THE HIT LIST

NIKKI URANG

Spencer Hill Press

Contact: Spencer Hill Press, PO Box 247, Contoocook, NH 03229, USA

Please visit our website at www.spencerhillpress.com

First Edition: November 2014
Nikki Urang
The Hit List: a novel / by Nikki Urang – 1st ed.
p. cm.
Summary: Aspiring dancer who was betrayed by her former partner must start over in a new conservatory where she becomes the focus of a game of sexual conquest.
The author acknowledges the copyrighted or trademarked status and trademark owners of the following wordmarks mentioned in this fiction: iPod, Frisbee, Fortune 500, Google

Cover design and interior layout by Jenny Perinovic

ISBN 978-1-939392-32-9 (paperback)
ISBN 978-1-939392-31-2 (e-book)

Printed in the United States of America

1

IN A WORLD OF MEDIOCRE TALENT, ONLY THE EXCEPTIONAL SURVIVE. THEY THRIVE OR WITHER, SOAR OR FALL, EXCEL OR FAIL — AND TO THAT, THERE ARE NO EXCEPTIONS.

I never should've agreed to do that stupid article. I shove the magazine back onto the shelf and pull another magazine over the top to partially cover it. Not that it will do any good. The bright red letters of the "Jeté" in *Jeté Magazine* are recognizable to half the students here. It's probably the most popular magazine at our little campus book store. Even hidden, my naive happiness taunts me from the glossy page.

My huge performance smile on the cover makes me look fake, even though it was genuine at the time. My blond hair was brown then, and it curls around my face and shoulders. Patrick's picture is farther down the page, hidden by the fitness magazine I used to conceal it.

Good. I'd prefer not to see him again anytime soon.

The feelings I thought he had for me were nothing more than a joke. I was only there to fill the void until he could move on to bigger and better things.

Without me.

I pull the magazine out again and snatch the last three copies off the shelf before I walk to the counter. No one else will have a chance to see it if I buy them all.

The blond girl at the register looks bored as she picks at her fingernails. Her Los Angeles Conservatory for the Arts T-shirt is tied at the back to offset the bagginess of the fabric. I set the magazines down on the counter, and she lazily scans each of them and pushes some buttons on the computer.

"This issue has been really popular. I've sold like twenty today already." Her eyes stay glued to the screen as she finishes the transaction.

That was a detail I didn't need to know.

She looks up to grab my credit card and freezes with her hand outstretched. "Hey, wait. You're her. You're Sadie Bryant," she says, pointing at my face on the cover. Her eyes widen as they scan me.

I say nothing and shift my bag onto my other shoulder and glance around. "Thanks," I mutter. I grab the bag and rush out of the door.

Four days into my fresh start and it's already ruined.

The bright California sun does little to lighten my mood. My dorm is in the main building across the quad. I just want to get there without anyone else noticing me from the article. Easier said than done since the sidewalks are filled with upperclassmen coming back to campus on move-in day. I dodge around students as I make my way down the sidewalk.

Trees grow randomly throughout the space. They're unnatural against the backdrop of businesses and buildings that line one of the busiest roads in the city. A fountain rests in the middle of the yard. Water shoots six feet in the air and cascades back down around the dancer standing at the center. The mirrored walls holding The Conservatory reflect the sun and throw it back across the surface of the water.

A group of girls walk down the sidewalk, leaving no room for anyone else. They split to walk on either side of me. The red head closest to me meets my gaze and frowns. She whispers something to her friend. They both turn to look back at me with confused expressions. As soon as I see the top of the magazine the red head pulls out of her bag, I turn back toward the dorms and walk faster. I refuse to meet anyone else's eyes. Too many people have already seen the article. Too many people already know who I am. I don't want to answer questions.

The article was supposed to be featured in one of the spring issues, but it got pushed back. I'd been counting on the buzz to die down over the summer before school started again. On par with my stellar track record of luck, it released on move-in day instead.

Laughter seeps out of the crowds toward me. When I look up, two blondes sit hunched together behind the magazine. They look up at me and then whisper.

So much for starting over.

My grip tightens on my bag. That article won't define me. I came here for a reason, to start over, to live my life how I want, to forget about everyone back in New York who had no problem forgetting about me first.

I can be the exception, the one who comes back from injury and a failed partnership to achieve greatness.

"Sadie!"

I whip around at the sound of my name. Brielle and Adam jog toward me. Brielle wraps her arm around my shoulders in a half-hug when she reaches me.

"Hey, roomie." Brielle runs a hand through her bangs to get them off her face. A few strands of her brown hair fall forward again to frame the edge of her cheek and curl around her chin.

"Hey, guys."

I pull out of her grasp and lean away from her. Brielle moved in this morning, but she acts like we're best friends already. I don't want to make it awkward, but I don't need friends here—especially not ones that I'll spend the entire year in competition with. Even the way she stands marks her as competition, with her posture and perfect turnout. Brielle's been classically trained for years, which ratchets her up a few notches on my competition meter. The whole reason I'd made the decision to come to The Conservatory instead of staying closer to home at New York Academy, the school feeding directly into the New York Ballet Company, was to get away from classical ballet. The only thing it symbolizes for me now is everything I've lost.

"So, I found something special this morning." Brielle pulls the magazine out of her bag and holds it up in front of her. "Look how adorable you are."

I sigh. I'm never going to be able to escape this. My face is everywhere. Which means my story is too. The past doesn't seem to want to let me go.

The article was supposed to talk about how Patrick and I were one step away from the New York Ballet Company. Except the interviewer came about a week too late. I'd already gotten hurt. I guess he did the only thing he could. He wrote about how Patrick was the new shining star at NYBC and pretty much painted me as a has-been.

"How did you even get that so fast?" I ask. I know it's popular, but not this many people should know about it yet. It just went on sale today.

Brielle raises an eyebrow, like that's the dumbest question she's ever heard. "Priorities, Sadie. I picked it up on the way to campus this morning."

Of course. Priorities.

"It's a good article." Adam takes the magazine from Brielle and flips through it. He's a little taller than me. Sections of his wavy hair cling together where his hair product wasn't applied evenly. His button-up shirt stretches tight across his broad chest.

Brielle puts her arm on Adam's shoulder and leans into me. "So what really happened with your partner? The article was kind of vague. Did he cheat on you? Is that why you left New York?"

I should be more prepared for this. I should have the answers to these questions rehearsed and be able to repeat them back in my sleep, whether they're the truth or not.

"I don't want to talk about it."

But I don't. I guess I hoped the whole thing would disappear.

Adam glances at Brielle, silent communication passing between them. I let them have their moment and continue toward the dorms.

It'd be easier if Patrick had cheated. At least then I would feel like he left me for someone else. In reality, he left me for himself and his career. He was the one who caused the hip injury that took me out for six months. He was the reason the New York Ballet Company didn't offer me a spot.

When NYBC offered him a place in their company, he didn't bat an eyelash before accepting, even though we were both supposed to go. Together. But he didn't care. My injury meant nothing to him. He didn't see how I fell apart as my career disappeared and I watched him get everything I ever wanted.

Adam nudges my side with his elbow. "Are you nervous about class tomorrow?"

I smile, grateful for the change in subject. "No, I'm actually excited."

I can't wait to get back into a routine again. It hasn't been that long since I was in the studio for rehearsal and I've been trying to get in some time every day during orientation, but it's not the same. I'm anxious to meet the teachers, learn new things, and to feel the familiar smoothness of the wooden barre under my hand again.

Brielle links her arm with mine. "I don't want to think about class until tomorrow. Let's go get lunch. It's Tuesday and the cafeteria has epic tacos on Tuesdays."

Adam smiles. "They are seriously amazing. Just you wait."

"Let's go eat then."

I take a step toward the main building when a Frisbee skids across the sidewalk and hits my left foot. Brielle picks it up and looks around for the person who threw it. Her face morphs into one of displeasure almost instantly at the guy jogging over to us. She looks like she's still going to throw it across the lawn in the opposite direction of where it came, but Adam grabs her arm and stops her. She sighs and drops her arm to her side.

"Hey, guys." Frisbee guy's brown hair clings to his forehead. He's shirtless and drops of sweat glisten on his chest. His bright green board shorts sit low on his hips, exposing his tanned skin and the V in the muscles on his stomach.

I drag my eyes back up to his face. He watches me curiously, but I force myself to hold his stare. I don't want him to think I'm weak. I might be new, but that doesn't mean I can't hold my own.

Brielle holds the Frisbee out to him. "You could have just waited for me to throw it back, Luke."

"Hello to you, too." Luke bends over and runs his hands through his sweaty hair a couple of times. He leans back again and puts his hands in his pockets. His hair falls perfectly into place.

How is that even possible?

Brielle ignores him and crosses her arms over her chest. "Are you ever fully clothed?"

"I figure it doesn't do anyone any good covering it up." Luke looks down at his chest. He takes a step toward her without taking his hands out of his pockets.

I'd be lying to myself if I said he wasn't attractive. Which gives me more reason to stay away from him. I don't need someone like him to cloud my judgment.

Brielle makes a gagging sound and steps away from him. "I think I just contracted an STD from all the manwhoreness pouring off of you right now."

I cover a smile with my hand, pretending to scratch my cheek. It's obvious he's just trying to get under her skin. And it's working.

A smirk spreads across his face. "You used to not be able to get enough of this."

She narrows her eyes. "Let's be clear on one thing. That was a long time ago and I wouldn't touch you now with a ten-foot pole."

"Don't be so sure about that." His smile broadens.

It's getting pathetic. He's trying too hard and she's not having it. He needs to just give up and leave.

Their conversation is interrupted by Luke's phone chirping. His thumbs glide across the screen as he returns a text message.

"Girlfriend?" Brielle's tone is venomous.

"Jealous?"

She looks like she's about to slap the smirk right off his face. I'm a little fearful for him. I don't know Brielle well enough to know if she would actually do it or not, but Adam doesn't look worried. He actually looks bored. Maybe this is normal?

"I'm sorry. I forgot. You don't *do* relationships."

He shrugs. The muscles in his arms glide against each other. I focus harder on the scene around us. Anything other than Luke's muscles.

A beat pulses through the air from a group of break dancers on the lawn across from us. I focus on that. On the piece of cardboard spread across the ground. On the vibrating sound waves caressing my skin as they pass.

"They're overrated, complicated, and unnecessary for what I want," Luke says.

Brielle takes a step toward him. "You're a pig."

Adam moves closer to Brielle, placing himself between her and Luke. His face has lost all traces of boredom. "We're just going to leave. We were on our way to lunch."

Luke's gaze shifts to me. "I'm Luke, by the way. Your roommate will never introduce us so I might as well."

He holds out his hand to me and I take it. His fingers close around my hand, while ocean blue eyes pierce into mine. The corner of his mouth tips up when my finger twitches under his.

His eyes are gorgeous, and the way his hand fits around mine is perfect.

Oh, my God, no. Just no. I can't do this again.

"Nice to meet you. I'm Sadie." I take a step back to release his hold on me.

He grins at my movement. It doesn't seem to faze him. "I've heard about you. You're the second best dancer in this school, but you'll have to work to stay there."

The statement catches me off guard and I stare back at him for a few seconds before answering. I may be new, but I'm not taking that.

"What if I don't want to be second best?" That's not what I came here for. I know he's just trying to shake me, but I can't stop my competitive side from emerging.

He leans forward and I have to take a step back to maintain my personal space. His grin widens. "You'll never be the best so it's useless to try."

"Why not?" It sounds like a challenge. One I would be happy to win.

He's taller than me and I have to look up to see his eyes under the hair that's flopped onto his forehead again. His smile has fallen somewhat. "Because then you'd be better than me."

"And we all know no one can ever be better than you," Brielle says, rolling her eyes. Adam laughs from behind me. He tries to cover it up with a cough, but he's not very successful. "I'm hungry. Let's go." Brielle walks down the sidewalk away from us.

Adam follows quickly behind her. I'd rather follow them than stay here with Luke. I take a step in their direction, but Luke grabs my wrist and pulls me back. My arm rests against his chest. It's not terrible.

"Los Angeles is totally different from New York. Let me know if you need someone *nice* to show you around." The warmth of his breath on my ear rivals the sun beating down on us.

He doesn't wait for my answer. Instead he walks the opposite way down the sidewalk. The muscles in his back move in all the right ways as I watch him walk away.

Yet another person who has read that article. It's fine. I can deal with this. It's not like I needed to start over anyway. Fresh starts are for dreamers.

2

The hallways are emptier after lunch now that most of the students have found their rooms. We pass a window on our way to the dorm room. Students fill the lawn, most just chatting. My eye lands on Luke and his friend, who are still playing Frisbee.

Luke runs to catch it, but abandons his efforts when a girl with dark hair walks past him in the opposite direction. He walks backward to continue talking to her. His friend throws up his arms in frustration of the abandoned game.

Adam walks back to me and leans closer to the window. "What are you looking at?"

"Nothing." I take a few steps, but they've stopped in front of the window.

Brielle scrunches up her nose. "Luke is such a pig."

"You really shouldn't let him get you going like that." Adam pushes off the wall next to the window and continues down the hallway. I fall into step beside him.

Brielle follows us. "I can't help it. He's an asshole."

"Maybe he's changed," Adam says.

I shrug. "He really doesn't seem that bad."

She's blowing this way out of proportion. It almost makes it seem like she wanted him to be worse than he actually was.

Her mouth twists into a grimace. "He hasn't changed and he *is* really that bad."

Adam raises his eyebrows and holds his hands up in the air. "Forget I mentioned it."

Brielle pulls a key out of her pocket and unlocks the door to our dorm. She lets the door drop on Adam after she walks through. He barely catches it before it hits him in the face. He glares at her back.

"His mom probably told him to tone it down." Brielle flops onto her bed. The click of her phone screen unlocking echoes in the room.

Why would his mom even care? This is college, not kindergarten. "Why?"

Brielle stares at me. She drops her phone on the bed to give me her full attention. "You don't know who his parents are, do you?"

I shrug and shake my head. "Should I?"

Adam drops the magazine he'd picked up from Brielle's nightstand. "Probably, since they're the heads of the department."

My mouth drops open. No freaking way. No wonder he thinks he's the best dancer here.

Brielle nods and picks up her phone again. "Right? Which pretty much gives him free rein to do whatever the hell he wants. He might only be a sophomore, but he acts like a senior. And he's been taking classes here for years, even if last year was his official first year."

"Even if he wasn't, it's not surprising he would find his way to you on the first day. Luke has hot blonde-dar like I have gaydar. You probably had his meter spiking the second he stepped foot on campus." Adam thumbs through the magazine from its spot on Brielle's bed. He flips too fast to actually read anything.

"Gross." Brielle throws a pillow at Adam. He catches it and throws it back at her head.

"Well, at least you won't be fawning over Luke this year so that'll be one less distraction. The rest should be easy for you." Adam traces lazy circles on her comforter with his finger.

"I don't even want to think about it anymore. I'm over it." Brielle grabs a pillow from her bed and wraps both arms around it.

Adam frowns and plays with her brown hair fanned across his legs. He twirls a bit around his finger and holds it tight for a few seconds before releasing it. The spiral curl loosens, but stays intact. "You just keep telling yourself that."

She glares at Adam and turns to look at me. "If you take one piece of advice at this school, it's not to get involved with Luke. He's nothing but trouble."

Adam waves her comment off. "She's exaggerating."

"No, I'm not."

From the little experience I had with Luke, he didn't seem as bad as Brielle makes him out to be. He actually seemed a little helpful by offering to show me around. He can't be that bad.

"How'd you spend your break?" Adam runs his finger against the back of Brielle's neck. She scrunches her shoulders up to protect herself, but he continues.

"What break? I can't take time off. Not after my chat with Miss Catherine at the end of last semester. Not if I want to dance in Fall Showcase in three months." Brielle moves to the other side of the bed, out of reach of Adam.

Fall Showcase was one of the selling points for The Conservatory. A chance to get in front of some of the biggest talent agencies in the country and possibly walk away with a job and a contract with one of them. I'll take it. If it means putting myself before everyone else I meet here, so be it. I'm done living my life for those around me. It's time I put myself first.

If I do well at Fall Showcase, I can secure my future again. I can prove that I'm not some washed up has-been who will never be as good as she once was. I didn't leave the classical ballet world because I wanted things to be easier, and I won't give up without a fight.

Adam crosses his arms. "It's not that bad."

"Miss Catherine made sure to tell me if my technique didn't improve, I'd be looking for a new school at the end of the year. She said I wasn't taking this seriously." Brielle slides off the bed and starts digging through a drawer, throwing clothes around randomly.

She sounds like she's serious about school now even though she might not have been last year. If I had met Brielle a year ago, our similarities would have been enough for me to be friends with her.

But it's not a year ago and I'm not here to make friends. I'm here to dance.

"I'm sure that had nothing to do with you showing up to class hungover all the time last year," Adam says.

I glance up at Brielle. She must have had a reason to act that way unless she likes throwing money down the drain along with her dancing career.

The glare she throws him brings new meaning to the phrase "if looks could kill."

"You got in here, so obviously you have the talent," I say. I meant it as encouragement, but she doesn't take it that way.

She looks at me like I'm dumb and I struggle to keep my face neutral. "They don't just look at technique in auditions. If they see potential in you, you're in. If you don't live up to that potential, nothing can save you, especially not Miss Catherine."

Okay, then.

Adam sighs. "Stop it. Seriously, you're fine. Just focus on why you're here. They can't kick you out if you don't give them a reason."

"I can't leave. If I leave, they'll be right and I swear to God, I will not let them be right about this." She slides off the bed and paces in the tiny walking space down the middle of the room.

A look of understanding passes between them. I chew on my lip. I want to ask her who *they* are and what she doesn't want them to be right about, but there's a reason she didn't elaborate.

Adam shrugs, playing off her statement, but his face remains serious. "Don't let them be right."

Brielle's face softens and she gives him a small smile. She grabs a nail file off her nightstand. "Here's my advice to you. Don't piss off the teachers. They're your best bet at making it into Fall Showcase. Don't be like me and have every single one of them on your bad side within the first month. Freshman year really counts. Don't blow it like I did."

I can't even imagine having teachers on my bad side. From the time I started dance, I've always been taught to be respectful. This means too much to blow it off. I've worked too hard and lost too much.

My phone whistles in my pocket. It's a nice distraction from the nerves that have started to twist in my stomach in anticipation for tomorrow. And maybe Mom texted me back after I called yesterday. But it's not her. It's never her. It's just a stupid email.

Whatever. Adam and Brielle discuss their plans for the night, and I glance at the screen.

The email is the newest post from the unofficial blog of The Conservatory run anonymously by some of the students. I subscribed to it a couple months ago in anticipation of coming out here. Aside from the boring gossip about who's dating who and who told off which casting director after a terrible audition, some of the posts have some useful information. Like new warm-up routines or which performances are playing at some of the lesser-known theaters in the area.

But the most recent post isn't like any of the other posts I've seen on the website. It's the rules for a game.

THE HIT LIST
September 3

Welcome to The Hit List: a game of sexual conquest.

We're back and bigger than ever in our third year. This isn't like the games you may have been a part of in the last two years. It's not just a couple of guys making a list of the hottest girls on campus. It's people voting on which girl is worth the most points every week. And weekly rankings of our guys to see who is scoring the most with our ladies.

Everything will be played out online. The Hit List is about to blow up the Internet and readers of this blog have a front row seat to all the action.

For those of you who pretend to have no idea what I'm talking about and for those of you who actually don't, let me explain. Over the next several months, a group of guys will be testing just how far each of them can go with the girls of their school. Points will be awarded based on the type of sex act. The hotter the act, the more points they'll get. The hotter the girl, the greater the chance they'll be worth bonus points. One guy will come out on top by scoring the most points. He'll win the money from the pool and bragging rights.

If you want to join the game, email me using the address in the sidebar. Sorry ladies, guys only. You'll have plenty of chances for fun if you make it onto our list. Here are the rules:

RULES

1. Initial buy-in to the pool is $50 and will take place on September 7. Subsequent buy-ins will take place every Friday and can be in any amount of your choosing.
2. Points accumulate from September 7-November 30. No points for past or future activities.
3. The guy with the most points accumulated by November 30 wins the pool and bragging rights.
4. All activity <u>must</u> be consensual between all parties involved.
5. Communication between The Hit Man and the Hitters will take place through emails only.
6. Hitters are in charge of keeping track of their own points and proof items.

7. Hitters are responsible for discreetly storing and destroying any proof or other trails leading back to The Hit List at the end of the point period.

8. Anyone found to be in violation of these rules will be removed from the score board immediately and will forfeit any money they have contributed to the pool.

9. You may not alter a girl's state of consciousness using drugs/alcohol without her permission. But if the girl gets that way on her own, she's fair game.

10. You must obtain some sort of proof of your conquest. See list of acceptable proof below.

11. Cock-blocking is a perfectly acceptable form of defense.

12. No coercion or bribes of any kind to get more points.

13. Use protection.

14. Above all else, have fun and get laid!

POINTS

First Base   + 1 point
Second Base   + 2 points
Third Base   + 3 points
Home Run   + 5 points

ACCEPTABLE PROOF

1. Underwear
2. Bra
3. Picture
4. Video
5. A well known item worn/used by your conquest

More details will be provided later, along with The Bonus Girls of The Hit List.

Until then, happy hitting!

~ THE HIT MAN

"What's this Hit List thing?" I ask, holding my phone out for them to see the email.

I can't believe I didn't know about this before I decided to come to The Conservatory. Three thousand miles means a whole lot less if I have to put up with a sex game all year. It's too late to transfer somewhere else. No one will have any openings at the beginning of the semester.

Brielle grabs my phone and holds it closer to her face to read the screen. "What are you talking about?"

Adam rolls his eyes. "Oh, that's like some urban legend. It's not actually real."

Someone's done an awesome job at breathing life into this urban legend. "Looks real to me." I cross my arms.

Brielle hands my phone back to me. "Where did you find this?"

I drop my phone on the bed and sit up to lean against the wall. "It's on The Conservatory blog."

She glares at me and pushes the power button on her laptop. A few clicks later, and the blog post is on her screen.

"What the hell? I seriously thought it was just a rumor last year." Brielle scrolls through the post.

Adam leans over Brielle's shoulder. "I liked this blog, too. The gossip was fantastic."

Brielle swivels in her chair. Her brown curls fly through the air at the movement and smack her in the face. She pulls at a few strands stuck to her lip gloss. "Is that all you ever pay attention to? There was some good stuff on there. And now some psycho with a sex addiction has taken it over."

He narrows his eyes at her, like he's deep in thought. "There are days I wonder what it would be like to have your brain, to know exactly how you reach these blown-out-of-proportion conclusions."

As if I didn't have enough anxiety about starting class tomorrow as the girl in *Jeté Magazine*, now I have to worry about if my name is used in this sex game.

That's totally cool. I needed a little challenge in my life.

I roll off the bed and grab my dance bag out of the closet.

"I'm going to the studio. See you guys later," I yell to them without looking back. I can hear their bickering even after I've shut the door.

Dancing is what keeps me sane. When everything else falls apart around me, I'll always have the studio. That's where I go to escape. If anything can help with the stress, it's dancing.

The classroom side of the school is quiet. A couple students wander through the halls. Two guys walk past me and one of them whistles. I keep my eyes trained on the ground ahead of me. Before the blog post, I would have assumed they'd seen the article. Now I'm not so sure.

I round the corner toward the studios. My mom's ringtone blasts through the silence, echoing off the walls. Two weeks isn't even a record for her, but it feels like it's been forever. She'd been on a business trip when I left and couldn't be bothered to come home to see her only daughter off to college.

I slide the answer button. "Hey."

"Did you make it to L.A. okay?" she says. My mom has never been one for formalities.

"Yeah, four days ago."

"Good. I didn't pay all this money so you could throw your career away again. Focus on your dancing and stay away from boys. You'll get back up to where you were before you got hurt, and you should have a job by the end of the year."

"I know." I don't understand how someone can be so overbearing and absent all at once.

We've had this conversation before and I hate it more every time. I don't need this from her. She's not even a mother the majority of the time. She's never had a lot of time for me, only swooping in to parent when it's convenient for her.

"I'm serious, Sadie. We don't need another situation like you had in New York. I told you not to get involved with that boy." Her voice is harder than it was a few seconds ago, like she's trying to drive her point home. As if I didn't get it.

My vision blurs, but I blink back the tears. I refuse to cry. Tears will only give her more ammo to use against me, and that's the last thing I need. "I know."

"Good."

And that's why my mom will never be the mother I need. She doesn't understand how hearing "I told you so" from her hurts more than Patrick leaving.

She hangs up without saying goodbye. Typical.

I toss my bag against the wall and hook my iPod into the stereo system. I let it shuffle through my dance playlist. I don't have a preference today. The only thing I want is to get lost in music and the movements.

A violin breaks through the quiet of the empty studio. The beat behind it is perfect for what I need. I fall into improvised steps easily.

My muscles relax as the air around my body heats up. I push off the ground with my right leg and bring my left leg up behind me. My arms move over my head. My hair brushes against the bottom of my foot and a tingle runs down my leg, but I hold the position in the air until my right foot connects with the ground again. My left leg falls slower, reaching the ground a few seconds behind.

The music drifts off and a new song starts, softer than the first. A flash of green in the doorway catches my eye. I turn to catch whoever has decided to watch my private rehearsal, but no one's there.

Maybe no one ever was. Just another illusion of someone who cares before it turns to dust.

3

The studio is a flurry of activity the next morning. Half the class is already there when we walk through the doors. A couple of girls whisper to each other just inside the door. Brielle slows as we pass them.

"I heard there's this new game called The Hit List and people are, like, killing other people over it. Like a real hit list." The girl's eyes widen as she tries to show her friend just how serious she is.

I open my mouth to correct her, but Brielle elbows me and takes a step toward them. The smile drops from her face and she looks completely serious as both girls stare at her.

"I heard someone legit got killed last night because they were playing that game. You better watch your back so something like that doesn't happen to you."

The girls hang on her words. The blond one leans closer as Brielle speaks, like it's the most fascinating thing she's heard all day.

The brunette's eyes widen like her friend's and I can see the outline of her contacts. "Come on, Noelle. You can't really believe that." She frowns in disbelief, but the worry lines on her face give her away.

Brielle crosses her arms over her chest and sticks her hip out. "It's true. I saw it."

"For serious?" Noelle's voice is barely above a whisper, like it's some big secret even though it was posted on a public blog.

"For serious." Brielle glances at me. She can't hide the smile at the corner of her mouth. The girls look at each other and nod. Their faces are just as somber as Brielle's was seconds ago.

If it wasn't so cruel, it might be comical.

"Thanks," one of them says, like Brielle actually did her a favor.

Brielle walks away. I follow her to a section of unoccupied floor and sit down.

"That was mean." I glance over at the girls who whisper fiercely to each other again. It's not their fault they didn't hear what the game is actually about.

She shrugs. "They'll figure it out."

I guess. Hopefully it's before someone tries to take advantage of them.

I stretch my legs out in front of me and lean forward. My left hip tightens momentarily, a side effect from my injury last year, but it's not unpleasant. It's the familiar feeling of loosening muscles. I love it.

Anxiety bubbles throughout the room. Or maybe it's just me. I resist the urge to bounce my legs to let off some of my nervous energy. A pulled muscle on my first day will not help.

A group of older women and men who I assume are the teachers stand at the front of the room. They watch as students enter the studio. I recognize one of the women from my entrance audition. She catches me looking at her and smiles.

Adam sits down in front of us. "Hey, ladies."

I wave in response. Talking takes too much energy right now.

"Morning." Brielle stifles a yawn.

"You better wake up fast. You know more than anyone that yawning equals boredom in here. And you better never let them think you're bored."

Brielle waves him off with her hand. "I'll be fine as soon as we start moving around."

I push myself farther into my stretch to rest my chest and stomach on the floor. From my position flat against the ground, I have a perfect view of Luke where he stands a little ways away from us. I want to move, but turning my head only gives me a view of Brielle's crotch. I sigh, staring ahead again.

A pretty brunette walks up to Luke and wraps her arms around his neck. She was probably the one he was texting yesterday. I want to ignore their conversation, but despite my best efforts, I can't. They're too close and not exactly trying to be quiet. He glances at me, and I roll my eyes, drawing out a smile from him. It's a little ridiculous that he seems to flirt with every girl he comes into contact with.

"Hey, Rachel." Luke's eyes rake up and down her body, flicking over to mine on occasion.

"I had fun last night. We should do it again soon." Rachel bats her fake eyelashes at him. She wants to look cute, but instead she comes off a little creepy and clingy.

She plays with the collar on his shirt. He reaches up to remove her hand, but she laces her fingers through his and holds him in place. They're like a couple from a romantic comedy. Except from the look on his face, he's only trying to get in her pants.

A smile pulls at his lips, but he tries to play it off. Whether the act is for me or for her, I'm not sure. "What are you doing this weekend?"

I didn't think it was possible, but she moves closer to him. She might as well jump into his arms. "Spending it with you, silly."

It's like a frickin' train wreck. I can't look away.

Brielle slides closer to me and watches the scene in front of us. Her leg moves behind mine so she can keep her stretch going while she takes in the entertainment.

Adam leans back on his hands and turns his head to see what we're looking at. "What are we doing?"

Brielle waves her hand at his face. "Shh, this is getting good."

He pulls his head back to keep from getting smacked in the face by Brielle. "Ooh, Luke's new wannabe girlfriend. I feel like we need popcorn."

We stare at them a little while longer as we warm up. She continues to touch him at every opportunity. His chest, his collar, his cheek.

Brielle makes a strangled sound at the back of her throat and moves away from me and back into her own space. "Gag me. You'd think with a sex game popping up she'd be a little more discreet. Apparently no one ever taught her how to play hard to get."

"Because you do that so well," Adam says.

Brielle grabs her water bottle and squirts it toward him. He throws his hands up to protect his hair, but the water sails by him and hits another girl in the back behind him. Brielle shoves her water bottle into Adam's lap and looks up at the mirrors. The girl behind us glares at Adam and moves to the other side of the room.

"Thanks a lot. I love making enemies on the first day." Adam's eyes light up with amusement even though his face is serious.

Brielle continues to stare straight ahead. "I don't know what you're talking about. That was all you."

Miss Catherine walks into the studio and all attention snaps to her. Conversations die mid-sentence and a hush rolls through the room. Luke moves away from Rachel and she's forced to release him so they don't get in trouble for talking. She looks frustrated as she sits down, like she can't bear to be separated from him for more than a few seconds.

"Welcome, students. I hope you all had a chance to warm-up because we're going to start class. All of the teachers will be with you this week to judge your skill levels. Once we can assess you, you'll be split up by ability next week. Let's get started with some barre exercises."

Miss Catherine claps her hands and students come to life around me, pulling themselves off the floor.

Barre exercises quickly turn into floor exercises. I line up behind Brielle and Adam. A boy I don't know stumbles and earns a few frowns from the teachers. His face turns a brilliant shade of red, but he continues.

Rachel moves to the corner to start the exercise. She sickles her foot instead of pointing it coming out of a piqué turn and the extension on her leap isn't even a full one hundred and eighty degrees. She's either off her game or she didn't warm up.

It shouldn't make me happy, but it does. Every imperfection by another student makes me one more step closer to the Fall Showcase.

Brielle and Adam both cross the floor without error. I step up to the corner, my feet finding fifth position automatically. The nerves fall away as I exhale. My muscles work from memory. It's a combination I've easily done hundreds of times. I'm confident the leap looks exactly as it should with my legs straight and toes pointed.

I finish and glance at the teachers. Several of them have smiles on their faces. I chew on my lip to hide my own smile. When I look up to make sure I don't run into anyone, I meet Luke's eyes. He looks impressed with my technique. I tuck a loose strand of hair behind my ear and his smile widens. I focus on the next exercise as I rejoin the line.

Brielle shakes her head at me, but doesn't say anything. I don't get what her problem is, until I see Rachel smile at Luke and tuck her hair behind her ear in the exact same way. My stomach flips as I make the connection. She thought I was flirting with him.

Just because I don't plan on having a relationship with anyone here doesn't mean I can't have a little fun. Flirting is completely harmless. The worst that can happen is I lead him on, but Luke doesn't seem like the type to let that happen.

The girl behind me in line finishes a moment later and the teachers applaud us. I focus on them instead of on the people around me.

The next three hours are more of the same. Floor exercises, barre exercises, putting on a show for the teachers, hoping to make it into an advanced class. When we're done, sweat drips down my temples and plasters my tank top to my back.

Luke's eyes catch mine for a second in the mirror before they flick back down to his phone, but he doesn't try to hide the smile on his face. I don't try to hide my look of indifference. His smile falls and his brow creases slightly.

Miss Catherine walks to the front of the room. Her eyes scan over students around me. "That's it for today. Before you leave, I have a quick announcement. This year, the teachers will be making a decision about which student has made the most progress through the semester. That student will spend next semester in London training with an assortment of teachers."

The classroom erupts into chatter around me. The chance to spend a semester in London is an opportunity most of us will never get again in our lifetime.

There's no way that dance article has any kind of reach overseas. London could really be my shot at starting over if I can't get anywhere in L.A. There are so many opportunities there that I could never even dream of getting to experience here. Like a shot to work with some of the best teachers in the world.

"Do you know how many people in this room would kill to go to London?" Brielle whispers beside me.

Adam wipes sweat off his face with a towel. "Get in line."

"I also wanted to let you know that we're doing things a little different with Fall Showcase this year. You'll all be dancing with partners. Partner rehearsal starts next week." Miss Catherine smiles.

Dancing with a partner was not in the brochure. No one told me it would be expected of me during my interview or my audition. There's no way in hell I'm dancing with someone else. I can barely rely on my own talent half the time. How am I supposed to rely on someone else's?

"Did you know anything about this partners shit?" Brielle asks, her whisper coming out more like a hiss.

Partners? They can't just spring this on us.

Surprise. Let me introduce you to the person who holds your fate in their hands. The person you need to dance well with in order to get anywhere in this business in the next year. Or maybe even the person who will drop you and then walk out of your life when you're at your weakest point.

I don't think so.

Adam shrugs. "Nope. I guess it was supposed to be a surprise."

"That's the worst surprise ever. What if I end up with a terrible partner?"

This can't be happening to me. I can't dance with a partner.

"I got a spot at NYBC. I start next week."

My foundation falls away as Patrick's words sink in, each stone crashing louder as my heart beats faster. "You're leaving?"

Someone steps in front of me, trying to get through the crowd to their bag on the other side of the room. Brielle pulls lightly on my arm, but I'm already off balance and I trip over my feet.

Falling. Toward the ground. Toward the end of my career.

Fire rips through my hip as Patrick tries to save me. But he can't stop the pain. He can't stop the falling.

Hollow sound fills the room, the kind in a movie when a bomb goes off. Except it doesn't fade after a few seconds. It gets louder as blood roars through my ears. Stars dance across the ceiling.

You can't see the stars inside the city. That's why Patrick brought me.

"It's simple out here. There's no pressure to be perfect all the time. The only thing you owe the stars is just to be you. You need to remember that every once in a while."

"Who needs stars when you have spotlights?"

I try to laugh, but the cold air is a shock to my lungs and my chest tightens. Small gasps are the only thing I can manage until my lungs adjust. Tears freeze at the corner of my eyes, tightening the skin around them. My eyelashes clump together.

Brielle frowns at me in worry, but no one else seems to notice my current meltdown. People chat around me as they stretch out their muscles in a cool down.

"Are you okay? You look like you're going to hyperventilate," she whispers.

"I'm fine." I slam the cupboard door, but my mom doesn't even notice. She's halfway across the apartment by now. It's not like she really cares anyway.

I shove the cake mix back onto the shelf. I don't feel like making it anymore. The whole point had been for her to notice.

Happy Sixteenth Birthday to me.

I'm going to die. I can't breathe. My heart feels like it's going to explode. The tears aren't frozen anymore.

Patrick opens the door, the smile falling from his face. "Why are you here? You know we can't practice together anymore. I'm not allowed to."

He acts like he can't tell I'm dying inside. Like the last two years didn't mean everything to my career, everything to me. A permanent stutter has taken up residence in my chest, like my heart is being shocked by everything that's happened between us over and over again. It reminds me how useless I am as a partner and as a friend. I'll never get it right.

I'll never succeed here, so why am I even trying? It's useless.

Brielle grabs my hand and places it in her lap, wrapping her fingers around my forearm directly above my wrist. Her thumb presses hard against my skin and my hand relaxes.

Patrick's hand touches mine tentatively, afraid that he's crossing one of my lines. "You don't always have to be the strong one."

I pull my hand back and let it fall into my lap. "One of us has to be."

Partnerships are never good once feelings get involved. It sucks because it's so hard to keep feelings out of them when you spend all your free time with the same person. And honestly, Patrick is one of the only people I'm okay spending all my free time with.

His green eyes sparkle from the dim lighting in my favorite restaurant. "Just this once, let it be me. Let me take care of you."

"You won't always be here." It's as close as I can get to telling him the real reason.

People leave all the time without a backward glance.

"I'll be here as long as you need me." He grabs my hand again. This time I don't pull away.

"And don't forget about our fundraiser this Friday. I expect to see you all there. You're dismissed." Miss Catherine walks out of the room.

"Mom?"

Silence.

She isn't here. Again. I don't know why I'm surprised.

I check her bedroom just to be sure. It doesn't look like she slept here last night. Considering I didn't even get an angry text when I didn't come home, I'm willing to bet she stayed out too.

I turn my iPod on and crank the speakers. The music fills the house with noise and takes away the emptiness for a little while.

I can't stand the silence.

Brielle leans closer to me. "Focus on your breathing. Shut out everything else around you."

"Breathe through the pain." Patrick breathes deeply through his nose and out through his mouth.

Because apparently an injury makes me forget how to breathe.

"You have no idea what this feels like," I say through gritted teeth.

I doubt he's ever been dropped only to have someone catch him by his leg at the last moment. He doesn't have a clue.

I pound my fist into the ground to offset the pain. No one else is in the studio to help. Our teacher went home a long time ago when we first started fighting. I wish she had stayed.

He grabs my face and I'm forced to look at him. "Focus. You'll get through this."

Brielle's grip is solid on my arm and I can feel my body begin to relax.

"I've got you. Trust me."

Famous last words. I'd believed them before I ended up on the ground. Patrick's never dropped me before, not even when we first started dancing together two years ago.

What does that say about him?

He can't be bothered to make sure I'm safe anymore. It doesn't matter as long as we pull off the moves. But we aren't pulling them off. We haven't in weeks.

What does that say about us?

I count my breathing, inhaling and exhaling to the count of four, and start to name the objects in the room to ground myself in the moment.

A chair. The barre. Five panels of mirrors. The stereo. Two windows overlook the courtyard. A pigeon sits on the window ledge.

There's no place I'd rather spend my last night in New York than in the windowsill of the dance studio. This is my home, more so than the empty apartment I'd rather not go back to.

The traffic below inches along. Horns honk as cab drivers get impatient. Bikers weave in and out of the cars on the edge of the street.

I'll miss the life of the city the most.

I pull myself off the ledge and walk to my bag on the other side of the room. It rests against a wall filled with colorful handprints. Earlier in the year, every student at the studio had a chance to add their handprint. It was a chance to add a piece of ourselves to the studio.

I press my hand against Patrick's handprint. The cold cement is rough beneath my palm. The handprint stretches up past my fingertips.

"Bye."

I'm not dying.

My heart rate slows as my breathing normalizes. The pressure recedes on my arm as Brielle loosens her grip. I open my eyes. Most of the students gather their things. Some have already left. Brielle lifts my arm and places it back in my lap. Sympathy clouds her eyes, though I'm not sure why.

She stands up and offers me her hand. "Come on. Let's go back to the room."

I let her help me up and follow her out of the studio. When we reach the dorm room, I flop down on my bed and cover my head with my pillow.

"Oh, no you don't," Brielle says, pulling the pillow off my head. She stretches her body out on her bed and props herself up on her elbow on top of her pillow. "Spill."

"What?" I know exactly what she's referring to, but I don't want to talk about it.

She sits up and crosses her arms over her chest. "You know what. You freaked the fuck out in the middle of the dance studio. What happened?"

"I was just really nervous about the first day of class. That's all." I refuse to break eye contact with her.

She sighs. "You're a terrible liar."

I stare back at her. "I'm not lying." I don't understand why she cares so much about this. It's none of her business.

She leans back against her pillows. Her arms uncross and she grips the edge of one of the pillows. "Fine. Don't talk about it."

I stare at the ceiling above my bed. I don't owe Brielle anything. She's nothing more than my roommate for the next year. I was serious when I promised myself I wouldn't put anyone before myself ever again. Brielle could easily end up just like all my other friends who moved on without me.

"I used to get panic attacks when I was younger. My shrink said it was from separation anxiety. Which is probably true. I was in therapy for years."

I frown, turning to look at her, but she stares down at her comforter instead. She looks younger, like she's just a scared kid.

I really shouldn't get into this conversation with her. We're bordering on friend territory. But I feel like I have to ask. "What were you separated from?"

She shrugs. "My parents were never around. My dad's a CEO for a Fortune 500 company and my mom's involved with real estate. When they weren't traveling for business, they were too busy screwing other people to stay at home and spend any time with me. I used to have a panic attack every time one of them left because I was afraid I wouldn't see them again."

It's sad to know someone else lived through what I did with my mom. Somehow it almost seems worse that Brielle has two parents. Knowing they would rather spend time with their affairs than with their child is heartbreaking.

I frown, watching the ceiling again. "That's terrible."

She laughs. "Yeah, I guess. I'm not really sure why I cared so much that they were leaving. When they were around, they'd make it a point to let me know how much of a disappointment I was. Why do you have to be a dancer, Brielle? No one ever made money dancing. Why can't you be a doctor? Why do you have to waste your time on a useless talent?"

I wince at her words. My mom never told me I was a disappointment, but she was usually too busy with other things to pay attention to me. For a while, she'd been grieving my dad's death. I was only a reminder of him so she made sure to stay away. Then she got promoted at her job and traveled a lot for that. I guess it didn't really matter. I was never home anyway. I spent every free second I had with my real family at the studio, even though most of that family moved on when they had the chance.

Brielle rolls over onto her stomach. "You know, they don't live that far from here. Maybe ten minutes, thirty in traffic. I haven't seen them in over six months. They couldn't even be bothered to come home when I was on break."

That's awful. What's the point of having a kid if you're not willing to spend any time with them?

I turn to look at her. "Who took care of you if they were never home?"

"I had a nanny. She was the one who used to take me to my dance classes, the first person who ever saw the potential in me. She's the reason I'm here." She smiles sadly.

"At least you had someone there." I meant for it to sound encouraging, but instead the words are filled with resentment. When my mom was gone, there was no one else.

She watches me. "Look, if you ever want to talk about it, I'm here. No judgments."

"Thanks."

I'm not sure I'll ever take her up on that offer, but it's nice to have. As much as I want to tell Brielle that I know exactly how she feels, I can't. It almost makes me feel guilty. It's not her fault that I've been screwed over so many times in my past. If things were different, maybe I'd give her a chance and let her in.

But things aren't different. And people always leave when given the chance.

The lobby of the school has been transformed to accommodate the annual Los Angeles Conservatory for the Arts fundraiser. It's beautiful. White and black silk tablecloths are draped over tall tables. Similar fabric covers the barstools at the temporary bar set up on the far end of the room. A makeshift stage with white and black satin bows sits on the opposite of the room. Familiar faces surround me as students work to put the finishing touches on things before the fundraiser starts.

Noelle pops up beside us. Her shimmery blue dress catches the light and throws patterns across Brielle's plum-colored satin dress and the table next to us. Noelle's blond hair is curled into spirals and flows down her back.

Brielle jumps, her purse knocking into my arm. "Jesus, where did you even come from?"

She smiles, not at all fazed by Brielle's tone. "You were wrong, you know. No one really died."

"No kidding." Brielle's face is flat.

It's kind of sad that Noelle took Brielle seriously. I feel like someone should tell her what the game is really about so she can prevent herself from being taken advantage of.

People move past us, hanging final decorations. I inch closer to Brielle to let a guy carrying a cooler through. He winks at me as he passes. Random.

"I just thought I'd let you know so you don't get in trouble or anything." Noelle runs her hand over the back of the chair.

Brielle's fake happy voice returns. It's scary how real it sounds. "Thanks. That's so kind of you."

More students have gathered in the lobby. The overhead lights dim around us and a spotlight lights up the main stage. It changes from white to blue.

"So don't kill anyone." Noelle shrugs one shoulder and bounces off to talk to another friend a couple tables away from us.

"I don't even know how to respond to that. I think I just got dumber. Is that possible?"

Adam narrows his eyes. "What the hell was that about?"

"Don't ask."

Some of the music students play songs and sing on the stage. Other students have started to dance. Rachel and Luke are close to the stage. Her back is pressed against him. His hands grip her hips as they move slowly to the beat. There's not even enough space for air to pass between them.

Brielle smoothes the satin fabric of her dress. "Come on." She doesn't wait for an answer and grabs my hand on her way to the dance floor.

Hours later, we haul ourselves over to a table, laughing hysterically from Adam's attempt at hip-hop. I don't recognize most of the students around us. A few kids walk past us and I'm about eighty percent sure they go to our school. Rachel grinds against a new boy up near the stage. Luke is nowhere to be found.

I rest my hand on the back of a chair and try to catch my breath. Brielle hops up onto a chair gracefully, careful not to flash the entire club. She holds her fifth drink of the night.

Adam grabs it and takes a sip. His face twists into a grimace the second the liquid touches his tongue. "God, Brielle, how did you even get alcohol?"

She giggles and looks toward the bar. "I know the bartender."

Adam shakes his head and tries to cover his smile. "Of course you do." He hands her drink back to her and pushes through the crowd toward a group of kids I don't recognize.

"Where are you going?" I yell after him.

"Let him go. Those are some of his friends from Pacific Harbor. See the cute one in blue? That's Jake, his sometimes boyfriend." Brielle leans on the table, her chest heaving and a huge smile on her face.

The music students from the school take turns singing the popular songs from the radio. There is no DJ tonight. Only them. And they look like they're having a blast. The bass pulses through my chest. Little shudders vibrate my heart.

"Hey, gorgeous," someone says behind me.

I whirl around and come face to face with Luke. He catches my elbow to keep me from colliding with him. I yank my arm out of his grasp, more out of habit than anything else, and grab the table for support. He narrows his eyes, but he's not mad. He seems more curious. He wears black dress pants and a slate gray shirt. The dim lighting darkens his eyes to a deep navy.

"She has a name, you know." Brielle glares at him from beside me.

"Would you like to dance, *Sadie*?" His eyes flick to Brielle as he says my name and he holds his hand out to me.

I shouldn't. I know I shouldn't. But it's just a dance. Nothing bad could possibly come out of this. I'm supposed to be having fun anyway. That's what tonight is all about.

I take his hand and he leads me out to the middle of the floor. The music slows as soon as we stop moving.

He spins me under my arm and pulls me against his chest before I have a chance to protest. My arm automatically goes to his shoulder and his hand finds the small of my back. My ballroom teacher back in New York would be so proud.

My hand rests loosely in his. It's nice to have a connection with someone after shutting myself off to everyone around me for the past six months. This is exactly what I need tonight. It's not like it means anything.

"How do you like L.A. so far?" His mouth is close to my ear, but his words are swallowed up by the music and the dull roar of the people around us.

There hasn't been a lot of free time since I arrived in L.A. I have yet to really see what it's like outside the school. But it's easy to see the atmosphere is more laid back than New York. "It's different."

He smiles and the skin around his eyes crinkles. "Better or worse than New York?"

I pause to think of the best way to answer. New York has Patrick and my mom, but it's home and despite how much I tell myself I need to be in L.A., I miss it. "Both."

"You seemed happy there." He shrugs and my hand slips lower on his arm. "At least, you did in that article with your boyfriend."

I laugh at how things have changed since then. "Yeah, well, that was a long time ago." I don't bother to correct his terminology. It doesn't matter anyway. He's got Rachel; we're just having fun.

Luke dips me backward and I can't help from laughing again at the ridiculousness of being dipped elegantly in the lobby of our school and talking to a boy I barely know. But as crazy as it feels, it's also a pleasant surprise. Never did I think I would have fun here outside of rehearsals. It's not why I'm here.

I shouldn't be enjoying it as much as I am. But for tonight, I don't really care.

Luke pulls me back against him. His hand finds the same spot on my back again, but this time he's closer. "You seem happy here, too."

"I am." And it's the truth. Even though he brought up New York, this is the most fun I've had since I got here.

"Good. Class will only get more intense. Remember to have a little fun every once in a while." The song ends and another one picks up, the beat a lot faster than the one we danced to. "I'll see you in rehearsal."

I smile and nod. It takes too much energy to yell above the music. He walks toward Rachel who sits with a group of girls from school at the bar. She wraps an arm around him and he leans into her side.

"There you are. I've been looking everywhere for you." Adam smiles as his arm slides around my back. "Dance with me."

I don't give Luke a backward glance as Adam drags me back onto the dance floor. He pulls me into his arms and leads me easily as the music slows again in the background, a sure sign that the fundraiser is winding down.

"What's up with you tonight?"

I frown up at him. I wasn't aware I was acting any differently. "What do you mean?"

Adam glances toward the bar where I'm sure Luke still stands next to Rachel. "You seem more relaxed. I just haven't seen you like this."

I shrug, not even sure how to answer him. "I'm having fun."

We turn so the bar is to my left. I can't help when my eyes travel to the spot I last saw Luke. But he isn't there.

Adam's chest shakes and I pull away to see his face. "What?"

"You like him." He laughs again.

I lean back and stare at him. "What? I do not."

He's crazy if he thinks that. Having fun and dancing with Luke doesn't automatically mean I like him. It was just dancing. That's like saying I've liked every person I've ever danced with. And *that's* crazy. I like dancing, not him.

"Yeah, okay." He tries to keep the smile off his face.

It's not like Luke would be hard to like anyway. He's nice and completely unlike what Brielle made him out to be.

I wait for Adam to say something in the silence, but he doesn't.

"It doesn't matter if I like him anyway because it's never going to turn into anything."

He looks down at me. "Says who?"

"Me."

I won't let the same thing that happened with Patrick happen with Luke. I can't let it happen. I don't know if I can handle another fallout like I had with Patrick.

Adam sighs and pulls me back against his chest. "I've known Luke for a long time and with all his faults, at least his intentions are clear. He's broken a lot of hearts, but it was never because he let a girl believe he wanted a relationship when he didn't. He's a decent guy if you can get past the commitment issue."

Commitment issues are a deal breaker for me. If I can't trust someone to be there for me, what's the point in even having a relationship?

He glances down at me. "Trust is always hard when someone hasn't given you a reason to trust them. I know what it's like to have someone move on without you. But at some point, you have to move on too. For yourself."

I stare up at him. Whether he's guessing or not, he seems to know a lot about my life. I believe Adam when he says Luke is a decent guy. But that doesn't mean I want anything to do with him.

The music students have stopped singing. Music plays from the stereo system. There are far less people here now than when we first arrived.

Adam notices it too and cranes his neck to look up at the stage. "I think that's our cue to leave. Let's find Brielle."

Adam grabs my hand and walks ahead of me as we search the lobby for Brielle. Ten minutes later, we find her making out with some guy against a wall. Adam pulls her away and pushes her toward the hallway leading out of the lobby. She giggles and waves at the guy, making a "call me" gesture to him as she attempts to stay upright in her heels.

We walk toward the dorms with Adam practically holding Brielle up so she doesn't fall over. I trail behind them. Brielle has clearly had more to drink since we left her earlier and Adam struggles to keep her on her feet and make forward progress at the same time.

I look backward into the lobby before I step through the door into the hallway that leads to the dorms. My eyes meet Luke's as he dances with a girl

I don't recognize. He smiles at me and I can't help the shy smile that crosses my lips.

But it's just a friendly smile. Because it was just a dance. Nothing more.

THE HIT LIST: THE GIRLS
September 7

It's been a week since the third annual Hit List games launched and guys are already starting to score. But let's face it. It's boring to watch our guys run around chasing the same point values week after week.

It's time to up the stakes a little.

This is the part in our show where I introduce our bonus girls. The bonus girls are worth more points if a Hitter is able to get them into bed. The first Hitter there gets to claim the points. After someone claims points, the girl will lose her bonus status and become like every other girl in the game.

Now, before this year, these girls remained anonymous until the very end. What fun is that? In no particular order, here are the lucky girls.

RACHEL BARRONS
SAMANTHA JAMESON
ASHLYNN JENKINS
NOELLE SANSTROHM
KATE WILLIAMS
BRIELLE WATKINS
JESSIE FREEMAN
REBECCA HEMSWORTH
COURTNEY TURNER
SADIE BRYANT

Relationships are not worth anything more than your happiness. Good for you for having sex with your girlfriend, but you're not getting points for it. If a Hitter happens to enter a relationship, he is still able to get points by running the bases with girls outside of his relationship. We won't judge you, but your girlfriend might.

Hitters cannot claim points for the same girl more than once. If you're going to bang the same girl all semester, you might as well date her. For those of you who think you can cheat the system, you might want to consider how pathetic that looks. Maybe that's why you don't have any points. Just saying.

Seriously. It's a game. Don't fuck with people's fun.

I hope you all continue to follow along. Starting today, anyone will be able to vote on the order of the bonus girls and who is worth the most points. You can only vote once a day, but you can vote every day if you want. The next post will have an update of the Hitters. Who's in the lead, who stands a fighting chance, and who's barely in the game? Come back to see.

In the meantime, happy hitting!

~ THE HIT MAN

4

Saturday is pretty open for the most part. Technically, there isn't class, but that doesn't stop me from going into the studio around noon. The studios are almost empty. I guess people would rather go out for the day instead of spend their free time dancing.

Fine by me. It allows me access to a studio I didn't reserve.

I turn the stereo on and jog in place to warm up my muscles before I sit down to stretch. When I'm convinced I won't pull anything, I flip the song to one of the old solos I learned in New York.

I prefer to be in the studio by myself. It's the only time I can really be me. I don't have to put on an act for other students or for the teachers.

Two hours pass. I barely notice. My muscles appreciate the familiarity of the routine. Since coming to L.A., everything has been new. It's nice to change it up, but sometimes I miss the way it was.

I pull myself into a pirouette. Something catches my eye as I spot the mirror and I let myself fall out of the turn. Luke stands in the doorway of the studio. His dance bag is slung across his chest.

I pick up a towel and wipe off my face. "Sorry. I didn't know anyone had this room reserved."

Maybe I should have reserved the studio, after all. I'd hate to be getting in the way of someone else's rehearsal that actually went through the right channels to get the room.

"I don't have it reserved. I was just walking by and saw you in here. You really are a great dancer."

I drop the towel back into my bag and pull the ponytail holder out of my hair. My hair falls down around my shoulders. "Thanks."

Luke pulls his bag off and lets it fall to the ground. He walks across the room and sits on the floor against the mirror.

I tuck my hair behind my ears to get it out of my face. I don't know what he's doing, but I don't really want to dance in front of him. I sit down in the middle of the floor and face him.

"It's quiet around here today." I don't know what else to say, but I feel like I need to say something. He just invited himself into my rehearsal.

"Take advantage of it. People are probably out enjoying the weather. It'll change in a few weeks and we'll all be fighting for rehearsal space on the weekends. It's always been that way." He runs his hand along the floor and wipes the dust on his pants.

"Haven't you only been here for a year?" How would he know what it's always been like?

He laughs and it echoes off the walls of the studio. It's a pleasant sound. "My parents used to let me use the studios on the weekends before I started class here. I've been coming here on Saturdays for like ten years."

Oh, right. I forgot they're directors of the department.

"The older kids used to teach me their routines. It was fun." His smile fades into a small frown.

Maybe it's not fun for him anymore. I bet there's a lot of pressure when your parents are big in the industry.

He picks at a blue spot on the floor. "I remember when they were painting sets in here one weekend. I think I was fifteen. I knocked over a can of paint and stained the floors. My mom was pissed." Amusement lights up his eyes.

I smile back at him. "I bet."

"She made me clean this entire floor. And then she wouldn't let me into the studio for a month." He shrugs. "I snuck in anyway. It's not like it was hard."

I laugh. I thought maybe last night at the fundraiser had been a fluke, but it's still just as easy as ever to talk to him.

He grins. "That's what she gets for keeping paint in the studio. Pretty sure she learned her lesson."

"I'm sure she did."

He watches me for a few seconds in silence. I study the room around me. I don't know why I'm afraid to meet his stare, but I am.

His phone vibrates against the floor and we both turn to look at it. He picks it up and swipes his finger across the screen. His smile slowly falls until he's frowning at his phone. The muscles in his arm clench as his grip on his phone tightens. If he squeezes any harder, he's going to break it.

"I have to go." His eyes stay glued to the screen.

"Um, yeah, okay. I should go, too." I don't know who pissed him off so much, but I'm not so sure I want to find out. I'm just glad it wasn't me.

He lifts his head up and his face relaxes as soon as his eyes meet mine. A small smile returns. "Well, Sadie Bryant, I'm off to enjoy the sunshine. Have a good weekend." He jumps up to his feet and grabs his bag. "Don't work too hard."

"See you Monday."

I don't want him to go, but I don't know how to ask him to stay.

He disappears through the door as I gather my things. I walk through the empty halls. If I'd asked Luke to wait for me, maybe he would have walked me back to my dorm.

And then what? It's not like I like him or he likes me. We talked for like two minutes in a dance studio. It means nothing.

I push through the door of my dorm room. Brielle sits at her desk with her computer open in front of her. She swivels in her chair to look at me.

"I have good news and bad news," she says. Her face is neutral. Apparently both options aren't that exciting.

I throw my dance bag onto my bed. Her news probably doesn't even apply to me, but I humor her anyway. "Okay."

She jumps onto her bed. "It's Saturday and we don't have class for another two days."

I raise an eyebrow at her and dig through my bag to find my clothes. They'll start to smell if I leave them in here until Monday. "I'm guessing that's the good news."

"Yeah. The bad news is that you're a target in the sex game."

I drop my bag. It thunks loudly onto the floor. "I'm sorry, what?" I didn't hear her right. There's no way she just said that.

"Lots of people are voting for you. So that's good news or bad news depending on how you take it."

"What?" I trip over my bag on my way to her computer. My hand comes down against the top of her desk so I don't fall on my face.

The Conservatory blog is open on her computer. The newest post fills most of the screen. She scrolls down to show me my name. She's listed a few spaces above me.

"What the hell? Aren't you mad about this? You're on there, too." I scan over the screen. It has to be some kind of sick joke. I never did anything to deserve something like this. Who would do that?

"Hell yeah, I'm mad about it. Some jackass just posted my name all over the internet so people can decide how many points having sex with me is worth." She shuts her computer and turns toward me.

"Who do you think did it?" I've only met a handful of people at this school, but I can't picture any of them doing this.

She opens the top drawer of her dresser and pulls out a tank top and some shorts. "It's not like we don't have plenty of options. Most of the guys here are dicks. I could see any of them doing it."

Obviously someone at The Conservatory has the balls to put this game out there. I wish there was a way I could somehow remove myself from it, but I know that will never happen.

"I'm going to go see if a studio is free." Brielle glances back at me as she swings her bag over her head and rests it across her chest. She chews on her lip.

I know she wants to say something and I'd rather she just do it. "What?"

She shrugs. "I wouldn't get involved with any of the guys around here if I were you."

I guess it's a good thing I already made that decision before I ever set foot in L.A.

———————

Monday morning comes too quickly. I can barely get out of bed. Every inch of my body hurts as I stretch to loosen my muscles. Fire shoots through my aching and overworked limbs. This is what happens when I push myself too hard.

Today will be hell.

I stare at the ceiling and debate emailing Miss Catherine to tell her I'm sick. That way I can avoid this whole partner thing and the entire male student body who may or may not be trying to have sex with me for points. Maybe I'll sleep the whole day. I relax back against my pillow. Sleep sounds so much better than leaving this room.

Brielle walks in with a towel on her head. "Morning. Are you ready for partner assignments?" She sounds excited.

"I don't really have a choice." It's going to happen whether I'm there or not. There's no escaping it.

She frowns. "No, I guess not."

I slide out of bed. "Let's just get this over with."

Standing in front of the mirror, I pile my hair on top of my head and swipe on enough makeup to make it look like I'm not exhausted.

Brielle looks like she's about to start skipping down the hallway on the way to class. She has enough energy for the both of us. Too bad she can't transfer some of her excitement to me.

Luke stands in the hallway outside the studio. He talks to a girl I recognize as one of the music students who was singing at the fundraiser on Friday. I slow my pace. Brielle slows beside me and I can see her glancing between Luke and me out of the corner of my eye.

Nerves twist my stomach as I consider whether I should say something to him when I walk past. It would be rude to pretend like I didn't even see him when I have to walk right by him.

Oh my God, I'm completely over-thinking this. I can say hi.

"Hey, Luke."

He doesn't answer me. Maybe he didn't hear me. It's not like I yelled it and he is distracted with another conversation. I open my mouth to say it again, but his gaze flicks up to mine briefly. Annoyance flashes in his eyes.

Wow. Apparently I was wrong.

Brielle huffs beside me and grabs my arm. "Whatever you're thinking, just stop. I heard he was playing that game last year, anyway. You don't want to get involved."

I walk through the door to the studio with Brielle, ignoring Luke and the music student. It's not like I needed him anyway. This just reaffirms my position on the whole stick-to-myself thing. If I don't open myself up to getting hurt, it can't happen.

I sit down next to Brielle and Adam and pull out my water bottle. It's empty. Dammit.

The water fountain is just outside the door in the hallway. I hold the bottle under the steady stream of water. Luke is still out here, but he's talking to a group of guys now instead of the music girl.

"She's definitely a hit. I bet she's worth a ton of points, too. If you don't do it, I will."

What the hell?

They're part of that disgusting game. No wonder he looked annoyed when I said hi. He was probably trying to arrange his next hit.

I can't believe I thought he might be a decent person. He's just another asshole like Patrick. He might even be worse. At least Patrick had some regard for other people before things ended between us.

I don't want anything to do with Luke.

I walk back into the studio and sit down next to Brielle, shoving my bag against the wall.

A frown creases her forehead. "You okay?"

"I'm fine."

I don't want to talk about this here. Especially since I know he'll be walking in the door any second and I know how much she hates him. We don't need a bunch of drama before class starts.

"You aren't allowed to be crabby, Little Miss I-Got-Into-All-The-Advanced-Classes," Brielle says, pointing at me. "You should be ecstatic."

I frown. "It's not that big of a deal."

Her face falls. "It's a huge deal for a freshman. It's a huge deal for me and I'm a sophomore."

When they emailed class assignments, I'd been over the moon. It was enough for me to get into The Conservatory, but getting into the advanced classes was only going to help my career.

Luke opens the door and his eyes meet mine. I look down at the floor, but it's too late. He heads straight toward us. I don't look up again, but I can feel him standing over me.

"Hey, Sadie."

Now he wants to talk? Absolutely not. I don't play that game. I won't talk to him only when it's convenient for him. And I definitely won't give him the opportunity to use me and dump me so he can get some stupid points.

I ignore him and focus on my stretching. He stands next to me awkwardly for a couple seconds before he moves to an empty spot on the other side of the room.

"What was that about?" Brielle doesn't look at me. Her face is against the floor as she stretches.

"Nothing."

Usually I have no problem shutting out everything else and focusing on dance during rehearsal. But today the only thing I can think about is how I've ended up on that fucking list.

There's no way Luke's little act at the fundraiser on Friday wasn't a way to try to get me to sleep with him. Pretend to be nice, pretend to have fun, pretend to be interested. He doesn't give a shit about me. I'm just another point value.

The longer I'm in class, the angrier I get. If this is what I'll be dealing with all semester long, how am I supposed to dance with a partner? How will I be able to have any kind of chemistry with someone if all I'm worried about is how many points they're trying to get?

There's no one at this school I'll be able to successfully dance with. That means I'll end up without a spot in Fall Showcase. And if I can't show them I'm getting better, I can kiss London goodbye.

That can't happen. I won't let it. I need Fall Showcase to prove to myself that my career isn't over after my injury. After Patrick.

Adam crosses the floor in front of me, his extensions amazing as usual.

Maybe I could partner with Adam. He's not wrapped up in this stupid game. He thinks it's just as bad as I do. And it's not like he would be trying to have sex with me anyway.

Class ends and I find myself walking alone to my next one. Brielle leans against the wall down the hallway talking to one of the music students. She glances up at me and I wave. She says something to the boy and walks over to me.

"Did you just give him your number?" I ask, unable to hide my smile.

She frowns, getting defensive. "Maybe. Why? Is that a crime?"

That's got to be the third boy I've seen her flirting with since this weekend. "How many guys are you going to date at once?"

"Who said anything about dating them?" She smiles.

I don't get how she can be so carefree about this. "You realize they're probably just after your points, right?"

She shrugs. "I can't take my name off the list. Might as well have some fun with it. Besides, not every guy in this school is involved with that game. There have to be some good ones."

Brielle links arms with me and we walk toward the next studio of the day. I'm about to follow her in, but an arm hooks around my waist and pulls me off to the side of the door.

"Why are you ignoring me?" Luke pins me against the wall with his arms on either side of me. "It makes me feel like you don't like me and I know that's not true."

He's close to me, but he's not actually touching me. It strikes me as odd. Other guys who have flirted with me usually touch my arm or my face, making me extremely uncomfortable. Luke knows next to nothing about me, but he seems to read some of my signals. Maybe he's more perceptive than I thought.

"I don't want to talk to you."

He takes a step closer to me and I step back into the wall. I'm trapped between brick and Luke.

His breath is on my cheek when he speaks again. "I just want to know why. I know you feel the connection between us. You can't deny it."

"You're a dick."

I have no doubt he's making a second attempt to earn points for me, but the good times are hard to ignore. He's not always like this. He was decent in the studio and at the fundraiser. If he could just pick a mood and go with it, my life would be so much easier. It doesn't seem like such a bad idea to be his friend when he actually talks to me.

The war rages inside me. I want fight or flight to take over, but there's a third option in this scenario— surrender.

His lips hover centimeters over my mouth and his shadow weighs on me like he's pressed against my body. He leans one forearm against the wall next to my head. His other hand remains flat against the wall above my shoulder.

My thoughts jumble together in my mind. I need to get away from here, away from him.

But my heart won't let go.

Part of me wants to be this close to him. The smell of his cologne mixes with the smell of sweat from the studios. I chose to leave my past behind when I left New York. I want to start over, but if he's only after me for this game, it won't be a fresh start. It'll be a replay of the pain I've already experienced. Except it'll be worse.

I stay—physically locked by his arms, mentally locked by his gaze, confused about what I want and what I should do. He sighs and closes his eyes. His lips graze my temple and then his breath is on my ear.

"I won't kiss you while you're attached to someone else, but do me a favor?" he asks, a smile playing at his lips.

"What?" My voice wavers, a combination of panic and attraction.

"Tell your boyfriend he's got competition."

He pushes off the wall and walks into the studio. I'm frozen against the brick. He's confusing as hell. If my interactions with him were a little more consistent, I wouldn't feel like I'm in a constant state of whiplash.

I don't understand his reaction. One minute he's ignoring me, the next he's got me cornered in the hallway asking why I'm ignoring him. None of this makes any sense.

Brielle sticks her head out of the door and stares at me. "Are you coming to class?"

I nod, staring at the opposite wall. "Yeah." I pull myself off the wall and follow her inside.

A double-sided portable barre stands in the middle of the room, ready for our technique class. I drop my bag under the barre and sit down next to Brielle to put on my pointe shoes, trying to shut out the world and focus on the next three hours.

I need to be strong. I'm officially on my own, and the only one who can ensure my success is me. I'll be so proud if I can make it through this, but it's hard to see November right now when I'm stuck in September.

Adam stops in front of the door to the studio and Brielle waves. Rachel pushes in through the doorway, hip checking him out of her way. He flips her off as she walks away from him.

Rachel stops beside me. "This is my spot."

"I'm sorry." I pick up my bag to move to another section of the barre. I don't feel like fighting with Rachel. It's easier to give her what she wants.

Brielle grabs my bag and throws it back on the floor. "Um, no. You know spots aren't assigned, and Sadie was here first. You'll have to find another spot."

I stare between the two of them. I don't care, but I don't want to get caught in a fight between Brielle and Rachel.

Rachel narrows her eyes. "You know this is the spot I used last year. You took these spots on purpose because you don't like me. It's not my fault Luke picked me over you."

I bite my lip and stare down at the floor. It figures that out of all the people in this school, I managed to worm my way in between these two and unwillingly joined Brielle's side in their battle against each other. Luke isn't even worth fighting over.

"Pick your battles." Patrick shoves a sweatshirt into his bag.

Is that what I am? A battle?

"Was it hard for you to pick NYBC over me? Because it seemed like you had a pretty easy time making that fucking decision."

This is unbelievable. He can't seriously tell me not to start this fight. I wasn't even the one who started it in the first place. He did the second he accepted NYBC's offer and left me in the dust.

He walks past me without looking at me. "Knock it off. You're acting like a child."

I'll show him acting like a child. I pick up his shoe and whip it across the studio. It hits the wall with a smack. "And you're acting like a giant douche bag."

Brielle raises an eyebrow. "You sound a little paranoid. You might want to get that checked out."

"You're such a bitch, Brielle."

My mouth drops open. I haven't spent a lot of time with Brielle, but even I've learned that she's feisty and it's probably not a good thing to piss her off.

Brielle glares at Rachel. "It's a fucking barre. Get over it."

"It's a fucking boy. Get over it," Rachel throws back. She stands there awkwardly for a second before she gives up and walks to another section of the barre.

Brielle drops to her butt in front of her own spot and sticks her legs out in front of her in a stretch, directly in Rachel's path. Rachel's toe hooks Brielle's foot and she pitches forward onto the ground.

Rachel's hands skid out in front of her and she cries out as she makes impact. She stays on the floor for a couple seconds before she pulls herself onto her knees. She turns to Brielle, her mouth open, and I brace myself for the string of curse words to follow.

But Adam rushes up behind her and grabs her arm to pull her up to her feet. "You should really be more careful. You don't want to hurt yourself on the first day of real class." He gives her a little shove away from us to get her moving again. She pauses, staring Brielle down, and for a second, I think she's going to lunge at her. But she doesn't and I breathe a sigh of relief.

"Your friend-making skills astound me," Adam says.

I can't help my smirk at his comment. It's absolutely true.

Brielle crosses her arms over her chest. "She started it. What are you even doing here? Last time I checked, you're not a girl."

"I was just passing through on my way to the boys' studio. I should go." He waves and heads toward the door.

"Later," Brielle says.

"Try to behave," he yells over his shoulder.

"Yes, sir." She salutes him.

I put all my energy into tying the ribbons on my pointe shoes, tucking in the bow on the inside of my ankle. If I focus on every single movement as I make it, I don't have to think about how my life is falling apart. And I don't have to worry about how I'll make it through the semester with a partner when one bad lift could end my career. My fragile hip won't come back from another injury.

I know my limits, but I don't expect anyone else to learn them, or trust anyone not to push them.

A woman I recognize from last week walks into the room and conversation quiets around me. Her platinum blond hair is styled in a pixie cut. Her black leotard and sweater stand out against her pale white skin. She doesn't look like she's stepped outside in the L.A. sun in the past year.

She walks to the front of the room and turns to watch us get ready for class. The remaining girls trickle into the studio. Only one space is open on the twelve-person barre. Girls around me warm up their feet and stretch in their shoes. I lift my leg onto the higher level on the barre and lean against my leg.

Rachel whispers to the girl next to her, Courtney, and they both glare at Brielle and then at me.

I ignore them. Brielle flips them off.

After about five minutes of watching us stretch, the teacher steps forward. "Ladies, welcome to your advanced ballet technique class. My name is Miss Laney. You will be required to wear pointe shoes for every practice. Even though we are a contemporary school, you need to maintain proper technique. Understood?"

The girls around me nod.

"Good. Let's begin. Spread out on the barre and make sure you have enough space. We're going to start with two demi pliés and a grand plié in first, second, and fifth positions, relevé in fifth position, hold for a count of eight and turn to the other side."

Soft piano notes drift from the speakers as the music starts. I push down on the tips of my toes one at a time. I haven't worn my pointe shoes as frequently here as I did in New York, but that's enough to make the skin on my feet less resistant to the unforgiving stiff blocks. I rest my hand lightly on the barre, careful not to wrap my thumb around it. Standing with my feet together, I open them at the toes, my heels glued together. My hips turn out and my feet stop just before they reach 180 degrees.

Everything stops. All the stressful thoughts, the worry about having to dance with a partner again, the bullshit with Luke and The Hit List, it's all gone. As soon as my hand connects with the smooth wood of the barre, I'm in my own world.

The entire class starts the exercise on cue without a word from Miss Laney. For so long, these barre exercises have been engrained in me, I could do them in my sleep.

And it's been my escape for as long as I can remember. When I can't stand the thoughts in my head anymore, I dance. Focusing on the movement, being told exactly what emotions I should be feeling, either by the music or by my teacher, feeling the physical pain and pleasure of exertion instead of the mental pain I've never gotten used to.

The one thing I can always count on when I dance is knowing exactly what I should be feeling during a performance. Barre and floor exercises keep my emotions in check as I focus more on the positions than the music. Choreography is a completely different story. I could be having the worst day ever, but dancing something happy makes me forget all about it.

Dancing allows me to feel something other than what's inside my head. That's my goal most of the time. When I'm doing floor work and barre exercises, I'm comfortably numb, content with focusing on muscle memory and the way it should feel if I'm doing it right. Every time I go into practice, I put in two hundred percent because if I'm not getting any better, then what's the point?

I finish on the right and rise up onto my toes in fifth position relevé. My right foot automatically pulls back against my left for support, as if a delicate thread holds them together. My arch rests against the top of my foot as my feet slide down against the bottom of my shoes and the stiffness of my shoes cuts into my foot.

I wouldn't trade it for anything in the world.

The rest of the class is filled with more barre exercises and floor routines. We battement, grand jeté, frappé, and pirouette until we can barely move. Miss Laney calls the end of practice as the sun falls behind the building across from the studio. The absence of natural light makes it seem later than early afternoon.

Sweat drips down my back. My face has taken on the lovely hue of being out in the sun all day. My feet are on fire, a sure sign that the blisters that have formed over the day have also popped. Every muscle in my body feels stretched beyond its capacity.

It's the best feeling I've ever had.

"All right, ladies. That's it for today. Thanks for a great class. Miss Catherine would like to see you all in the main studio for partner assignments in fifteen minutes." Miss Laney smiles and walks out of the room.

"I guess it's time." Brielle shoves her shoes into her bag and stands beside me. "Let's go."

She heads out of the studio, but I hang back. I have to talk to Miss Catherine, convince her to let me have Adam as a partner. I won't survive with anyone else, especially not Luke.

If I don't speak up, I'll be stuck with someone I can't stand.

It's now or never. After today, I have no chance of getting Adam as a partner. I find her office and knock on the door.

"Come in."

Opening the door, I step inside. Dance posters line the walls of Miss Catherine's office, all featuring her as the subject. I take a few steps forward. She looks busy.

"Sadie, what can I do for you this afternoon?" She sits at her computer, typing something furiously on her keyboard.

I press my fingernails into the palm of my hand. It's not that hard. I can do this. If I want to survive here, if I don't want my plans to fizzle out and die, I have to do this. "I was wondering if I could talk to you."

She frowns. "I don't make a habit of meeting with my students without prior arrangements. I'm very busy, but I have a few minutes open right now. Have a seat," she says, pointing at the chair in front of her desk.

I manage a smile and sit down in the chair.

"What's on your mind?" Her eyes are hard. She'd rather be working on whatever it was she was doing instead of talking to me.

My words come out in a rush, not at all like I practiced in my head in the hallway. "I know we're getting partners today. I just wanted to talk to you about it."

She glances up at me quickly before focusing back on her computer. "You've danced with a partner before. You have nothing to worry about."

I play with an invisible spot on my tights. I want to tell her what my concern is, but I can't bring myself to tell her about my life. She doesn't care about people leaving, about my trust issues, about my injury. It will only add to her doubt of my abilities.

"I haven't partnered in a really long time and I just think it would be better if I could partner with someone I'm starting to get comfortable with. Like Adam."

She narrows her eyes at me. "Are you asking me if you can partner with Adam?"

I take a deep breath, unsure I should even answer her question. Her tone scares me and I don't want to dig myself in any deeper than I already have.

She folds her hands on the desk in front of her and continues without my answer. "I told you the first day of class we don't give breaks. If I allow you to partner with the person of your choice, I have to allow that same consideration to every other student in this program, and I can't do that. Even if I could, the partners have already been chosen. This doesn't just affect you. It affects every other student here."

I look down at my hands in my lap, unable to look her in the eye any longer. This was a huge mistake. "I understand."

"Do you? Because it doesn't look good on your part, asking for special treatment in the second week of class. Keep in mind we don't just look at technique and abilities in a dancer when we're considering someone for London. We consider the dancer as a whole, including how agreeable they are." Her eyes flick to her computer for a couple of seconds.

My cheeks burn. I want to be as far away from here as possible. What even made me think this would work in the first place? This conversation will spread like wildfire to all the teachers and no one will want to work with me anymore. I've just turned into the high maintenance, needy dancer. Awesome.

She doesn't bother to look at me anymore, focused instead on a piece of paper lying on her desk. "If that's all, you can go. You can't afford to be late for class right now."

I walk out of her office. I never should have talked to her in the first place. Such a stupid mistake.

Brielle catches me in the hallway. "Did you just talk to Miss Catherine? What's wrong?"

"I don't want to talk about it." I keep walking.

"Is there ever anything you do want to talk about?" She crosses her arms over her chest, like she's expecting me to spill my guts for her now.

I glare at her. "Sometimes."

"Sadie?"

I turn at the sound of my name. Owen, a guy in my dance history class, jogs up beside us.

"Hey, how are you?"

I smile. "Good."

I don't know him that well. It's weird that he's making an effort to come talk to me outside of class.

"I was wondering if you wanted to go to dinner this weekend."

My smile falls. The Hit List hasn't even been around that long and I'm already sick of it.

He looks nervous. "I'm not part of that game, if that's what you're thinking."

Brielle laughs beside me. "Does that actually work?"

He looks offended. Maybe he really isn't part of it. He could just actually want to date me.

"She's not interested." Brielle pulls me toward the studio.

Owen doesn't say anything back. He shuffles back down the hallway the way he came.

I watch him walk away, but wait until he's out of earshot to say anything. "That was mean. He might not really be playing."

She raises an eyebrow at me. "Did you want to go out with him?"

"No." I don't want to go out with anyone.

"Okay, then."

Brielle turns into the studio we're in next. I follow her and sit down on the floor to stretch to keep my muscles warm.

This is it—the partnership that can make or break me. The odds that it'll be the latter are too high for me to think about.

Luke sits behind me, but he faces away from me, completely absorbed by his cell phone, like he didn't just pin me to a wall. Rachel tries to get his attention by telling an animated story about her bikini mishap on vacation, but she's failing miserably. His eyes remain glued to his phone. Courtney sits on the other side of the room, equally enthralled with her phone. They seem to be playing a suspicious game of phone tag.

I can only assume that he's flirting again. I've never seen someone flirt as much as him in my entire life. And he seems not to care that everyone he flirts with constantly sees him with someone else.

I mean, really. It's not like we don't have standards.

Miss Catherine talks with another teacher near the front of the room. They look casual, like they're not about to ruin my life.

"I have the partner assignments I know you're all eagerly waiting for." Her eyes find mine, but I look away.

If I'd stayed in New York, none of this would be happening right now. I wouldn't feel so defeated. New York may not hold the fresh start I wanted, but right now, L.A. doesn't either. Maybe there's still an option to transfer somewhere.

It's easier to run than it is to deal with all this shit. That's what my life has become. Running from one problem to the next.

"Sadie."

My head pops up when I hear my name and I hold my breath.

"Your partner is—" She glances down at her clipboard before her eyes flick back up to mine.

It's possible I won't be completely screwed by this whole thing. Maybe Adam was already chosen as my partner.

Please be Adam. Please be Adam. Please be Adam.

"Luke," she says, smiling.

You've got to be kidding me.

THE HIT LIST UPDATE
September 10

Welcome to the first point update posting of The Hit List. Each of our guys has been assigned a number for the time being. If our girls knew which guys were participating, the game wouldn't be any fun.

#4	3 points
#10	2 points
#2	2 points
#6	1 point
#9	1 point
#3	1 point
#12	——
#11	——
#7	——
#1	——
#5	——
#8	——

As far as the girls go, here are their weekly numbers. There has been a ton of voting activity in the polls this week, but here are the standings as of right now. Whatever position a bonus girl is in when a Hitter scores points for her determines the amount of points that Hitter will receive. So if someone claims Rachel while she's on top, they'll receive the max of fifteen points.

Rachel Barrons	23%
Brielle Watkins	19%
Sadie Bryant	15%
Jessie Freeman	11%

NIKKI URANG

Rebecca Hemsworth	8%
Noelle Sanstrohm	6%
Ashlynn Jenkins	5%
Courtney Turner	5%
Samantha Jameson	5%
Kate Williams	3%

Remember to keep voting to change up the positions of our girls and how many points they're worth. Come back next week to find out who has taken the lead, how many points the guys have racked up, and which girls have fallen.

In the meantime, happy hitting!

~ THE HIT MAN

5

The studio I'm using to practice with Luke is right down the hallway. Rachel and her friends sit in the windowsill outside the studio. She holds the latest issue of *Jeté Magazine* in her hands. I keep my head down, hoping I can disappear around the corner without them seeing me.

But I don't have that kind of luck.

"'Neither has danced without the other for two years. One wonders what kind of effect this separation will have on their dancing.'" She makes direct eye contact with me as she finishes quoting the article. Her brown eyes burn with dislike for me. I'd like to think it's jealousy, but I think it's just her.

I keep walking, not giving her the satisfaction of a response. She won't continue if I don't encourage her.

It's clear that our separation has only benefited Patrick. The only thing it's gotten me so far is a lot of unwanted attention.

Rachel kicks her feet against the wall below the windowsill. One of her friends jumps down and steps out in front of me. I sidestep so I don't run right into her. She follows me down the hallway as I walk.

"From what I've seen, she was the weak link in that partnership. I mean, look how well he's doing. He was lucky to get out when he did." Rachel shoves the magazine at one of the other girls.

She's right. I was the weak partner. But I'm determined not to let that happen here. I have to make this partnership work.

"Don't you have something to say, Sadie?" She smiles and the rest of the group turn to watch me.

I stop and close my eyes as I take a deep breath. There are so many things I want to say to Rachel, so many things that would wipe that fucking smile right off her face. I don't want to stoop to her level, but that doesn't mean I won't.

"You don't know what you're talking about, Rachel."

She grins like she knows a secret. "I know no one wants you. Not Patrick and especially not Luke."

She thinks it's an insult, but she doesn't know that I don't want them either. Patrick can go to hell and she can keep Luke. She doesn't even know the whole story. All she knows is something she read in a magazine. How would she feel if she were left at her most vulnerable time by the partner she loved more than anything else in the world?

"Why do you even care so much?" There are so many other things she could be focused on right now. Like Fall Showcase. Or her name being on The Hit List.

She narrows her eyes at me. "Stay away from Luke."

"Maybe you should tell him to stay away from me. It's not like I put my name on that stupid list." I'm starting to see why Brielle hates Rachel so much.

"Maybe someone put you on that list for a reason." She stares intensely at me for a couple seconds before she shrugs and smiles. Her playful attitude returns to her face, like she doesn't have a care in the world. "Or maybe they did it as a joke, because who would seriously work that hard to sleep with you?"

My hands clench into fists at my side, my nails digging into my palm. Patrick didn't want to keep working with me so he left. Luke is persistent right now, but he'll get sick of the game quickly. Rachel's right. No one wants to work that hard.

And I don't want them to. I don't want any of that. I don't want a boyfriend or a friend with benefits or some other unspecified relationship. I don't want to be part of this game.

I round the corner to the sound of Rachel's laughter. I need to focus on the task ahead of me. As much as I don't want to think about partnering with Luke, I want to think about Patrick even less.

A boy stands beside a girl farther down the hallway. He touches her face and she smiles. "You deserve so much better than him."

They look cute together.

Until another very angry student interrupts the moment by punching the first guy in the face. "Are you fucking kidding me, Justin? Did you seriously just try to cock-block me?"

Justin lies on the ground, rubbing his jaw where a brightly colored bruise has already started to form behind the cut that drips blood down his chin.

"What the fuck is wrong with you, Derek? Your name's not on her. She's fair game."

Derek looks like he's ready for another round of punches. "Does she know we wanted to nail her for points?"

"She does now, genius." Justin scrambles off the floor and lunges at Derek.

A teacher catches Justin before they make contact again. Derek steps back against the lockers with his hands raised. He's crazy if he thinks the teachers will believe he had nothing to do with this. A couple more teachers run down the hallway to help with the situation. The first teacher pushes Justin toward an office. Derek follows with a smirk on his face.

I stare in horror at the girl across the hallway. A tear runs down her cheek before she runs away. This whole school has gone bat shit crazy over this game.

Luke flirts with some blond chick outside our studio. She giggles when he tucks her hair behind her ear. He doesn't seem at all disheartened by my rejection. He's flirted with every single girl I've seen him talking to since I met him.

I storm past them, sick of seeing flirting everyway I go, and push through the doors of the studio. Luke glances at me, a frown creasing his forehead. "Later, Candace." He follows me into the studio.

Candace giggles again. "Bye."

I roll my eyes.

"Hey, it's about time you got here," Luke says.

"There was a distraction on my way here." I don't meet his eyes because I don't want him to see how angry I am, but I'm sure he can hear it in my voice. It's not like he was doing anything important before I got here anyway. I don't want to deal with any male at this school. They're all playing that game and it's sick.

Luke paces the floor on the opposite side of the room. He won't cross the invisible line in the middle of the room. "The teachers like us to be warmed up before they get here."

"Okay." I'm not in the mood for Luke and I refrain from telling him exactly what I think of him.

My phone vibrates against the side of my arm, through my bag. I pull it out and stare at the number I should have deleted a year ago, but I could never bring myself to do it. Patrick.

How's L.A.?

No "Hi." No "Sorry I haven't called in all this time." Not even a "Hey, how's your hip doing after I dropped you?"

"How's L.A.?" Fucking pathetic.

I don't even know what to say to that. He was dead set on forgetting about me before I even left New York. Why the hell does he suddenly care about me now?

I shove my phone back in my bag and set it down in the corner of the room, out of the way. Luke walks to the stereo system and plugs in his iPod. I head to the front of the room and sit down, blinking back the tears.

My hips and legs tighten as I stretch out my muscles. I take a deep breath and focus on the feeling. The cool floor feels nice against my skin and it helps to calm my racing heart and relax my muscles, allowing me to push further into the stretch.

Luke walks to the stereo. "You better make sure you're on time from now on. I need you to help me win Fall Showcase. Which means you need to be on time and give everything you've got in rehearsal."

I stare at the imperfections in the floor beneath my face.

"How's L.A.?" It blows.

Latin beats fill the small studio. Half the song is in Spanish and I don't understand it. I wonder if Luke played it intentionally. He glances back at me, flashing me a brilliant smile, and sits close to me to stretch. I refrain from rolling my eyes at him. It's not a question anymore. Clearly, he did.

The song is on repeat and it plays five and a half times before our teacher comes in. Finally. I'll be singing it in my sleep.

"I'm Miss Tasha. I'll be your partner teacher." She holds out her hand for me to shake. "Nice to meet you, Sadie."

Miss Tasha has short blond hair. She's small, but her muscles are toned. She's probably stronger than me. She looks younger than most of the other teachers, probably in her early thirties.

"Miss Tasha," Luke says, nodding in her direction. "You're looking lovely today."

Miss Tasha rolls her eyes at him, like she expects nothing less coming from Luke, but a faint blush rises to her cheeks. She's flattered.

"Seriously? Is there anyone you won't flirt with?" I'm so sick of him. I wish I could push him down the stairs.

Luke looks at Miss Tasha. "Someone's feisty today."

I'm about to tell him exactly how feisty I am when another guy walks into the studio. I swear I saw him taking class here last week even though he looks like he should have finished school a few years ago. He wears a pair of black shorts and a black tank top, but he removes the shirt within five seconds.

At least I'll have something nice to look at today.

Luke is off the floor in less than two seconds. He looks at Miss Tasha. "Why would they put Brandon with us?"

Brandon smiles. "Someone has to make you work this year." He glances at me, his eyes leaving my face and focusing on other parts of me for far too long.

Brandon's a full head taller than Luke. His shaggy blond hair hangs down below his forehead, almost concealing his blue eyes. The tension between them crackles. Any more and there would be sparks flying. Not the good kind. The kind when rock strikes metal and the resulting spark creates a fire that devastates everything nearby.

"Brandon is my senior assistant this year. He'll be helping choreograph." Miss Tasha plugs her iPod into the stereo and grabs the remote so she can control the music. "Here's what we're going to do. I'll have you watch us dance first, then we'll start on the choreography. I want you to get a feel for the dance and the emotions and the music before that. Sound good?"

Luke speaks for both of us. "Yeah."

I walk up to the front of the room and sit down with my back against the mirror. Luke sits next to me. If I move my leg slightly, I'll be touching him. My muscles tense as I try to stay completely still. I don't want to have to explain moving farther away from him so I stay put. The heat from his leg radiates against my thigh and I cross my ankles, hoping to get some sort of relief.

"The concept of this dance is about a boy who is falling in love with a girl, but the girl is trying to work through some major issues. The boy won't let her fall and continues to love her. He fights to stay in her life and he promises not to give up on her or their relationship."

Because why not? Everything else is going so well in my life. Things needed to get a little harder for me.

I have to force myself not to roll my eyes as my heart stutters at the similarities this dance shares with my real life. Why couldn't the concept be us hating each other? I can handle that.

Miss Tasha presses a button on the stereo and guitar chords fill the air. I'm familiar with the song, but I never imagined myself dancing to it. Miss Tasha and Brandon start to move. Brandon is there to support her for every lift, catch her every jump. The choreography melds together so well, the dancers in perfect sync with the music, with the emotions.

Patrick doesn't kiss me when he enters the studio. He used to touch me at every opportunity. A kiss before rehearsal begins, his fingers graze the skin between my tank top and my shorts as he leads me to my starting position, a squeeze of my hand before he separates from me. It's almost a superstition at this point. We do little things at every rehearsal, things he hasn't done in the past week.

"What's wrong?"

He smiles, but the skin around his eyes doesn't crinkle. "Nothing."

I'm not stupid. We've been dancing together for two years. He can't hide anything from me. I know him better than I know myself.

The routine we've done a million times is a disaster today. He can barely look at me, like I'm the one who did something wrong. But I haven't done anything. He's the one who's changed. He's the reason we're falling apart.

They finish as the music dies off.

"Now it's your turn," Miss Tasha says.

This is going to be horrible.

"We'll go through it slow. You have nothing to be worried about. I've seen you dance." Brandon's reassurances are lost on me. He'll never be able to make me believe I can do this.

Luke walks to the middle of the floor and I follow slowly. This is it. The moment we find out if I'll be able to pull this off. I'm not confident that this will end well at all.

When I'm a couple steps away from Luke, I turn around to face the mirror so my back's to him.

"You need to be closer than that." Miss Tasha puts her hands on my shoulders and walks me backward until Luke's body is pressed against my back.

I close my eyes and take a few deep breaths. My body is completely rigid and my hands clench into fists at my sides.

"Where are you going?" My arms hurt from the crutches, but I hobble over to him while he gathers up his stuff.

"There's no reason to even stay here. You can't dance. We're not partners anymore, Sadie. Let it go." He doesn't look at me as he wanders through the studio collecting various things that have somehow managed to end up here.

I think he does it on purpose because he knows I can't follow him. I haven't gotten the hang of this whole crutches thing yet.

I stop in the middle of the floor, turning every so often to keep my eye on him. "It's so nice to hear that I mean nothing to you."

He sighs, running his hand through his hair, and drops the shirt he's holding into his bag. "It's not like that and you know it."

"Then what is it like, Patrick?"

He drops the bag and walks back to me, taking my face between his hands. For a second I think he'll kiss me, and my heart jumps in my chest.

He leans in and kisses my forehead. Like I'm his friend. Or his fucking little sister.

"Good luck." He grabs his bag and disappears out of the studio.

I hear his footsteps on the stairs, making his way down to the street. He can't be leaving. This can't be happening. I fight through the pain and move as fast as I can with my injury.

Just before the steps, one of the crutches comes down on my pant leg. It slides out from under my arm and there's nothing close by to grab onto to keep myself from falling. I land hard on my injured hip, crying out against the intense pain. I try to get up, but the pain is too much. Instead, I curl in on myself, sobbing against the floor, wishing life had gone differently.

I hope he hears. I hope he comes back.

But he doesn't.

He's gone.

"How's L.A.?" I don't even know what that means, but apparently it's the best he can do. I doubt he even cares. He's playing at some game to get something out of me after all this time. Maybe he found out about the fucking game and wants to collect some points for himself.

"Sadie, relax." Miss Tasha grabs my left arm and swings it back and forth, trying to loosen my muscles.

My arm loosens against her grip. She doesn't notice that every other muscle in my body is still tense.

"Better. Okay, Luke, I want you to put your left hand on her stomach and your right hand on her chest, just below her throat. This will be your starting pose."

Luke's hands slide against my skin. They're softer than I remember. My heart rate spikes as I meet his eyes in the mirror and see the affection in them. Not the kind that we fake every day with the people we dance with to make it look real. The real kind of affection, like he cares, like what he's feeling is real.

Patrick looks at me and the world falls away. It doesn't matter that we're in rehearsal or that there are a handful of other people in the room.

This is the reason I dance with him. When he looks at me, I feel loved. He doesn't look at anyone else that way. It's like if he lets me out of his sight, I'll disappear.

He always finds me. Whether we're on the stage or out in the city. And he always looks at me like that. Like I'm the only one he sees. Like I'm the only one he'll ever see.

We finish dancing and he frowns at me. "Are you okay?"

"Never better."

I can't handle Luke's look anymore and my gaze shifts down at our feet in the mirror. Sweat beads on my forehead and slides down my temple. I'm trapped between Luke's body and his hands.

I'm fine. I can do this. It's just a dance. I don't have anything to worry about.

My body betrays my thoughts. I inhale for the first time since Luke touched me. Everything sounds hollow around me, like I'm in a tunnel. Black dots close in on my vision as my lungs fight for more air and I gasp for breath, but Luke's hands act like a vice around my lungs, preventing the air from going in.

The studio is cold today. Maybe because it's snowing in New York. Maybe because I haven't talked to Patrick in fifty-eight days.

I need to get over this. I need to get over him. But every day this studio breathes life into the memories and it's like he never left. It might be time to find a new studio.

The door opens behind me. My heart flutters in anticipation. "Patrick?"

Miss Leah shakes her head. She smiles like she knows how my heart breaks over and over again every time he doesn't show up for our rehearsal. But she doesn't know. She could never know.

I know he's not coming. He hasn't been here in two months.

It's too late. My body's already shutting down.

Brandon frowns at me. "Are you okay?"

I shake my head no. If I talk, I'll start crying and freak everyone out.

Luke tries to help me, but I jerk away from him. I need to get away from him. The room spins around me when I take a step. I trip and my hands fly out to catch myself as Luke's arm wraps around my stomach.

"Brandon, go get a cool washcloth," Miss Tasha says.

Brandon's feet pound across the floor as he runs to the door.

Luke walks me to a chair and I collapse into it. He pushes my head down between my legs. "Take deep breaths."

He kneels beside me and rubs my back. I don't want him to touch me, but the nausea that overwhelms me makes it hard to move away.

The door opens again and seconds later a cool towel is placed on the back of my neck. It feels heavenly.

"I heard she worked really hard this weekend. She's probably just worn out from that. Plus, it's really hot in here. No wonder she almost passed out. Can we get a fan to circulate some air?" Luke sounds annoyed, but I don't think it's directed at me.

How does he know I worked all weekend? I try to focus on my breathing and push the thoughts out of my head. The tightness in my chest releases, the nausea disappears. I pull myself up into a sitting position. Luke's hand falls off my back and I meet his worried eyes.

His eyebrows pull together in a frown. "Are you okay?"

"Yeah, sorry." I move to stand up, but he pushes down on my shoulder and I sit back down hard.

He doesn't move his hand from my shoulder. "Stay there for a couple of minutes. If you get up too fast, you'll end up on the floor."

"We'll just take a break for ten minutes or so and then start again. Brandon, can I talk to you in the hall?" Miss Tasha asks. She shifts her weight from foot to foot, looking nervous.

They leave and I'm left alone with Luke. I'm painfully aware of how close he is to me again. I want to run out of this room, but I know I can't because if I leave now, I'll never be able to come back. I'll be on my way to New York with my dreams shattered. Again.

"What's going on?" Luke asks. He continues to rub my back.

"What do you mean?" He doesn't need to know. It's none of his business.

Except that it is because this affects him.

"You almost passed out twenty minutes into rehearsal. I know you can do better than that. What's going on?" Luke leans back against the mirror, his arms crossed over his chest.

"Nothing. I just have a lot on my mind." I can't tell him. He wouldn't understand.

"Well, you better figure it out pretty fast. You won't last here if you do this in every practice." His stare is icy, a complete change from the way he looked at me when his hands were all over me.

I throw my hands up in the air. "I'm so sick of you. One minute you're nice and the next you're a total asshole. I'm well aware that you're just trying to get points for me, but I'd think you'd actually want me to like you before I did. Or do you really just think that highly of yourself? That girls will fall all over you because you're an asshole to them? It's not a turn on."

Luke's brow creases. "What are you talking about?"

His feigned innocence does nothing for my mood. "Don't be dumb. You know exactly what I'm talking about. You're playing that stupid game."

He can't seriously expect me to believe he isn't. There's no way. No one would really be dumb enough to believe that.

"What game? You're confusing the hell out of me." He laughs when he says it.

The sound makes me want to rip my hair out. "That fucking sex game."

He shrugs, his eyes wide. I guess there's something to be said about his persistence to maintain the lie that he doesn't have anything to do with the game.

"You know what? Forget about it." I'm done with this. We're not going to work.

I turn to walk to my bag to get my water bottle, but his fingers close around my bicep and he whips me back around to face him. My hand reaches out for his shoulder to steady myself.

"Look, I know you just met me, but you need to trust me. I'm not going to drop you. If you keep freaking out, someone's going to get hurt and it's probably going to be you. Try a little harder." It sounds like a threat, but I'm not sure he meant it that way.

For someone who said he wanted me, he's doing a fantastic impression of someone who doesn't give a shit about my feelings. He has no idea how hard it is for me to dance with him. Not that he would care even if he knew. "Screw you. I am trying. I don't need to trust you. I don't even need to dance with you."

"You don't have to like me, Sadie. Hell, you don't even have to tolerate me, but you do need to dance with me. There aren't any other partners." He takes a step closer to me, like he really wants me to get the point. "Do you want a chance at Fall Showcase? Or in London? Because you sure as hell aren't showing it, and I'll be damned if you fuck up my career with your bullshit."

Luke doesn't understand how badly I want those opportunities. And he doesn't understand that part of the reason is because I don't know how to not be a dancer. Dance has defined me for so long, if I left, I wouldn't have anything. He doesn't understand that my fear over what would happen to me if I quit, if I gave up right now, is the only thing that's keeping me in the same room as him.

His fingers tighten around my arm. He's trapping me here. I don't have a choice. I need to get away.

I wrench my arm out of his grasp. "Don't touch me. Don't even talk to me. I want nothing to do with you unless I'm being forced to spend time with you in this studio."

He glares at my arm like it burned him when I pulled it away. "No one is forcing you to be here. If you want to succeed then suck it up and dance. That's your only option if you're going to stay."

It's not my only option. There has to be some way around this. I can't dance with him. We just proved that.

Luke throws his hands up in the air, clearly frustrated with the situation and with me. "If you miss New York so much, why don't you just go back?"

I'm sick of fighting. I just want to forget. "Maybe I will."

I don't understand. An hour ago, he had me pressed up against a wall, ready to kiss me, but now it's like nothing happened between us. Well, that's fine with me. I prefer not having my world turned upside down whenever he's around.

He doesn't know how much his words hurt. L.A. is just another place for me to feel out of place. Another place to feel like I don't belong. I back toward the door.

Patrick was right. I don't know why I even bother to try. Things aren't ever going to go back to the way they were.

Luke yells my name, but I run before he can catch me.

Running keeps me safe. People can't leave you if you can outrun them.

THE HIT LIST UPDATE
September 12

Greetings from The Hit List. I'm just going to jump right in with the reason I'm posting before the week is up. Consider this a friendly reminder because I will only say it once. A lot of our girls are starting to work with partners for an upcoming show, which will require long hours and excessive touching. If you enter a relationship with any girl, I don't care if she is on the list or not, you cannot collect points for her. If you want to cheat on your girl and go after other girls to collect points, that's your prerogative. Frankly, I don't give a shit either way.

Now that we've gotten that out of the way, here are the latest poll standings, just because I'm nice.

Brielle Watkins	18%
Rachel Barrons	16%
Sadie Bryant	15%
Courtney Turner	12%
Noelle Sanstrohm	11%
Rebecca Hemsworth	7%
Jessie Freeman	6%
Samantha Jameson	6%
Ashlynn Jenkins	5%
Kate Williams	4%

As always, happy hitting!

~ THE HIT MAN

6

How's L.A.?

If I tell Patrick the truth, I'll look pathetic. But he probably wouldn't care either way.

I type out a response without thinking. If he knows I'm unhappy, maybe he'll answer me back again.

L.A. sucks. Wish I were home again. How's NYBC?

My phone vibrates as the call screen wipes out my message. I don't want to fight with my mom today, but if I don't answer I probably won't talk to her for another month. When I called her earlier, I'd actually felt like chatting.

Sometimes it's nice to give her a taste of her own medicine and ignore her for a while. Except she doesn't care. She'll just hang up and forget all about it in less than five minutes.

"Hi, Mom."

"Sadie, I'm in a meeting. What did you need?" She sounds rushed, like she doesn't have time to deal with me.

But that's not new. That's just her.

This was such a mistake, but I can't just hang up. "Nothing. I just thought I'd see how you were doing."

People talk faintly in the background. Apparently her meeting continues without her. "Can we talk later? I'm right in the middle of something." Her voice continues, but she's quieter, like she pulled the phone away from her ear. I can barely hear what she says to the person she's talking to, but it freezes the blood in my veins.

"No, I won't accept that. I can't even buy another apartment with that kind of money." Something rustles against the speaker and she's back with me. "Sadie, I have to go. Call me later, okay?"

Anger surges through me. "You're selling the loft?"

She sighs into the phone. "I don't need that much space. With you in L.A., it's the only thing that makes sense. Don't worry about your stuff. I'll pack it up and put it in storage until you need it."

"I don't care about my stuff. You can't just move. What if I want to come home?" A very real option until now. I can't go home if I don't have a home to go back to.

"We'll talk about this later." Her voice takes on a forceful tone, but I'm not a little girl anymore and it's useless on me now.

"Answer it."

We sit on the couch in my living room. I fumble with the phone, finally getting it on speaker and setting it on the coffee table so we can both hear.

"Hello?" My hands shake. I slide them under my thighs to stop it, but it doesn't really help.

"Sadie? This is Eleanor from Jeté *Magazine. I wanted to talk to you about doing an article with you and Patrick."*

Out of all the things I expected, this was definitely not one of them. I grin, looking over at Patrick. "No freaking way."

"Excuse me?"

Patrick picks up the phone frantically. "She means yes. That would be a yes."

"No, we'll talk about it now. I grew up in that loft. You can't just sell it."

The letter feels heavy in my hands. I'm going to vomit. The cold tile on the wall of the bathroom does little to calm my nerves. I slide my finger under the edge of the envelope.

We are pleased to inform you that you have been accepted into Los Angeles Conservatory for the Arts.

"Where will I go when I come back to New York? That's my home."

"I'm not going to argue with you about this. We'll talk later." She hangs up before I can say anything else.

I'm so glad I'm a part of a family where my opinion doesn't mean shit.

My email pings. Miss Catherine never has anything nice to say when she sends emails. I don't know why I expected her to.

I need to see you in my office tomorrow morning before class. Leaving rehearsal early will not be tolerated.

I don't want the reminder of how much I'm screwing up at The Conservatory. Another email replaces it as soon as I drag it to the trash. I can't escape The Hit List. Another damn update. I hope the rest of girls involved aren't as dumb as The Hit Man thinks we are.

The comments underneath the post are similar to the other posts. Guys cheering him on and telling him to "tap that ass." Girls wondering what makes them so different from the girls chosen as the top ten. I'd gladly give them my spot. Other girls criticize him for promoting sex as a chess game in which girls are just pawns.

I don't know why I'm even still subscribed to the damn blog. It obviously won't be talking about anything useful anymore.

Today sucks. If I could get away with sleeping for the rest of the semester, I would do it in a heartbeat.

My phone beeps with more incoming email. The drafted text to Patrick pops back up on the screen. I delete it and throw my phone across the room. I don't need that temptation again.

Someone bumps into the door. It's either Brielle or someone not paying attention to where they're going. A key turns in the tumbler and Brielle pushes through the door, balancing her dance bag, her book bag, and an iced coffee as she tries to get into the room.

"Hey, where were you? You were gone when I went to check the studio." She sets her coffee on the end table and looks over at me.

I turn to look at the ceiling again. I don't even know what to feel anymore. I don't really care about anything right now.

"You okay?" She tosses her dance bag onto her bed. Unzipping it, she takes out a water bottle and her iPod and tosses them onto her pillow.

I don't look at her when I answer. "Fine." My voice sounds hollow.

She raises an eyebrow at me. "You don't look fine."

"I am."

I'm fine with partnering Luke. I'm fine with Patrick texting me. I'm fine with my mom selling the loft. I'm fine with being a sex object on some list. And I'm fine with knowing I'm screwing up every possible chance of making it to Fall Showcase or London.

I'm just fine.

"Fine." She shoves a sweatshirt in her dresser more forcefully than she needs to and it rattles her makeup on top.

I glance over at her. Her face scrunches up and her eyebrows pull together. I chew on my lip as I war with myself. If I tell her, it just opens me up to hurt. But I already hurt so much.

"People suck."

She sits down on the bed next to me. "Dang. What happened?" Her smile falls into a look of concern.

I shake my head and run my hand along the wall, feeling the imperfections in the paint. "A lot of things. My mom is selling our loft. Patrick texted me. It's all just dumb."

She looks over at me and shrugs, a sad smile on her face. "People suck."

I smile back, feeling the understanding between us more in those two words than in any other comforting words she could offer.

"Hey, did you hear about those two theater kids that got expelled today?"

"No. Why?"

"Apparently they were fighting in the hallway." She flops onto her own bed and stares up at the ceiling.

There couldn't have been more than one fight today. "I'm pretty sure I saw that on my way to rehearsal. They were trying to sleep with the same girl. Then one got mad at the other and they were throwing punches."

She turns to look at me. "Holy shit. That's insane."

"No kidding." I lean back against the wall. The Hit List needs to just disappear.

"I've heard some crazy shit about that game." Her eyes widen.

"Like what?" I roll onto my side and prop my head onto my elbow.

"Like the things some of those boys have done. I heard one of them slept with like five girls in one night. I have no idea who it was though."

I crinkle my nose. "That's gross."

How can people do that? It doesn't take any kind of connection to have sex, but it should. Are they that desperate for status that they're willing to do whatever it takes for the points?

She shrugs. "I think it's kind of fun to be at the top of the list."

"Why?" I can't even imagine why that would ever be a good thing.

"Think about it. You have tons of guys trying to be with you. You'd basically be able to get them to do whatever you want. You have power." She rolls onto her stomach.

"No, thanks. I don't want that kind of power."

No one should want that kind of power. It's sick. And it's not any better than the boys playing the game.

"I've been trying to figure out who's behind it. There are so many options. For instance, Luke."

I sigh and roll onto my stomach. "What makes you think it's Luke?"

She narrows her eyes. "Have you met Luke?"

Has she? The real Luke, not the one that flirts with every girl he comes into contact with. The one who tries to get to know me outside of that stupid article. The one who does his best to take care of me after I almost passed out in rehearsal.

"I don't think it's Luke."

She lies on her stomach and kicks her legs back and forth. She kicks faster as light dances in her eyes. "Okay. How about Nathan? Have you met him yet? He's a dick, too."

"No."

One of her legs hits the wall. Someone in the room next door knocks back and she glares at the wall behind her. "No he isn't behind it, or no you haven't met him?"

I bury my face in my pillow. I don't want to talk about this anymore.

"I guess it could be him. I still think it's Luke though."

I hold up my hand. My head feels like it's going to explode. "Please stop." It's bad enough that I can't seem to escape the topic of The Hit List outside of my room, but I shouldn't have to deal with it here.

"Fine. How was rehearsal?"

I roll my eyes, not really excited that out of everything, she chose to talk about this instead. "Terrible. I almost passed out."

She narrows her eyes at me. "Why?"

"I think I forgot to breathe." It doesn't help that I've been worried about everything since I got to L.A.

"How exactly did you forget to breathe? That's like an automatic response. You shouldn't have to think about it." She stares at me like she's expecting something more believable.

But I don't have a better answer. "I'm not really sure, but I wouldn't recommend it."

She slides off the bed and walks to her computer. "You're stressed. You shouldn't be this stressed."

I couldn't agree more. "I'm fine. I'm just adjusting."

"I know it's hard to dance with someone new and this might sound insensitive, but you kind of have to get over it."

I glare at her. Just because we had a moment of sharing doesn't mean she knows anything about me. "You're right. That sounds extremely insensitive."

She sighs. "That's not how I meant it. If you're having problems, we need to find someone else you can dance with. Then you can practice and be okay when you're in class."

She makes it sound so easy. Because I have so much extra time in my ten-hour days filled with dancing and other classes. Those few spare minutes at night when I half-ass my homework don't really matter. I'm sure I could spare some of those.

"I don't have time to dance with someone else. And I don't need to dance with someone else."

Luke's my partner, and like it or not, I need to get over my shit and just dance with him. No matter how hard it might be for me.

She shrugs. "Fine. No one's going to say anything about it. Not everyone gets along with their partner, but we all need to rehearse."

It's tempting, but there isn't anyone else I'd want to partner with. Being with Luke isn't the issue. It's having a partner at all. I just don't want to do it.

"Adam would probably be willing to help you out, if you want. You just have to ask." She swivels back and forth in her chair.

It's not a bad idea. I'd already requested Adam as my partner anyway. She could have come up with something worse.

"It's just a thought. You don't have to. I'd prefer not to have to break in a new roommate when you end up leaving because you can't figure this partner stuff out, but whatevs." A look of indifference crosses her face, but I can see the little worry lines creasing her forehead as she stares out the window.

It won't hurt me to try. Hopefully.

As much as it annoys me to admit that I might have to depend on someone else again, my need to do well in L.A. overpowers it. The longer I struggle with Luke, the faster London slips through my fingers. The sooner I'll be forced to deal with what I'll do when I don't have dance anymore. I pull the door open and stare out into the hallway.

"See you later." The corner of her mouth tips up briefly.

I don't acknowledge her. If I stop now, I might not ask Adam at all. He's my one chance to get this right. I don't know what I'll do if he doesn't want to help me.

Adam's room is down a different hall than ours. He opens the door as soon as I knock. "Hey."

I glance into his room, trying to gauge whether I'm keeping him from doing something. "Can we talk?"

"Yeah." He looks back into his room at his roommate. "But let's go out. James is trying to study."

"Hey, James." I lean into the doorway and wave at him while Adam grabs his cell phone off his desk.

He waves back at me and jumps off the bed. "Hey, Sadie. I was wondering if maybe you wanted to get dinner sometime?" He looks down at his feet when he's finished talking, obviously nervous.

Adam coughs beside us as he tries to muffle his laughter. I elbow him in the ribs and his laughter turns to real coughing.

"That's really sweet of you, James, but I'm so busy I don't really have time to date. I'm sorry." It's not really a lie anymore, but I feel kind of bad saying no. James is probably the sweetest guy that's asked me out in a long time. And the offer seems genuine coming from him. There's no way someone as nice as him is involved with the people behind The Hit List.

James's face drops. "Oh, that's okay, just thought I'd ask."

"I have the studio reserved tonight. Let's go there." Adam pushes me out into the hallway.

I stumble over my feet and glare at him.

He closes the door behind us. "You know, James isn't playing that game. So if you did actually want to go out with him, it's not like he'd try to use you for points."

"How do you know?" It's hard to give anyone the benefit of the doubt when it comes to The Hit List. James genuinely seems like a nice guy and if Adam thinks he's not involved, I feel a little safer. But not safe enough for a date.

Adam shrugs. "I've known him for a while now. He's not the type."

I follow Adam through the now familiar halls. They're dark and empty, with only every third light illuminated. I'm glad Adam is with me and I don't have to walk through here by myself. It's creepy.

Two girls from the music department walk toward us down the hallway. One is in a class with me. She's hard to miss with her bright pink hair. They talk quietly to each other, but as they get closer, I can make out their words.

The brunette I don't recognize plays with a strand of her hair as she walks. "I just don't understand why he hasn't called. It was amazing. I would think he'd want to do it again."

I can only imagine why she's upset. Probably another victim.

"I saw him flirting with Betsy today in Intro to Theater. Maybe it wasn't as amazing as you think." The pink-haired girl shrugs. She doesn't look concerned about either her friend's or Betsy's well-being.

I glance at Adam, but he doesn't give anything away. I'm not even sure he's paying any attention to them. The girls continue to walk down the hallway and their voices get too quiet for me to hear any more.

Luke's roommate, Nathan, approaches us from the opposite direction. He would be attractive if I'd never spoken to him. His green eyes were the thing that drew me in, but then he opened his mouth.

His black hair is a mess. He's either just come from rehearsal or from some girl's room. He gives me the head nod when he's a couple feet away. His sleazy smile gives me the creeps. "Hey, sexy. Want to come over later?"

Eww. Not in a million years.

I grimace. "No, thanks. I'll pass."

"Suit yourself. It's only a matter of time before you give in to this." He lifts his shirt and gestures to his abs.

No. That's just sick. I don't want anything to do with him ever.

Adam curls his lip. "Didn't you get chlamydia last year from sleeping with some random girl?"

Nathan smiles and winks at me. "I think that random girl was her roommate, but don't worry. I have a clean bill of health now."

He's about as far from attractive as he can possibly get. "Something to be proud of."

That's probably all he has to be proud of.

"You know where I live." Nathan rounds a corner down the hall.

Adam stares at the hallway where he disappeared. "It's unnatural how much you and Brielle get hit on."

"It's because of that game. These guys are running around trying to sleep with every girl on campus."

I don't even understand how they would get someone to sleep with them after everyone in school found out about the game. No one is that desperate. And if they are, they need higher standards.

He stops walking and looks at me. "You know, not every guy at this school is playing that game. Some of them might actually be interested in dating you. Like James."

"Could have fooled me."

Brandon is in the studio when we arrive. He looks like he's almost finished. A towel drapes around his neck and a tank top sticks to his chest, the visible skin flushed from his workout.

Adam puts a hand on the door to push it open.

"Shouldn't we wait until he's done?"

"I have time reserved. We're fine."

Brandon raises his hand in a wave as we enter the studio. "Hey, guys. I was just leaving."

"Hey," Adam says.

I give Brandon a small wave. The last time I saw him, I was passing out. Not exactly the best first impression for one of the people who gets to vote for me for Fall Showcase.

"Are you feeling better?" He wipes his face and throws the towel over his shoulder. His brown hair is slicked back against his head, but a few spikes stick up here and there.

Adam frowns at me, confused, and it takes me a second to remember that he doesn't know I almost passed out today.

"Yeah, thanks. It's just been a rough week."

Brandon slides his iPod into the pocket in his pants. "Well, get used to that. You're going to have a lot of those around here."

Adam laughs. "I wish I could say he was lying." He puts an arm around my shoulder and pulls me into his side.

It's awkward, but I'd rather be closer to Adam than Brandon. I don't pull away.

"I wouldn't worry so much if I were you. From what I've seen, you stand a good chance of making it into Fall Showcase and of being in the running for London." Brandon picks up his stuff and walks toward the door.

I turn to watch him. I like it better when there's distance between us. He gives me a weird vibe. "Isn't it a little unfair that the seniors get to judge who makes it into Fall Showcase? Why wouldn't you all just vote for yourselves?"

Brandon takes a drink of his water. "Seniors get a free pass to Fall Showcase."

"Of course." I guess it makes sense that they should automatically be in one of the last shows they'll get in front of the talent agencies.

"I look forward to seeing you in rehearsal, Sadie." Brandon pushes through the door and disappears into the hallway.

Adam whistles as the door closes behind Brandon.

"What?"

Adam is hard to read. His face is guarded and I can't tell what he's thinking. "Just be careful. If you're worried about anyone playing that game, it should be Brandon. It wouldn't surprise me if he's the brains behind the whole thing."

"What are you talking about?" Something about Brandon rubs me the wrong way, but despite that, he's been one of the nicest people in L.A. so far.

"I'm not saying not to trust Brandon because I'm sure he can be really nice, but he and Luke don't exactly get along. I don't think he would toy with you just to get to Luke, but you never know." He grabs my hand and pulls me into the middle of the studio.

"That's crazy."

What difference would it make anyway? Luke doesn't like me so why would it affect him in the least if Brandon pays me any attention.

Adam laughs. "I never said it wasn't. Just watch your back. There's been a target on it since you got here."

"So I've noticed."

It feels like people have been against me from day one. I wish I could convince myself that I'm blowing everything out of proportion. But Adam's right.

"I worry about you and Brielle since you're both on the top ten list. I shouldn't have to worry this much about people."

I laugh. He must not see half the shit that Brielle does. "I don't think you have to worry about Brielle. She seems like she can hold her own. And she's playing her own game by leading them on."

His brow pulls together in confusion. "She wasn't always like that. She was really shy last year when she started here. I don't know what happened, but it was like a switch got flipped. The city got to her, I guess. She started caring more about sleeping around and partying than going to class. That's what got her in trouble with Miss Catherine. I just don't want to see her have a breakdown because of this game."

I don't want to see that either. I can't handle it if we both go off the deep end. "She'll be okay."

"What about you? Are you okay with everything? Is it weird that everyone knows you already?"

I shrug. I'd rather no one knew me because I probably wouldn't have ended up in the game, but there's nothing I can do about that now. "People can be weird about it, but I'm fine."

"Well, if it's any consolation, I liked the article about you in *Jeté Magazine*."

"It's not, but thanks." It's a constant reminder of my failure. And now it's a constant reminder that everywhere I go in the dance world, everyone will already know about me, making my fresh start impossible.

"What did you want to talk about?" He sits down on the floor, stretching out his legs.

He looks sincere and it makes me want to tell him about everything, but I don't think I'm ready to do that yet.

I take a deep breath. "I need help partnering."

He runs a hand through his hair and gives me a crooked smile. "You've done it before. It's kind of like riding a bike. Once you start getting into it again, it'll all come back to you."

If only it were that easy. I would give anything for that to be my problem. "That's not the issue. I know I can partner. It's not like I lost it in the last year."

"You're confusing me. You can't partner, but you can?" He looks like he's trying to do calculus in his head.

I sigh. I need to tell him enough so he'll understand, even though I don't want to tell him anything at all. He deserves some kind of explanation if he's willing to take the time to work with me. It's rude to expect him to help me with no reason why.

"I haven't partnered with anyone since my injury. The whole reason I got injured in the first place was because a lift went wrong."

"You're scared."

I can't meet his eyes. I don't want to see the pity. I never wanted people to feel sorry for me.

I don't want to talk about this, to tell him that I'm scared I'll get hurt again, to tell him Patrick shattered any future trust I would ever have with another partner.

"What if I get hurt again and I can't dance anymore?" It's a very real possibility.

He laughs. It booms off the walls and lightens my mood a little. "No pressure."

I shove his arm playfully. "I don't think you'll drop me."

"I'll help you in any way I can, but at some point you're going to have to dance with Luke." He looks up at me from his position on the floor. There's sadness in his eyes.

I'm well aware of that, but the thought of a repeat of today's rehearsal is sickening. "I just want to be able to get used to lifts again without him."

Walking to the stereo, he turns the music up. "Let's take it slow. Dance with me. No choreography, just us." He stands up straight when he comes back to me. It makes him look more confident.

He wraps his arm around my waist and grabs my right hand with his left. We dance around the studio, using every inch of space. He's good at improvising and he pulls me into small familiar lifts from time to time. It reminds me of dancing with Patrick before everything fell apart and he left. Familiar and safe. The way it should be with Luke.

The song ends and he pulls me into a hug. "You did great, Sadie. So, now the question is—"

"Why can't you dance like that with me?" Luke asks from the doorway.

7

Luke leans against the doorframe of the studio. He pushes off against the wood and walks toward us. I'm frozen in Adam's arms, but Adam solves that problem for me when he steps forward between me and Luke and his arms fall from around me.

I silently curse at him for eliminating my buffer against Luke. I feel like I've done something wrong, but I shouldn't. This is probably the best thing I've done for myself in months.

"Hey, Luke," Adam says.

"Hi." Anger rolls off Luke's body in waves.

He has no right to be angry.

"I'm just going to go," Adam says, picking up his bag. "Watch yourself, Morrison."

I plead for Adam to stay with my eyes, to help me explain, but I know he can't. He turns back to me once he's behind Luke and mouths the words "talk to him."

Yeah, right.

Adam disappears into the hallway and I'm left alone in the studio with Luke.

"What are you doing here?" I cross my arms over my chest. Anger is the only thing I have. If I can stay angry, I won't get hurt.

"I could ask you the same thing." His eyes burn into me.

I see the jealousy he's feeling, but I don't care. I'm doing this to be a better dancer. Whatever it takes. That's what I told myself before I left New York. Whatever you have to do to make your dream come true, do it without regret. Whatever it takes to make it to Fall Showcase and London. Whatever it takes to keep dancing.

"It's not a crime to dance with someone else." My right hand finds my hip, my other clenching into a fist at my side.

"It is when it interferes with our partnership. You know he's gay, right? He doesn't want to get in your pants no matter what you do. I mean, you can't possibly be that dense." He smirks at me, knowing his words have cut deep.

He's just crossed a line he's not coming back from. Not everyone gets involved with someone from the opposite sex because they're interested in some sort of sexual relationship. It feels cheap that he would even suggest something like that.

I glare at him. "Fuck you, Luke."

He runs his hands through his hair and takes a deep breath. "Can we start over? I'm sorry I said that stuff to you earlier. This year is really important to me. I can't afford to screw it up."

He couldn't screw up if he tried. He'll always have the safety net of his parents to pull him out of whatever situation he gets into. If I screw up this stage in his life, he'll still have his talent and his parents to fall back on.

"Your parents are head of the department. I don't think you have anything to worry about." They wouldn't let him fail.

"Which makes it that much harder to break into this business. People look at me like I'm some spoiled little rich kid," he says, pointing at his chest. "My parents are in charge of the dance department at one of the most prestigious performing arts schools in the country and the only reason I got in is because I'm their child."

I frown. He may have an in with his parents being who they are, but it still took some sort of talent to get him where he is. Talent I've seen. Talent that makes him one of the best in the school. "That's not true. You're an amazing dancer."

He smiles bitterly. "No one sees that. Not the talent scouts. Not the people who are out there offering jobs. They see my parents' name. They see I have raw talent, but I don't have the best extensions and sometimes my turnout isn't there."

I smile at the criticisms he holds against himself because I've been there. One flaw in an otherwise breathtaking performance is always the focus of attention. A sickled foot, a bent knee, a missed count.

People are paid to find flaws in us. It doesn't matter how hard we try, there will always be something and it's hard to be okay with that. It's hard not to take every thing they say to heart. It's not just injuries that destroy dancers. It's imperfections.

The little things are a dancer's downfall. Because when someone wants to find something wrong, they will. We're not perfect, and we never will be.

"They see flaws that my parents' child should have left behind by age ten. They focus on every thing that sets me apart from being just like them. I had access to some of the best teachers in the world. I should be perfect."

I can see the pain in his eyes even though he tries to cover it with anger. He sounds so deflated, like these people have the power to decide who he is.

My heart bleeds for him. He strives for perfection, but he's only human. I learned a long time ago that internalizing every flaw, every criticism, slowly sucks the life out of you if you don't create a balance. Dancing becomes a chore. And the day that happens is the day you should walk away.

"It's not always about perfect technique. You've got to have heart, too."

The dark blue in his eyes turns to ice and he crosses his arms over his chest. "Well, that's definitely your area of expertise. I hear my parents talk about you. I've seen your audition tapes. You don't just dance, you shine. I can't take my eyes off you as soon as you step out onto the floor. Hands down, you're the best dancer at this school."

I stare at him, daring him to add a sarcastic comment about how I'll never surpass his talent, but it doesn't come. I want to tell him about my own struggles in New York. About the time a teacher told me I could never be a ballerina at the age of eleven because I didn't have the body type and recommended I take diet pills. Or the time when I was fifteen and a director told me I didn't have thick enough skin to make it in this world because I cried at an audition when he called me fat. Or the time last year when I wanted to give up on my dream because the last person I ever thought would leave me did.

But I can't. I can't be vulnerable with him. He may trust me enough to share his fears, but I refuse to let someone in like that again. I will never trust anyone enough for that.

"I thought you were the best dancer at the school." My goal is to throw his words back in his face, but when I meet his gaze, I don't find the usual cocky attitude I've gotten used to from Luke. Instead, he looks a little lost and more than a little scared.

I shouldn't have said it.

He shakes his head, a sad smile on his lips. "We both know that's not really true. I've gotten used to playing the part. I'm successful by association. I get jobs because of my parents' positions. That's my form of success, and I can't afford to lose it. If I can't maintain that, I won't have anything left." His words are soft, so soft that I'm not sure I heard him right. His eyes search mine for some sign that I understand him.

This is exactly why I can't trust him. "You don't love dancing, you love success. If that's the case, you'll never be truly successful because the minute you step out on that stage, the whole world will know dancing isn't the most important thing in your life."

He takes a step closer to me and runs his hand through his hair. "You don't get it. This is what I want. I want to be the best. I want to deserve all the shit that appears for me at the snap of my parents' fingers. I don't want to live under their shadow anymore, and I need the best dancer at The Conservatory to help me get there."

I can't help my smile. It's validating to hear, especially since I feel like I'm doing something wrong every time I'm around a faculty member.

"How can we fix this partnership?" His eyes plead with me.

I'm not sure I even want to fix it. Trusting him won't make my life any easier. If anything, it'll make it more complicated. "It's not my business whether or not you're playing the sex game, but you need to stop trying to play for me if you are."

He sighs and rubs his palms against his eyes. "I've told you. I'm not playing that game. What are you really worried about?" He scans my face as I try to look as impassive as possible.

"I don't want to talk about it."

He runs a hand through his hair again, clearly frustrated with me. His hair stays pushed back away from his face this time. "Do you trust me?"

I stare at him, my jaw tightening as his brow creases. "No."

"That's how we fix this. If you won't open yourself up to any kind of relationship with me, then it's no wonder you can't trust me." He takes a step closer to me.

A humorless laugh escapes my lips. "I don't want any kind of relationship with you."

"You already have one. We're partners."

He's right and nothing I can do is going to get me a new partner at this point. I have to at least try to work with him. I'll regret it if I don't.

"I'll try to dance with you, but I don't want to be anything more with you than partners."

I can handle this. I can control my own emotions. I can make sure this partnership doesn't turn out like my last one. After all, not every partnership leads to a romantic relationship. People dance together all the time without feelings getting involved.

I'll dance with Luke. I'll even give him the benefit of the doubt and believe that he isn't playing the game. He's just a flirt. He doesn't want anything from me and all I want from him is a partnership to get me to Fall Showcase and London.

As long as I remember that, I should be fine.

———————

Sleep is my enemy.

I thrash against my blankets for the third time in the last ten minutes. I don't know why I'm even bothering anymore. It's just after midnight and I should have been asleep hours ago, but now the only thing I can focus on is how I need to be up in five hours to be at rehearsal on time.

Brielle is fast asleep in her bed on the other side of the room and I'm careful not to wake her as I grab my iPod and shoes. I don't waste time changing clothes. I'm already in shorts and a tank top and for what I have planned, it's perfect. Stepping outside our room, I slide on my flip-flops and walk down to the lobby. I don't care that we have a ten o'clock curfew. No one's out here to catch me.

Back home when I couldn't sleep, I would sneak out to the fire escape and work on my technique. Barre exercises set to the tune of New York City traffic are the most relaxing things in the world. It won't be the same here, but it might help me fall asleep.

The steady hum of cars from the freeway drifts into the open space. I turn on the music and the opening piano notes from "Clair de Lune" take over my senses. Using the brick wall as a barre, I fall into the comfortable rhythm of the exercises I mastered years ago and have committed to muscle memory.

The moonlight reflects off the now-still water in the fountain and onto the grass in front of me. The hustle and bustle from the city has gone indoors for the night. I'm alone. It's peaceful in the darkness, and I can pretend like I don't have a million things to worry about.

It's been so long since I've danced just for me. I walk out onto a patch of grass next to the fountain and slip off my shoes. Tucking my iPod into the jogging strap wrapped around my bicep, I start to dance.

It's freeing. My tension falls away as I focus on pointing my feet at every opportunity or pulling up into a deliberate flex with my knee bent to break my lines. I pull myself into a pirouette. Blades of grass break beneath my foot from the friction.

I step out into an arabesque penchée and grab my leg behind me with my right hand to pull it up. My left arm stays in front of me for balance. I close my eyes, reveling in the tingles in my hip as I push myself just past my flexibility.

The foot I'm standing on grips the grass and dirt beneath me, but I'm facing down a slight incline and I can feel my body slightly shift forward as my muscles work to keep me upright. It's hard to catch myself in this position and I fight with my balance to stay standing.

A breeze floats through the courtyard, tickling my face with my hair. I shiver against the sensation. My center of balance shifts and I'm forced to let go of my leg so I don't face plant on the lawn. My right leg lowers a little to balance out my body as my right arm falls forward.

A flash of movement in front of me catches my attention before two strong hands grip mine and hold me up. I look up to see Luke, his hands still firmly clasped around mine to keep me from falling. I drop my leg behind me and he lets go of my left hand. He raises the other one above us both and twirls me.

"Where did you come from?" I watch him, but he doesn't say a word.

He pulls the ear buds from my ears and removes my iPod, tossing it onto the grass a few feet away from us. Without missing a beat, he continues to lead me through the choreography we'd learned during audition week. It wasn't designed to be a partner dance, but it works when Luke makes the changes. And even though we fumble through some of the steps and transitions because he's improvising as we go, it's okay. For this moment, I can forget about everything else that's happened between us. In this moment, I just dance.

The eight count in my head becomes our music. His hand travels down my arm and onto my cheek as he takes a step closer to me. His thumb swipes across my cheekbone as my hands find his waist, silently pleading with him to stay.

He steps past me. His hand moves to my neck and I lean backward to stay close to him, to maintain contact. His hand lowers with me and he holds me up by the back of my neck, my torso and thighs parallel to the ground. I rise up onto the balls of my feet. My toes dig into the dirt. Arching my back, I roll up to a standing position and turn to face him again.

His hand finds mine when he turns toward me and with his fingers threaded through mine, he pushes me back once again until my hair brushes the grass beneath me. Pulling me forward, he leans toward me and I jump to wrap my legs around him. My arms lock behind his neck and I curl my body as close to him as I can. His arms close briefly around my back before he straightens them out behind me. My legs fall and my body uncoils as I hang off him, his arms under mine. He holds me off the ground, but flat against his chest. Slowly, I feel his arms close around me again.

He holds me for longer than the dance allows, and I take it as a cue that we're done. But he doesn't release me. I stay suspended in his arms as time passes us by in the moonlit courtyard. He watches me, barely far away enough to move his face in front of mine.

I glance down at his lips. I want him to close the distance, but he doesn't. His eyes never leave mine as the rise and fall of our chests slow, never saying a word, never breaking the moment. I can feel his heart beat against my skin. It stutters and I know he feels exactly the same way.

I can't feel this way about him. And as if my body has suddenly caught up with my mind, my heart races for a whole different reason. We're not supposed to be like this, not close to each other, not like we're more than partners. He notices as my body stiffens. His hands slide down to my waist and he sets me back on the ground.

"I told you we could make this work." His eyes sparkle with pride.

My mind is clearer without his body pressed up against mine. Half a dance doesn't mean anything. It definitely doesn't mean I can trust him. Out of everyone here, if he gets the opportunity to step out of his parents' shadow, he'll take it without a second thought.

I take a step away from him, letting the cool air wash over my slick skin. "We can't dance together, Luke." I sound breathless.

He shakes his head, a sad smile breaking on his lips. "We just did."

He walks away from me, never giving me a backward glance, leaving me alone in the cold moonlight with an empty heart.

8

Miss Catherine looks up from her computer, her piercing eyes staring through me. I'm not in the mood to be scared of her today and I stare back passively. The only thing that's been on my mind this morning is dancing with Luke.

I've never been this tense. Dancing with Luke had taken some of the stress away for a little while. Even though I won't admit it to him, we danced amazingly last night. It confuses me.

I shouldn't be able to dance that way with Luke. The only other person I could do that with was Patrick, but I had a connection with Patrick. I try to ignore it and call it something else, but maybe I have that connection with Luke, too.

No. I can't have that with Luke. I can't have that with anyone.

"I'm sure you're aware you're here to master your talent. I shouldn't have to remind you that attending class is the best way to do that," Miss Catherine says.

I'm not in the mood to keep my attitude in check. "In all fairness, there was a reason I requested Adam as my partner. I have issues dancing with people. That's why I haven't been doing it."

She narrows her eyes at me. "You will partner with whomever this school deems is the best partner for you. If you don't like it, you're free to leave. Do you want to leave, Ms. Bryant?"

She knows I don't. I take a deep breath. I can't be rude. I'll get myself thrown out of school.

"No."

"Good. You need to work on your discipline. Your dancing will improve greatly."

"Okay." I have discipline. I'd like to see her show some restraint after dealing with her son and being up all night.

"I'm pulling you and Luke out of your other classes today to make up your missed practice yesterday. Miss Tasha and Brandon had to rearrange their schedules for this, so you should make sure to thank them."

I stare at the wall next to me. "Fine. Can I go?"

She waves a hand at me to dismiss me from her office.

"One more thing."

I turn back around to face her and she looks up from her desk.

"Lose the attitude, Ms. Bryant. It doesn't suit you and it will get you nowhere in this business."

I smile bitterly at her, wrench open the door, and stalk out of her office.

Rehearsal will be hell with the mood I'm in. I don't want to put up with anyone at the moment, least of all Luke.

Luke stands ten feet away from the door of the studio and smiles when he sees my expression. "Looks like you had a nice chat."

"Shut up." I don't bother to wait for him as I walk toward the studio. I would settle for taking out my anger on him instead of his mother, but it's probably best if I don't. As long as he doesn't push me, I should be fine. Which means it'll probably take less than ten minutes for me to snap at him.

He runs to catch up to me. "I know she's not the nicest sometimes, but she really does know what she's talking about."

I whirl around on him and he has to step to the side to keep from running into me. "Were you eavesdropping?" It's bad enough that I have to spend most of my time with him, but he doesn't need to know everything that's going on with me—especially when it involves me getting scolded by his mother.

His eyes widen with terror. "No, I just assumed she said something you didn't want to hear since you stormed out of her office."

I take a deep breath. I need to get away from everyone right now, but I can't. I need to practice or I'll get in more trouble. I'd rather dance with Luke than get called to Miss Catherine's office again. "Let's just get this rehearsal over with."

Miss Tasha and Brandon are already in the studio when we arrive. Brandon smiles at us, but Miss Tasha looks annoyed that she has to be here.

It only takes fifteen minutes of warm-ups for Tasha to start in on us.

"Okay, this is how it's going to work. You two," she points at us, "have royally pissed me off with your issues. I don't have time for it. You don't either if you have any hopes of making it through tryouts." She looks between the two of us until we nod. Her hands find their place on her hips. If she's already starting that then it's going to be one hell of a practice.

"We missed one practice. We're fine," Luke says.

She takes a deep breath, like she's trying to forget she heard him, before she continues. "You're going to stay in this room until you figure your shit out. If either of you leave before rehearsal is over, I will make sure you don't have a chance in hell of making Fall Showcase. And you can kiss London goodbye. Do I make myself clear?" Her fingers drum against her hip bones.

I hope we can avoid rehearsals like this in the future.

"Crystal." I'm starting to wonder if they put something in the water here to make everyone a raging bitch.

She stares at us for a couple seconds, like she's trying to be intimidating, before she turns around and motions for Brandon to come over to her. "You have fifteen minutes to warm up before we start on choreography," she says, looking back at us.

I glare at her back. Her stare isn't intimidating. It's annoying.

Luke grabs my hand and pulls me toward the center of the room. "If we dance like we did last night, there won't be any issues."

Patrick touches my hand. It doesn't hold the warmth it once did. We're not dating anymore. We're not partners. We might as well be strangers.

I pull my hand away from him. He doesn't even have the decency to look hurt by it.

I rip my hand away from Luke instinctively, not even aware I've done it until I see the hurt in his eyes.

"Sorry." I say it more out of habit than anything else. I don't actually mean it, but I'm glad I said it because his face relaxes. It's going to be hard enough to do this without me making it worse.

He points at my arm. "That's what Miss Tasha is talking about. We need to fix that."

"I don't know how to fix that." I don't know how many times I have to tell him.

"That's a lie. You did it last night."

I know it's a lie. Somehow dancing with him last night made me drop the wall around my emotions. Somehow he made me feel something for him that I had no intention of feeling. He flirts with every girl in this damn school. I can't like him. "That was an accident."

Brandon stops his conversation with Miss Tasha. "I'm sorry, does talking help you warm up?" He waits for one of us to say something. "I didn't think so."

Dick. Adam might be right about Brandon.

"I have an idea," Luke whispers.

I watch as he pushes the chairs back up against the wall and moves the barre out of the middle of the room. I have no idea what he's doing, but I don't like where this is going.

He reaches his hand out to me. "Get up."

I glance over at Miss Tasha. She watches us curiously, but she doesn't say anything. Luke's hand is still in front of me. I stand up without touching him.

He frowns and drops his hand. "We'll start small."

I don't trust anything about what he's doing, but I'm almost curious about what he wants to try. I should probably feel flattered that he hasn't given up on me yet, but I'm starting to feel like a project.

Luke holds out his hand. "This is how you learn to trust me. Take it when you're ready."

I hesitate for a few seconds before I slide my hand into his.

His fingers thread through mine and he grins down at me. "Good," he says.

He's treating me like a child and it's more than a little frustrating, even though he's not doing it to annoy me. He wants to make this partnership work.

The only way that's going to happen is if I allow myself to let go, to trust someone. I did it last night, but I have no idea how. I've held onto the idea that I'm on my own for so long now, I don't know how to change it.

Luke leads me up to the mirror. He pulls me in front of him and steps behind me to take the position at the beginning of our routine. He drops my hand and stands with his arms at his sides. I watch his body to figure out what he's doing.

"Look at me."

My eyes snap to his in the mirror.

"I promise you I will never hurt you. I will never make you do anything you don't want to do. All you need to do is say the word and we'll stop everything, but you have to believe it's going to be okay."

I'm at the edge of a cliff. The only way down is to take a step off the edge. That step is a blinding free fall, full of terror and panic and waiting for the second the parachute opens to save me before I crash into the rocks below.

Luke is trying to show me another way. A slower descent with footholds that require me to trust him, believe that he knows what he's doing and he won't let me fall, that he won't hurt me.

I close my eyes and brace myself for a crash landing as I take the first step. "Okay."

He smiles at me. "I want you to step backward so you're right in front of me. Just like yesterday."

I desperately want this to work. I want to be able to dance with a partner again because I know I do my best when I have someone else on stage with me. I don't break eye contact as I nod my head. "Okay." My voice is small and I clear my throat, hoping it will help.

There's no turning back from this. As soon as I take that step, I'm telling him my trust is building. As much as I keep telling myself I can keep the two separate, I can't. Some part of me has to trust him if I have any hopes of making it here.

Miss Tasha watches us silently from the front of the room, Brandon by her side. I tune her out. It's unnerving the way she doesn't take her eyes off of us.

I step backward until I'm almost touching Luke. I take a deep breath to calm my nerves, and then move closer so that my back presses flat against his chest and stomach.

"When you're ready, put my hand on your stomach," he says, raising his hand in front of me and watching my reaction in the mirror.

"Okay." I feel confident. I can totally do this. I can overcome this.

His chest rises and falls against my back in even breaths. He's not in a hurry. I take his hand in both of mine and slowly bring it to my stomach. His palm is warm against my bare skin. My muscles tense for a couple seconds before they relax. I stare down at his hand. My own hands cover most of his and he threads his pinkie through two of my fingers. I meet his gaze in the mirror as a slow smile spreads across his face. I can't help my matching smile.

He moves his hand to my chest as slowly as I moved his other hand. My heart rate spikes as his hand comes into contact with my skin.

"Your heart's racing." His brow creases.

"I know." I find his eyes in the mirror and take a deep breath. My heart needs to relax. I need to calm down. I don't want to think about why my heart is racing because I know it has more to do with the boy standing behind me and less to do with my trust issues.

"Can I try something?" he asks.

I take a deep breath. Now or never. "Yes."

"Miss Tasha went through the whole dance with me after you left, so I know the choreography. I know what comes after this. You spin back under my arm so you're behind me, but I still hold onto your hand. I pull you back in front so we're face-to-face, turn you around again, and lift you so you're arched over my shoulder before you slide down the front of me. Do you think you're up to that?"

"I want to try it." I'm not sure I'll be able to let him lift me, but I need to do this for me.

"We'll take this one step at a time, okay?" He watches me closely.

I nod. It's surprisingly easy to have a little faith in Luke.

His hand slides off my stomach and grips my hand. "Ready?"

"Yes." I'm so ready.

He pushes me gently as he raises his arm so I can easily turn under it. I straighten my arm for a few seconds before he pulls me back to him and I crash against his chest. We're face to face, my body pressed flat against him, his hands on my hips. But I can handle it.

"Turn around."

I do as he says, every inch of me between my stomach and my back touching him as I do. I catch his eyes in the mirror again.

He holds my gaze. "Ready for the lift?"

I smile at him. My body shakes, but it's not from fear. "Completely."

His hands tighten on my waist, my signal to jump. He lifts me up and I arch my back over his shoulder, my hands over my head in fifth position. For the briefest of moments, I worry about him losing grip and allowing me to crash to the floor, but he doesn't. He holds me there for a few seconds before he lets me slide slowly down his body. It takes a couple of seconds for my feet to hit the floor again. He doesn't remove his hands even after I'm on the ground.

I turn in his hands and grin up at him. "I did it," I say, flinging my arms around his neck and hugging him tight.

"You did. I'm so proud of you, Sadie." His arms circle around my waist. The warmth in his eyes disappears in an instant. "I think we should take a break. I don't want to push you too much today. We still have a lot of work to do."

"Yeah, okay." I thought we made a ton of progress, but maybe I wasn't working hard enough or fast enough for him.

He runs his hands up my arms and removes my hands from his neck. The action sends shivers up my spine, but they're good shivers. I jerk my hands back so he doesn't notice.

Miss Tasha claps from the front of the room. "Can I please see more of that in rehearsal? Because that is exactly what I'm looking for. The steps weren't great, but that's the chemistry I expect."

It takes a lot to please Miss Tasha. I'm glad I lived to see the day when she was pleased with something I did.

"Take a ten-minute water break and then let's come back and learn this choreography."

I glance at Luke. We haven't even done that much. I'd rather just keep going than take a break now. But he seems to have different thoughts because he grabs his water bottle and walks out of the studio.

I slide my front leg out and lower myself into the splits to keep my muscles stretched. Halfway through the break, I switch to the other side. Luke doesn't come back until exactly ten minutes has passed. He barely acknowledges me when he walks by. I don't get his sudden mood swing. We were doing great.

"All right. Let's go." Miss Tasha walks to the center of the room to stand next to us.

The choreography is brutal. I'm so anxious about being close to Luke that I continuously trip over my feet. Luke isn't any better, botching the choreography in his own ways. His goofy smile doesn't match the mood of the dance at all. My hands shake every time I have to touch him. My heart goes crazy every time he touches me in return. I lose my center in a pirouette and fall out of it, stumbling into Luke in the process. He catches me before I fall backward.

And it pisses off Miss Tasha.

"What is wrong with you?" she asks after the third time we run it. "This is not what I asked for. Again." She paces the front of the room as the music starts again. Her pacing makes me even more nervous.

We're just as rocky as ever, like we've forgotten all our previously learned technique. I refuse to practice the lifts. That's an accident waiting to happen. It feels safer on the ground. Instead I mark everything, barely letting Luke touch me.

"Okay, stop. Stop. Stop. Stop." Miss Tasha pauses the music. She rubs her forehead with her fingers and points toward us without actually looking at us.

Brandon takes the hint and walks over to us. "Let me show you how it's supposed to look," he says to Luke. He raises his eyebrows when Luke doesn't move.

Luke looks annoyed, but he steps back.

Brandon steps behind me, ready to show Luke the lift we'd been marking for the past hour. His hands find my thighs and he slides them slowly to my hips, making me extremely uncomfortable. I want to step away, but I'm afraid Miss Tasha will yell at us again. One thing's for sure, though. There's no way in hell I'm letting him lift me.

"Assistants don't have the same rules as teachers, you know. We can date other students." His hand brushes against my butt and he holds it there too long.

"What the hell?" I ask, pulling away.

But Luke saw it too. He grabs my arm and pulls me away from Brandon. The momentum makes me stumble. Luke stands chest to chest with Brandon. He breathes heavy. Brandon looks unfazed.

"Hands off." Luke looks furious.

Brandon laughs and gives Luke a little shove away from him. "Or what? You'll tell Mommy?"

Miss Tasha pushes her way between the two of them. "I don't care what's going on between you two, but I can promise you I don't have time for your bullshit. You want to fight? Take it out of the studio."

"Gladly." Luke shoves Brandon's shoulder. Brandon's smirk drops and he looks murderous.

I reach out and grab Luke's wrist, surprising us both. But he doesn't take another step. Instead, he watches me, like he's afraid I might break. I run my hands over my hair to push back the fly-aways that keep sticking to my face.

Miss Tasha holds her head in her hands. Brandon's one second away from attack mode. He shifts from foot to foot and glances between Luke and me.

"Just go. Go get some sleep, go get a brain transplant. I don't care. But when you come back tomorrow, you better be ready to work." Miss Tasha walks out of the studio with Brandon.

I turn to Luke to ask what the hell happened between us in that moment, but I don't get the chance.

"I'll see you tomorrow," Luke says. He grabs his bag off the ground and heads to the door.

"Okay." I frown at his back.

Things were supposed to be better after we danced. But they're not. At this rate, it doesn't feel like they'll ever be better.

⊢————⊣

Nutrition class is the last place I want to be after everything that happened in rehearsal. I never want to see Brandon again after the way he treated me. But I need to talk to Luke. I need to know what's going on between us.

Class doesn't start for another couple minutes. I watch the students around me. Kate, another freshman in the dance department, waves at me from across the room. I smile at her.

A group of girls sit up in the front of the classroom. They're a combination of theater and music students. I don't really know any of them, but their conversation gets louder until they're yelling at each other.

"I can't believe you. How could you sleep with my boyfriend?" Jessie stands up, moving closer to the girl she's talking to.

World War Three is about to break out in nutrition class over a boy.

Rebecca holds her ground. She stands up and pushes her chair out of the way. "It's not my fault. He came onto me. Maybe if you were nicer to him, he wouldn't be hanging around other girls."

How can they not see this is all because of The Hit List? They shouldn't be mad at each other, they should be mad at the boy that's causing the issues between them.

Miss Taylor walks into the room. "Ladies, break it up or I'll break it up for you."

The girls separate, but continue to throw hateful glances at each other from their seats.

I keep my head down for the duration of class. I don't want to get involved in anyone else's drama. I have enough of my own to worry about. When it's finally over, I rush back to my dorm room without making eye contact with anyone. I'm not in the mood for conversation.

Brielle sits on her bed and listens intently as I run through the events of the day with her.

"That's nothing. I heard there's a girl giving it up to the highest bidder so she can pay off her student loans," Brielle says.

"You're joking. Is she aware that's prostitution? And how much does she think she's going to get?"

Unbelievable.

"The girls in this school are crazy." Brielle flips through a gossip magazine.

I frown. "They wouldn't be so crazy if they didn't have to deal with this game. Maybe I should talk to Miss Catherine about it."

She bites her lip. "I don't think you really want to do that. You'd pretty much blacklist yourself in the community. Your best bet is to just let it go and don't get involved yourself. Just don't sleep with someone from the school. Problem solved."

"How many guys do you think are involved?" I ask. She has to have a better idea than I do. She's flirted with half the guys on campus.

She takes her eyes off the magazine for a couple seconds to look at me. "Who cares?"

"I do, considering everyone I talk to seems to have some sort of involvement. Luke and Brandon almost got into a fight after Brandon felt me up in rehearsal."

Brielle stares at me with her mouth open, like I've forgotten basic math. "I'm pretty sure that had nothing to do with the game on Luke's part and everything to do with the fact that he likes you and he was trying to protect you from Brandon."

"Whatever."

"I've seen the look he gives you. He thinks you're hot. And because of that, you should avoid him at every opportunity," she says.

I can't hide my smile from her. "He does not. And how am I supposed to avoid him when he's my partner?"

I'm not sure whether or not I want the words to be true. I think part of me is hoping it is. The other part is terrified of what that means. Things could get really complicated really fast if I start to care about him as more than a partner.

Brielle's eyes widen. "Sadie Bryant, you like him, don't you?"

I do my best to relax my face and look as indifferent as possible. "Okay, so maybe I don't really hate him, but that doesn't mean I like him."

She raises an eyebrow at me. "I want you to remember that I told you from the beginning that he was a jackass because this can only end badly. But if you really want to go for it, then you should. Maybe he's only a jackass to ninety-nine percent of the female population."

"Thanks?" I'm not sure how to answer that. It sounds like she's giving me her permission to date him, but that's not what I want. I just want to be able to dance.

I don't even know if I like him yet, let alone trust him.

"It doesn't really matter. Everyone I end up liking has a tendency to leave for better things. So what's the point?" I stare at my pillow so I don't have to make eye contact.

Her voice is quiet when she speaks again. "Not everyone leaves in the end. Sometimes you just have to give people a chance. Give them a reason to stay."

THE HIT LIST UPDATE
September 30

It's time for another update post. Our Hitters are starting to get into the swing of things and two of our lovely ladies have fallen from the game. You'll see their names crossed out along with their point values. The rest of the ladies are still available for votes. As for our guys, their standings are listed below.

#10	16 points
#1	11 points
#3	9 points
#4	8 points
#16	8 points
#5	7 points
#2	7 points
#14	6 points
#13	6 points
#6	4 points
#7	3 points
#9	3 points
#15	1 point
#11	1 point
#12	1 point
#8	----------

Brielle Watkins	25%
Sadie Bryant	19%
Rachel Barrons	14%
~~Rebecca Hemsworth~~	12 points
Samantha Jameson	11%

Noelle Sanstrohm	10%
~~Courtney Turner~~	9 points
Ashlynn Jenkins	9%
Jessie Freeman	7%
Kate Williams	5%

As always, have fun and happy hitting!

~ THE HIT MAN

9

"Get it together, Sadie," Miss Tasha yells for the third time in less than fifteen minutes as I mark another lift with Luke. "You can't keep marking things if you ever hope to get it right for tryouts."

I want to flip her off, but that won't go over well.

It's been two weeks since we learned the choreography. Tension has only increased since Luke and Brandon's standoff. Brandon makes me uncomfortable and I'd prefer if he weren't in class, but I don't have a choice. He's assigned to us and I can't change him any more than I can change Luke.

I don't trust Luke any more than I did then and we're nowhere near as polished as we should be by now. I always chicken out after a few seconds of Luke touching me, so I mark most of the lifts. I know it annoys all of them, but there's nothing I can do about that.

"Glare at me all you want. Tryouts are in twenty-five days. And if it were up to me, I'd cut you both in a heartbeat. Stop marking shit and dance full out. We have one more shot before practice is over. Make it count. Let's take it from right before the lift." She rewinds the music a couple of eight counts.

I count it out in my head. I don't need to worry about this. We've done it before, we can do it again.

Right on cue, I launch into Luke's arms, turning in the air so I face away from him when he catches me. My feet find his thighs as my body curls in and I straighten my legs to stand on his thighs. His hands close around my hips. I focus on calming my breathing. We can't fail. I can't fall.

The lift isn't new. We've done it a hundred times and I don't expect this time to be any different.

That's my first mistake.

My foot slips against the fabric of Patrick's shorts. He corrects it quickly, but the damage is done. I overcompensate for the change in balance and my upper body sways.

Patrick isn't fast enough. When I lean forward to protect myself, he grabs whatever he can. My hip shreds before I hit the floor.

My second mistake was believing he would stick around for my recovery.

Breathing is the least of my worries when Luke shifts slightly underneath me. Fear closes in around me.

He's going to drop me.

My mind goes into overdrive as I plan an escape route from the lift with the least amount of damage to myself. I lean back slightly so I'm angled to drop right to the floor on my feet instead of on my face. My feet slide off Luke's thighs before I'm ready. His hands slip from my hips and he catches me around the waist before I hit the floor. Disappointment shoots through me and every failure in the last few weeks weighs heavy on my heart.

Luke releases me immediately and takes a step back. "You were fine. I was just getting into a better position. There was no chance I was going to drop you."

Miss Tasha throws her hands up in the air. "I give up. You two are useless." She stalks out of the studio.

"Well, that was rude." Luke stares at the door as it bangs shut behind her.

I sit down in a straddle, letting my muscles cool down in a stretch so they don't tense up. "She's right. I'm useless. I'm never going to be able to do this." Tears form in my eyes and I press the heels of my hands against them. I'm tired and I'm stressed.

"You just need to have more faith."

"And how do you propose I do that?" I ask, waiting for his miracle solution that I know he doesn't have. If he did, we wouldn't be in this situation.

He smiles and holds out his hand. "Let's go for a ride."

"I'm not in the mood. I want to stay here and practice." I stand up without taking his hand and brush the dust off my butt.

He walks toward the door. "You're going to be practicing by yourself then. I need a break."

I shouldn't go. We need to practice more, but practicing without Luke is pointless. I already know I'm good without him. If I go, I'm stuck wherever he decides to take me. But the break sounds nice and it's been a while since I've gotten off this campus. "Fine, but I need to change first."

I change quickly because I'm excited to get out of the school for a while. It has nothing to do with the fact that I'll be spending the day with Luke outside the studio. Absolutely not.

He isn't back when I'm done getting ready so I walk to his room. I'm almost there when I hear the soft sounds of someone crying. A girl sits on a bench in the hallway. Her tears fall onto her shirt. A collection of darker dots has formed where they fall. She glances up at me and starts to wipe frantically at her tears, as if she can erase the evidence of the mascara rivers on her cheeks.

"Hey, are you okay?" I sit down on the bench next to her.

She continues to wipe at the tears that don't seem to be stopping. "I'm fine."

"Do you want to talk about it?" She is anything but fine. It feels rude to just leave her here when she's obviously upset.

She takes a deep breath that sounds more like a bunch of little gasps as she tries to gain composure. "I slept with this guy. Turns out he just wanted some points in that fucking Hit List game."

I should have guessed that was the issue. I wonder how long it will continue before something devastating happens.

"I'm sorry. That really sucks."

She glares at me. "Yeah, it does."

I reach out to put my arm around her shoulder and give her a little comfort, but she leans away from me. "Have you thought about going to the faculty and telling them about it?"

"Are you crazy? For what? So I can be called a narc by every other person at this school? So I can ruin everyone's *fun*? I don't think so."

I shift on the bench. I don't know what to say to make her feel better. "It might make it better. Maybe some of the guys will get in trouble. I heard a couple got expelled for fighting."

She rolls her eyes. "Why don't *you* tell someone? I hear people talking about you all the time. You're almost on top of the polls week after week. They all want you. Every single guy playing that game."

I don't want to believe that the guys I interact with on a daily basis could be playing, but I know some of them are. Still, there are some decent ones in this school. There aren't enough spots for guys playing to make up the entire male student body. "Not everyone is playing. The good ones can't help that this game is going on, but there are good ones out there."

"Like who? Luke Morrison? Come on. Do you really think he's interested in your brain?" She raises an eyebrow. Her arm falls across her lap like she doesn't have the energy to hold it up. Probably because she's so shocked at my naïveté.

"He's not playing." I fidget with the loose armrest on the bench.

He can't be. Everything I've built with him over the past few weeks would be a lie if he were playing. I refuse to believe that's a possibility.

It kind of makes sense, though.

She laughs bitterly. "Is that what he told you? You're stupid if you believe that."

Maybe I am stupid. It wouldn't be the first time I believed good things about a person when they turned out to only care about themselves.

I take deep breaths while I try to ignore what she says. He's not playing. I have to believe that. The second I start to question it, everything goes downhill. The second I think he's lying, this partnership is dead.

She stands up and crosses her arms. "If you guys are really into each other then why aren't you dating?" She waves her hand through the air and doesn't wait for me to answer. "I'll tell you why. He can't get points for you if you're dating."

She walks away, leaving me close to tears on the bench. I'm so glad I stopped to see if I could help her.

Shake it off. It's not worth getting upset over this. He's not playing.

I head toward Luke's room again. I won't let what this one girl said ruin my day. We'll still have a good day off campus. I'll make sure of it.

I lean against the wall outside his room and drum my fingers on my arm. Maybe he'll take me someplace special. Like out to dinner or something.

My fingers freeze mid-drum. I don't want to go out to dinner. That would make this some kind of date. And this is definitely not a date.

A boy from my music class walks toward me. I smile to be polite as he gets closer, but he takes it as a different meaning.

He stops in front of me and brushes his bangs out of his eyes. The piercings in his lip and eyebrow reflect the fluorescent light in the hallway and the unknown band shirt he wears is ripped in a couple places. "You're Sadie, right? We have music together."

I smile. "Yeah. I'm sorry. I don't know your name," I say, still trying to maintain my manners even though he's giving me a creepy vibe.

"I'm Mike. I'm a theater student." He holds out his hand, but I don't take it and he runs it through his hair like that was his plan all along. He just looks awkward. I should really learn not to engage with anyone. Or even be polite, for that matter. Just because I'm nice to people doesn't mean I want to have sex with everyone I meet. Maybe if I'm a bitch to everyone I see, they won't bother approaching.

"So, I hear dancers are really flexible." He winks at me.

I don't even know how to dignify Mike's comment with a response. It's degrading and he deserves to be punched for it, but I'm classier than that. I settle for staring back at him, making him feel as uncomfortable as possible. He doesn't leave.

Instead he shuffles nervously from foot to foot. "How's your day going?"

I roll my eyes, ready to walk back to my room. Luke will figure it out eventually. The door opens beside me and Luke steps out. He stands next to me and swipes my hair off my shoulder, kissing the bare skin next to my tank top. "She's taken. Sorry, bro."

Warmth spreads down my arm. I shake my arm behind my back to get rid of the feeling. I think he was trying to help, but it was anything but helpful. It made me feel like I belonged to him. Which is so not the case.

Mike looks between us a couple times. "Well, it was nice to officially meet you. I'll see you in class."

Luke steps away from me as soon as Mike is out of earshot. "I'm really sorry, but I could hear him through the door and I thought I'd help you out. I didn't mean to say we were dating, it just kind of came out."

He can't get points for you if you're dating.

I feel like someone pushed me into a pool. I can't breathe. I can't find the surface. Everywhere I turn, I'm faced with the feeling of Luke's lips on my shoulder. "It's fine. Don't worry about it."

"Are you ready to go? If you don't want to, it's okay, but I promise I won't do anything like that again."

My heart stutters as I nod. "No, let's go."

I follow him out of the building. I shouldn't be hurt by his promise, and I don't want to be. But I can't help feeling a little disappointed that he felt the need to promise it in the first place.

———

We stand on the Hollywood Walk of Fame, surrounded by stars. People wander between each of the monuments. Some just look. Others take pictures.

"We don't have time for this. I could be doing a million other things right now and none of them include staring at names on a sidewalk," I whine.

With everything else feeling so much more important, it's hard to be impressed by a bunch of stars. Luke grabs my hand and pulls me forward through the crowd.

"We're here for more than looking at names on a sidewalk. This is what I use for inspiration when I'm feeling like a failure. Do you know how many people on this sidewalk failed or were told by someone important they would never succeed?"

I don't want to let go of his hand so I follow him. I ignore the tiny voice that tells me to let go while I still can. We dodge a couple taking pictures and a group of people crowded around one particular star.

He stops in front of John Lennon's star. Paul McCartney's star is ahead of us a couple feet. A little girl runs up the sidewalk, weaving in and out of the crowd. Her older brother chases her. A teen girl stops next to us and takes a picture with her phone before moving onto another star.

"What do you know about The Beatles?" Luke asks, drawing my attention back to him.

"Everyone knows who The Beatles are, Luke." I know they weren't dancers so I'm not sure why it matters right now. I sigh and cross my arms.

"They were told by a record label that they had no future in show business when they were just starting out. They went on to sell millions of records. What do you think would have happened if they believed that guy and quit?" His thumb rubs circles on my hand.

It makes it hard to concentrate. I don't care about names on a sidewalk when he does that. I don't care much about anything because I can't think when he touches me.

I know what he's trying to do and I smile, grateful he cares but confused about why he's going through the trouble for a friend. "They wouldn't have seen their dream come true."

"Exactly."

He walks down another half a block. He doesn't release my hand, but his fingers slip a little when he increases speed. I jump forward to solidify our connection again. His fingers tighten around my hand and my heart flips.

He stops in front of Elvis Presley's star. There's a crowd gathered and we have to wait a few seconds to get up close to it. He looks so happy while we wait. He catches me looking at him and squeezes my hand.

I wish he'd stop doing that. But not bad enough to pull my hand away.

"Elvis was fired after one performance at the Grand Ole Opry because the audience didn't like his style. The manager told him to go back to his truck driving job in Memphis."

The little girl who ran past us earlier looks up at Luke in fascination. He smiles down at her. The silent exchange does something to my heart, but I push the feeling down. My trust in him is building and I wouldn't want to compromise that with something other than a friendship and partnership. Besides, he's made it clear that's all we are.

He walks faster to the next one. My hand is still glued to his. His energy is contagious and when he breaks into a run, I run too, a smile on my face.

We stop in front of another star.

"Fred Astaire." I swing his hand in excitement.

"Arguably one of the best performers ever." He lets go of me and I feel a pang of disappointment. Maybe he wouldn't have noticed he was still holding onto me if I hadn't started swinging our hands.

"He's the reason I took my first tap class." I pull out my phone and take a picture of the star.

I used to watch *Blue Skies* with my grandpa and dance around his living room to "Puttin' on the Ritz." I'd been captivated by the sounds Fred Astaire could make with his shoes and begged my parents to let me take a tap class if I promised to keep up with my ballet. It turned into one of my favorite classes before I dropped it to focus on preparing for a career in ballet and contemporary.

I'd always wanted to get back into tap, but I never have time for anything outside ballet. Maybe I could find a class to take over break between semesters.

"So what terrible thing was Fred Astaire told?" I ask, knowing where Luke's going with this.

He smiles. "He was told by a casting director that he was balding, couldn't sing, and could only dance a little."

I stare at the star beneath us. In the grand scheme of things, my issues pale against the things these people have overcome. No one has ever told me I don't have talent. In fact, I've been told on multiple occasions that I'm talented. And if I could get that message to my brain and give up a little bit of control, I might be exceptional.

I glance at Luke, but he isn't looking at me. He might be the only person who cares enough about me to take me out here and tell me these things. And for reasons I can't comprehend, he doesn't want out of this partnership.

He could get mad every time I force him to drop me because I struggle too much. He could get annoyed every time I pull away from him after we've just made progress. He could get frustrated every time Miss Tasha berates us for not doing our best, when he clearly is doing everything he can with what he's got. But he doesn't do any of those things. He's patient with me. He cares about me.

Luke's fingers thread through mine. I stop focusing on the bad things. Things are good with Luke right now and I want them to stay that way.

He tugs on my arm. "Come on. I have one more thing I want to show you."

Over an hour and a bus ride later, we're standing in Venice Beach. Luke winds through the crowded sidewalks without releasing my hand. We stop in front of a graffiti-covered wall. It's a mess with spray paint everywhere.

I crinkle my nose. "You brought me to look at gang art?"

"It's not gang art. Did you even look at it?"

I squint, looking closer at the images in the sunlight. The brilliant colors form letters and words stretching across the cement. Famous quotes turned into works of art in curvy, bubble, and block writing. It's beautiful.

Luke watches me as I stare. "It's called the Wall of Inspiration. The street performers started writing on it a couple years ago. The city tried to clean it up, but it's become a huge attraction for tourists, so they leave it. You have to have a permit now to add to it. Good thing I picked one up yesterday," he says, smiling at me.

He pulls a can of spray paint out of his bag and hands it to me.

"What do you want me to do with that?" I ask, looking down at it. Despite what he's just told me, it seems sketchy to spray paint a wall in the middle of L.A.

He shrugs. "Add your own inspiration. Whatever you feel in this exact moment."

I shake the can and step up to an empty space on the wall. Whatever I write won't measure up to the beauty that already exists in this space. All these people who come here looking for inspiration don't need to hear false words from someone who can't practice what she preaches. But maybe I can change it. Maybe, starting today, I can make a promise to myself to change, to do what I love, to succeed. I drag the spray can into cursive letters over the wall, stepping back when I'm done.

"I won't give up," Luke reads.

"It's not just inspiration, it's a promise. One that I hope to keep." Something I should have been telling myself since day one.

I don't want to give up on myself or on Luke. He's made serious effort in this partnership. It wouldn't be fair to either of us to give up on it now.

He smiles. "I'll help you keep that promise any way I can."

I grab his hand, already knowing it's safe. "I'm counting on it."

He's been doing it all along, since the first time I fought with him about our partnership. He's been there every step of the way, whether I wanted him there or not. And I have no doubt he'll do everything in his power to help me keep my promise.

He leads me down the sidewalk and we stop to get ice cream before continuing on to find an open bench. I stare out at the ocean.

It's a terrible day to be sitting on the coast. Rain pours down around us. It's not supposed to be this cold in the summer. I shiver and pull my knees closer to my chest to get warm.

Patrick drapes his jacket around my shoulders and wraps his arms around the outside of it. I'm trapped against his body. It's warm and I lean back against his chest to get closer to the warmth, closer to him.

He leans his chin against my shoulder. "Better?"
"Better."

My throat closes as I remember exactly why I shouldn't get involved with Luke. Nothing will keep him here. I'll get attached, maybe even fall in love, and then he'll leave. It'll be worse the second time. And all the recovery time in the world won't heal those wounds.

"Truth or dare," Luke says. He takes a bite of his ice cream cone.

I look over at him. "I hate that game."

"I'm not going to make you kiss a stranger. Just pick one." He raises his eyebrows at me, as if to tell me he's harmless.

Right.

I stare at the ground, nervous about either pick. A dare could mean doing something embarrassing, but the wrong truth could reveal way more than I ever want.

He sighs. "Fine, I'll go first. Truth."

There is one thing I've wanted to know since I met him, but I'm worried it's too much right off the bat.

"You're not going to offend me. Just ask." He looks out at the ocean.

A couple of kids skate by on roller blades and skateboards. A baby cries somewhere behind us. A husband and wife play at the edge of the water with a toddler.

I look up at him. He better know what he's doing. "Why does Brielle hate you?"

He laughs. "I hope she doesn't actually hate me."

I roll my eyes. "Okay, why does she *dislike* you?"

"We hooked up last year. She wanted something more and I didn't. That's how I get most of my enemies." He nudges my shoulder with his, a smile on his lips. "Except you. You hated me because I flirted with you."

I smile, knowing it was so much more than that. "Your turn."

I look down at my lap. I'd rather be embarrassed than have to open my soul to him, especially after what he's just revealed. "Dare."

He turns so he faces me on the bench. "Why don't you trust me?"

Not happening. He hasn't earned that story yet. He might not ever earn that story.

"That's not a dare."

His eyes pierce into me. "I dare you to tell me why you don't trust me."

For a brief second, I consider it. Things might be easier if I told him about New York, about Patrick and my mom, about the friends who left me behind. He's opened up to me about hurting Brielle, so maybe he would understand.

Or maybe he wouldn't.

I look out at the ocean, straddling the line between past and present. "I can't."

The sounds of Venice fill the silence between us. It drags on as both of us eat our ice cream. I want to change the subject, but my brain won't focus on anything other than the boy next to me.

"Do you think you'll ever trust me?" He stares out at the water.

Do you really think he's interested in your brain? You're stupid if you believe that.

I don't answer him. I don't know how. If I say no, I'll hurt him. But if I say yes, I might be lying. I don't want to give him false hope that this partnership will ever work out the way both of us want it to. So I don't say anything.

He turns to look at me, not questioning me. His look tells me everything his words never could. Reassurance that we'll be all right. Faith that we can do this, even if I don't fully trust him yet. Hope that one day we'll get there.

But beneath the emotions written on his face, he can't mask everything he doesn't want me to see. Hurt that I don't trust him enough. Disappointment that we'll never get there. Realization that he can't fix me.

His not-so-secret emotions tell me I should have said something, anything. I want to tell him why I didn't, but he turns away from me to stare back out at the water.

The moment's gone.

I should have said yes.

THE HIT LIST UPDATE
October 13

The week you've all been waiting for has finally arrived. The top girl in our polls has been taken out of the game. It's a shame that we lost her so early in the game, but second best is still available. Keep voting to see your favorite girl in the second place spot. And remember, the top spot may be gone, but we've still got six girls in the game.

~~Sadie Bryant~~	15 points
Brielle Watkins	29%
Samantha Jameson	23%
Rachel Barrons	17%
~~Rebecca Hemsworth~~	12 points
Noelle Sanstrohm	13%
~~Courtney Turner~~	9 points
~~Jessie Freeman~~	8 points
Ashlynn Jenkins	12%
Kate Williams	6%

#2	22 points
#18	21 points
#10	19 points
#7	18 points
#15	17 points
#19	16 points
#1	16 points
#5	15 points
#11	13 points
#17	13 points

#3	12 points
#14	12 points
#4	11 points
#12	11 points
#6	9 points
#13	9 points
#16	8 points
#9	5 points
#8	----------

Happy hitting!

~ THE HIT MAN

10

"You look adorable."

"I look like a five-year-old." I stare at the tiara Brielle insists I wear. I don't even know why I'm doing this. It's my birthday. I should have a say in whether I wear a stupid plastic crown all day.

"People should know to treat you like a princess. It's your eighteenth birthday. That only happens once." She walks up behind me and plays with my hair.

"You'll get mad if I take it off, won't you?" I make eye contact with her so I can see how she really feels. I don't want to hurt her feelings.

She pouts at me in the mirror. "Maybe."

It's not going to hurt me to wear it. "Fine, I'll wear the damn tiara."

She smiles and claps her hands, doing a fantastic impression of an excited three-year-old. We're a perfect pair today.

"Let's go. We're going to be late."

She rushes me out the door and over to the studio. Most of the students in our class are already here. I'm the only freshman in this class. It used to be awkward, but years don't mean a whole lot here. Technique has nothing to do with how old we are at this point in our lives. We find a spot and spread out. Brielle sets her bag in an open space to save room for Adam.

Courtney and Rachel sit near us and I can't help but listen to their conversation.

"He's been trying really hard. I figure it's time to reward him for it." Courtney giggles as she slides on her shoes.

Brielle leans over to me. "Am I hearing this right? Is she seriously bragging that she's about to be used for sex?"

I try to give Courtney the benefit of the doubt. "Maybe she doesn't want to get hit on anymore?"

It could happen. There wouldn't be a point to sleeping with a girl anymore if she had already been used for points.

"Yeah, I don't think so." She waves at Courtney to get her attention. "Probably something you shouldn't be bragging about."

Brielle's voice is loud and half the students turn to look at her. Courtney glares at her.

Rachel whips around. "Were you included in this conversation? I didn't think so."

"Was I talking to you? I didn't think so." Brielle turns back toward me. "I'm just trying to help her out."

"At least your name is still on the list." Rachel says it to Courtney, but she glances at me for a second, anger gleaming in her eyes.

Courtney and Rachel continue their conversation, their backs to us.

"What do you suppose that means?" We're not crossed off the list either. It doesn't make sense.

"Who knows. Ignore her."

The rest of the chatter in the room is back to its original level. No one stares at us anymore.

Luke talks to Cara, but he doesn't even give me a sideways glance. He hasn't talked to me outside of class since he took me to Venice Beach and the Hollywood Walk of Fame almost two weeks ago. And in rehearsal, he's practically a zombie. He's still patient with me and does a great job hiding his frustration. But I know it's there. Just like it was there when I refused his dare.

Cara reaches up and wraps her arms around his neck to pull him into a hug. He goes willingly. With his arms around her back, he looks up at me for the first time.

I look away the second his eyes meet mine. I don't want to watch him flirt with her.

It's bad enough to think that I've pissed him off because of my issues. I don't want to think I've pushed him right into her waiting arms.

"So what do you say to dinner? We can do anything you want after." He whispers something in her ear.

She gasps and smacks him in the chest, but her smile never leaves her face. "You're dirty."

You don't do relationships.

And just like that, I've pushed him so far away during the time we've been dancing together that he's not coming back.

Do you really think he's interested in your brain?

When I glance back in their direction, he's separated from her.

"Trouble in paradise?" Brielle asks. She leans forward on her elbows between her legs and looks up at me.

I watch other students in the mirror. Most of them look tired, but happy, and I wonder if any of them struggle as much as I do, if they know what it's like to be afraid to let go. "He's mad at me."

"Should he be?" She rocks her hips gently forward and rolls into a center split.

I really don't want to have this conversation in the middle of the dance studio with everyone else around. "Don't bounce. You'll pull something."

She glares at me. "Don't change the subject."

I sigh. I should know better than thinking she would drop it. "Probably."

"What'd you do?" She leans forward again with even pressure and looks up at me.

What didn't I do? It's such a loaded question and I'm not sure how to answer it. Since I started here I've had a panic attack at his touch, struggled when he wanted to push me out of my comfort zone, and refused to trust him when I had no reason to believe he would hurt me.

"I'm frustrating."

I know I am. I just thought maybe he'd work to earn my trust a little harder. I thought maybe he was done flirting with every girl. I thought he was done with that game.

Clearly I was wrong.

"You should work on that." She lies down on the floor between her legs, reaching her arms over her head.

"Gee, thanks. Good talk." Even something along the lines of blowing my chances at Fall Showcase or London would have been better than that advice.

"Anytime."

Adam rushes in right behind Miss Jasmine, barely on time for class. Miss Jasmine narrows her eyes at him and he mouths "sorry." He sits down between Brielle and me to stretch.

"Are you ever on time to anything?" Brielle asks, her face still against the floor.

He slides his bag across the floor and it smacks into the wall below the mirror. "I wasn't technically late. Class hasn't started yet."

Miss Jasmine whistles above the chatter. "Okay, let's get started. Line up in the corner. We're going to run some floor exercises to warm up."

I walk to the corner with Brielle and Adam. I don't want to be here right now. I'd rather be in bed avoiding everything. Screw Fall Showcase and London. I just want to survive the next two weeks before tryouts.

"We'll start easy. Piqués across the floor. I want excellent turn out, people. I don't want to see sloppy mistakes. If you give me mistakes, be prepared to give me fifty push-ups." Miss Jasmine starts the music, not giving anyone a chance to reply or ask questions.

"Lame," Brielle whispers. "She needs to get laid if she's uptight about piqués."

Adam chuckles. "I'm sure there's someone around here that would be willing to take care of that. Even if she's not on the list, she's worth points."

Brielle scoffs and hits him in the arm. "Gross. You're talking about a teacher."

That was exactly the mental image I wanted to start the class with. I focus on my turnout and practice piqués in line while I wait for my turn.

Miss Jasmine claps her hands. "Courtney, I saw that sickled foot. Fifty push-ups. Go."

Courtney looks pained and wanders off to the corner.

"Shit just got real. She's not screwing around," Adam whispers.

I step up to the corner and wait for Rachel to clear half the floor before I start. I stand in fifth, my arms rounded into first position. I'm not giving Miss Jasmine a reason to call me out.

But she does it anyway.

"Sadie, what are you wearing?"

Brielle answers for me. "It's her birthday. I told her she had to wear it."

Miss Jasmine doesn't bat an eyelash. "Do you wear everything people tell you to wear?"

I want to say yes, just to see what she'll do. But push-ups are the bane of my existence. It's not worth it. "No."

Miss Jasmine watches me in silence for a second. "Happy Birthday, Sadie. Now take it off and piqué."

I pull the tiara out of my hair and slide it across the floor. Taking a deep breath, I point my toes whenever they leave the floor, turn my hips out as far as I can without hyperextending, and keep my standing leg as straight as possible. Miss Jasmine frowns at me the entire way across the floor, but seems satisfied enough when I get to the other side.

Thank God.

Brielle makes it across without invoking Miss Jasmine's wrath and stands next to me along the wall. "If I knew she was going to throw a fit about a fucking tiara, I never would have asked you to wear it."

I wave her comment off with my hand. "Don't worry about it." I'm over it.

Rachel pushes off the wall and steps behind a couple people until she's next to us. "It's kind of sad that you slept with Luke. You know he's taken, right?"

"By who? You? If he's so taken, why is he sleeping around?" Brielle crosses her arms over her chest.

It takes a few seconds for what Rachel said to sink in. "Wait, what do you mean I slept with Luke? I didn't sleep with anyone."

"That's not what The Hit List tells me."

"I don't care what anyone tells you. *I'm* telling you I didn't sleep with anyone." My voice is louder than I expected. I glance up to find Luke watching me. Did he hear what I said? Shit, half the class probably heard me.

Did Luke lie and somehow claim points for me? He's the only one I've been close to. Why would he do that? I know he's mad at me right now, but there's no way he would ever do something like that. Nerves twist in my stomach. I'm not one hundred percent sure I believe he wouldn't try to hurt me. I've given him enough reasons to.

Rachel shrugs. "If you say so." She moves back to her place in line.

Miss Jasmine continues to watch dancers cross the floor. She has no idea what just happened. She can't hear the thump of my heart over the bass of the music.

"Was it all just some kind of game to you? To see how long it would take you to get into NYBC?"

Patrick sighs into the phone. I miss the way his sighs would flutter the hair by my ear, but that was before things fell apart, before things were different. Before I found out I was living a lie.

"You could at least answer me." I deserve that much. After everything he's put me through, he can tell me what happened to us.

"What do you want me to say?" The tension strains his voice.

"I want you to tell me the truth." Even as I say it, I'm not sure it's what I want. The truth has the power to break me more than I already am.

"You want the truth? Fine. I started dancing with you because I knew it would help my career. It's easier to get noticed when you have a pretty girl by your side. Is that what you wanted to hear? Are you fucking happy now?"

My grip tightens on the phone. *"The fact that you think that would make me happy proves you never gave a shit about me in the first place."*

Something rubs against the receiver and I can almost see him in front of me rubbing his hands over his face. *"I'm sorry. I didn't mean it. Can we forget this happened?"*

"You know what, Patrick? Go ahead. Forget everything that's happened in the last two years. Forget about me."

I don't wait for his answer. I whip the phone across the room. It shatters against the wall on the other side of my bedroom.

I'm done with lies.

"Come on, guys. You have two weeks until tryouts and right now none of you are impressing me. We're going to have a pretty unhappy audience if we don't have any performers," Miss Jasmine yells above the piano music.

I glance over at Luke. He watches the front of the room while he holds a relevé position.

Two weeks.

"Do you think you'll ever trust me?"

How do you trust someone that keeps giving you reasons not to?

Fourteen days.

"Why don't you just quit? Find something else to do with your life that doesn't involve dance. Then you don't have to worry about your hip anymore."

Patrick doesn't realize that giving up dance is the scariest thing I've ever had to think about. Dance is my existence. It's what I tell people when they ask what I want to do with my life.

"What else would I do? Dance is my life."

Without it, I'm lost. I don't have any idea what I would do. I have no other interests. There is no other career path I would enjoy. This is it.

Without it, who am I?

Patrick meets my gaze in the mirror from the other side of the room. "Maybe it's time to find a new life."

Patrick followed me to L.A. without ever stepping foot here. He's successfully wormed his way back into my life. Every reaction I have to Luke is because of him. Every time I freak out, it's because Patrick couldn't be a decent human being after I got hurt. Every time I pull away, it's because Patrick didn't stay.

Pulling away doesn't make me weak. It makes it impossible for Luke to leave. He can't leave me if I never had him to begin with.

I don't even know if I believe that anymore. It feels like he's leaving. Every cold shoulder, every awkward silence, every touch given to another girl makes it worse. I'm in this thing deeper than I ever thought I could be. Maybe I do trust him even though I tell myself I don't. And maybe I do care even though I've convinced myself I can't.

Except now someone is trying to say they slept with me. Luke is the only one who makes sense.

Who would believe anyone else? I spend all of my free time with him.

My ears buzz from a lack of oxygen. I can't think. My brain can't even figure out how to survive right now.

Brielle has a death grip on my arm. Luke watches the whole scene with something like concern in his eyes. Miss Jasmine watches us and words come out of her mouth, but my brain can't connect the meanings. She speaks a foreign language.

Brielle's hand comes down hard on my back and the instinct to breathe kicks in. She pulls me across the floor to the doors and out of the room. Miss Jasmine follows us out into the hallway.

"What do you think you're doing? You can't leave class," Miss Jasmine says.

Brielle takes a step in between us. "Are you for real right now? She's fucking blue. She needs a minute."

I put my hands on my knees and suck air into my lungs. The burn is a welcome relief.

Miss Jasmine looks flustered as she glances between us. "Fine. Five minutes. Then I expect you back inside."

She turns to walk back into the classroom, but the door bursts open and Luke runs out. His gaze falls on me. Time stops as I take in his expression.

No hurt. No disappointment. Just worry for me.

He takes a step closer, but he's not even close enough to reach out and touch me. "Are you okay?"

As much as I want to be happy about it, I can't. My mind is a jumbled mess. I don't know if he really cares. I don't know if I really care.

Brielle glances at me before she looks at Luke. "I got this, Morrison."

He doesn't take his eyes off me while he waits for my answer.

I stand up straight and lean against the wall. I don't need help from anyone. I especially don't need his help, not when I can't figure out what I feel.

"I'm fine."

Luke's eyes stay locked on mine for a few more seconds. He runs a hand through his hair. "Okay. See you back inside." He pushes through the doors.

Brielle sits down on the floor in the hallway. "I really wish you would stop doing this. It scares the shit out of me."

"You and me both." If I could control it, I would, and I'd choose to never feel like this again.

"It was that game, wasn't it? The reason you freaked?" She looks up at me from her place on the floor.

I rest my hands against my knees to breathe deeper. "I don't really enjoy people spreading rumors about me. Especially when those rumors involve my sex life."

She frowns. "I'm sorry."

"I'll be fine." I want to get away from people for a little while, but that's not going to happen. I have to go back to class.

She looks skeptical, but nods after a few seconds. "Try to put it behind you. Don't worry about what those people think. Nothing they say matters anyway. As long as you know what's real."

A few more deep breaths and my lungs feel normal. I nod at Brielle and she opens the door to go back into the studio.

I lie on a blanket in the middle of the quad and listen to music on my iPod. I shouldn't feel like shit on my birthday, but I do. I've pushed Luke too far for him to be like himself around me anymore. I've done a pretty good job pissing off all the people who hold my future in their hands.

My life is a disaster.

I pull out my ear buds to watch the commotion in front of me on the sidewalk. Two students stand close to the entrance of the school fighting.

"You're such a bastard. I can't believe I ever slept with you." She takes off down the sidewalk away from him.

He jogs to catch up with her. "It's not like I did it because you were worth bonus points or something. I would have done it even if you weren't."

The crack of her hand across his cheek echoes off the wall beside them and I flinch.

She keeps walking. He stands stunned in the middle of the sidewalk, a red handprint on his cheek.

My phone vibrates against my side. I drop it when I read the screen. She never calls me first.

"Hey, Mom."

"Sadie?" She sounds more confused than me.

"Yeah. Who did you expect to answer?" I probably don't want to know the answer to that question, but it's out of my mouth before I can stop it.

She sighs. "I must have dialed you by accident."

Of course. Because who would just expect their mom to call on their birthday?

"I won't keep you then," I bite out.

Something shuffles against her phone and I picture her moving it to her other ear and holding it with her shoulder while she looks for a piece of paper in her bag. "What's with the attitude?"

Like she even has the right to ask.

"Nothing. I'm just stressed. Things aren't going the greatest with my partner."

There's silence for a few seconds before her voice comes back strangely calm. "You're dating someone?"

"No, Mother. I'm not dating anyone."

She would think that.

I hear her intake of breath, getting ready to berate me for being rude to her. I end the call before she has the chance and toss the phone back on the blanket.

L.A. was going okay for a while, but now everything is falling down around me. I don't have anyone I can talk to about this. Patrick was my go-to for everything bad in my life.

Not anymore. He doesn't care anymore.

But he could. He did text me asking how L.A. was going.

I grab my phone off the blanket. Without thinking about it, I type out a reply to Patrick's text from last month.

I hate L.A. The people suck. I want to come home. I miss New York. I miss you.

I stare at the words on my phone. I shouldn't send it. He was trying to be nice. He doesn't actually care. He probably just wanted to know why he hasn't heard from me in so long since I called him or texted him all the time before I left. He just never answered before.

I can't send it.

I delete the draft before I convince myself it's completely okay to send it.

"Fuck." I drop my phone back onto the blanket and rest my head in my hands.

"Rough day?" Adam stands at the edge of the blanket.

I lean back to look up at him. "You could say that."

"Can I sit?" He gestures to the blanket.

"Sure." I slide over to give him room.

We sit in silence for a few minutes. I watch people walk by on the sidewalk down by the street. The fighting couple is done. Traffic has slowed as the evening drags on. A guy throws a Frisbee for his dog in another section of the lawn. A girl has an easel set-up nearby and she works to capture the coloring of the sky as a storm rolls in on the horizon.

"I heard someone lied to get your name crossed off The Hit List." His eyes follow the dog as it runs across the lawn and back to its owner.

"You saw the post?" I didn't think he followed that blog anymore.

He shrugs. "And I heard a couple girls talking about it in the hallway."

Fabulous. Now I'm a new source of gossip. I can't win here.

He cocks his head to the side and squints his left eye to block out the sun. "Honestly? I wouldn't worry about it too much. Fall Showcase is coming up. People don't have time to be messing around with that game. It'll just fade away once everyone's focus shifts."

I hope he's right.

The conversation drifts into silence again. A breeze has picked up and it blows at the edges of the blanket. The corner flips over my leg and I kick it off. The sun has reached the horizon. It was still pretty high in the sky when I sat down.

"What's going on with you and Luke?" Adam plays with a piece of grass.

That seems to be the million-dollar question.

I sigh. "I don't even know. We're all over the place."

He rips the blade of grass into smaller pieces and sprinkles them back onto the lawn. "Luke's being dumb because you're not like every other girl he's gone after."

"And you know something about the girls he usually goes after?" I run my fingers over the scraps of grass on the blanket.

"I used to be really good friends with Luke. We grew up together. He was a good guy before he found out he could date eighty percent of the girls in L.A. without a problem." He tosses the remaining pieces of grass back onto the lawn and leans back on his hands.

It's hard to picture Luke before he was a flirt. That's what I know him as. It wouldn't be normal for him not to flirt with every girl he saw.

"You're a challenge to him and he doesn't know how to deal with that. The feelings he has for you probably scare the shit out of him."

They scare the shit out of me too, but I can't tell him that. "How would you know?"

"Do you remember Jake? He was at the fundraiser." Adam turns to look at me, crossing his legs and leaning back on his hands.

I don't know why we're changing the subject. I'm so hung up on my own problems right now. I don't think I can handle Adam's, too.

"Brielle said he was your boyfriend."

He laughs. "Something like that."

"Who is he, then?"

"I met Jake years ago when we were both still in high school. He did some acting and we met during a class. We had an instant connection, got along really well, and started dating. We dated through high school, but when we went off to college, he said he didn't want any attachments because he didn't know what would happen over the next few years."

"Ouch."

I don't want to hear this story. It feels too much like Patrick. I can't handle listening about how Adam was left heartbroken because Jake didn't love him as much as he thought.

"Yeah. So, anyway. Jake doesn't really define himself as anything."

Shitty things happen to the nicest people. It's just not fair.

"Jake slept around a lot his first year of college. Boys. Girls. It didn't really matter as long as they could give him what he needed." He leans forward and brushes off his hands. He looks so sad as he talks about Jake leaving him on the sidelines to go do whatever he wanted.

I frown. "Wait, so I don't get it. Aren't you guys off and on?"

He smiles and runs a hand through his hair. It falls back to its original spot as soon as his hand is gone. "We talk religiously once a week. Every few months when he's tired of his life, he'll come back to me. And it'll be great for a few months before the cycle starts over."

"Why do you put up with it?" I can't believe Adam would let Jake walk all over him while sitting around waiting for him to come back. There are so many other options out there for him.

His smile fades. It's easy to tell their situation doesn't make him happy. "I have to trust that he'll come back to me. It's a balancing act we've got going. I let him do what he needs to do and he always comes back to me eventually. It might not be perfect, but I'll take it."

That's crazy. I don't think I could ever have that kind of relationship with someone. Not that I can have any kind of relationship with anyone. I always find ways to screw them up.

"We choose who we trust, Sadie. People have to earn that trust, but we give it away, too. At some point, you have to decide if it's worth holding yourself back. What are you missing out on? Maybe your trust will be abused, but you never really know until you try."

I know he's right. I know I have to start showing Luke that I can trust him. I just don't know how. But if I don't start soon, Fall Showcase is going to be a disaster.

Adam smiles at me before pushing himself up off the ground. "I'm going to go find Brielle. Have a happy birthday."

I smile up at him. "Thanks, Adam."

If I don't learn to trust Luke, then the only one I'm hurting is myself. I'm killing my chance at a future with dancing. And I'm ruining his chances, too. I won't be able to live with myself if I'm the reason he doesn't get into Fall Showcase. He deserves that much.

THE HIT LIST UPDATE
October 13

It appears that we've had a case of mistaken identity. One of our girls was accidentally crossed off the list prematurely. It's been corrected below to show who is still available for points. On the plus side, our top spot is open again!

Brielle Watkins	29%
Samantha Jameson	23%
Rachel Barrons	17%
~~Rebecca Hemsworth~~	11 points
~~Noelle Sanstrohm~~	10 points
~~Courtney Turner~~	9 points
~~Jessie Freeman~~	8 points
Ashlynn Jenkins	12%
Kate Williams	6%
Sadie Bryant	0%

There you have it. Good luck and happy hitting!

~ THE HIT MAN

11

The sun shines through the studio window as people wander the streets below. It feels wrong that it should be so bright when I'm having such a shitty morning.

"Are you okay?" Brandon stands beside me. I didn't even hear him enter the studio. "You look a little pale."

"I'm fine. Just a little stressed."

"I hear sex helps reduce stress."

Jesus Christ. Of course he would know that my name is back on The Hit List.

I hold up my hand. "I'm not interested. So stop. Stop with the lingering touches. Stop with the sexual remarks. Just stop."

His face contorts to one of barely controlled rage. "You're not even worth this." He walks across the studio.

"Good. You don't deserve anyone's points anyway. Leave me the hell alone." I don't think he heard me, but I don't really care.

A backpack slides across the floor behind me. Luke.

"Hey." His voice is softer than usual. Maybe it's because he hates me. Or maybe because he's not sure how mad I am after I saw him blatantly trying to get points for someone.

"Hey." I don't want to give him the satisfaction of knowing how uncertain I am.

"I'm sorry about yesterday," he says, rubbing the back of his neck.

I shrug, trying not to show any emotion. He doesn't know that I blamed him for my name getting crossed off The Hit List. Now that it's come out as a mistake, I feel guilty for even thinking he would screw me over that way. "It's fine."

"No, it's not." He leans against a chair.

"It's seriously fine." I'd rather just forget about it and fix this partnership. We still need to dance together.

"So, yeah, I'm sorry," he says.

Miss Tasha walks into the room at that moment. Brandon trails close behind.

"Please tell me that today's practice is going to be the best you've ever had. You guys are already behind everyone else. We can't afford to lose another day. At this rate, you'll never be ready for Fall Showcase tryouts in less than two weeks." She crosses her arms over her chest and pushes her hip out. She reminds me of Brielle when she gets impatient.

She's technically talking to both of us, but she looks at me for most of her little speech. I get it. I'm the one that screws up rehearsal the majority of the time.

"I don't see why we would have any problems." I'm determined to prove to all of them that I can do this.

Brandon smiles at me and I glare back at him. If he gets handsy today, I may punch him.

I step farther out of Brandon's reach. Even after everything I've been through with Luke, Brandon is worse, in my opinion.

He grins back at me. "I'll stand in for Luke if you need me to."

"Yeah, I bet you will." Luke steps in between us to give me a barrier.

Miss Tasha uncrosses her arms and clasps her hands together. Brandon and Luke turn to look at her. "Great. Then let's get warmed up so we can run through choreography and make this routine the best it can be by four."

I can feel it, today is going to be a good practice. Our partnering is going to be amazing. We're going to nail this.

"Let's do this." Miss Tasha presses a button on the remote.

It doesn't matter that I've told myself this will be okay and that we'll do well. The second Luke steps behind me, my heart slams against my ribs.

"What are you waiting for?" There's an edge to Miss Tasha's voice already. Three hours is going to feel like three years if she's like this for the entire rehearsal.

"Just wait." Luke matches Miss Tasha's tone.

Miss Tasha looks like she wants to say something to him, but doesn't. She huffs and walks to the front of the room to watch us in the mirror.

"You can do this. Don't worry about her. Take your time." He runs his hand along my arm.

I shiver at the touch. I don't want to like the way it feels, but I'm sick of lying to myself. But that means that I might be okay with the idea of liking Luke. I don't know if I'm willing to admit that to myself yet.

Luke watches me with concern. I can't tell if it's normal partner concern or if it's girl-I-care-about-as-more-than-a-partner concern. Does it really matter?

I want to say no, but I know the answer is yes. How is this happening to me again?

I take another deep breath, but all the oxygen in the world can't keep my lungs from seizing. Luke's hands find my chest and stomach. The heat of his palm through my tank top sends little chills outward across my skin.

"Okay, I'm ready." As ready as I'll ever be, anyway.

Miss Tasha nods and pushes play. The music fills the studio and I start to dance with Luke. Every touch feels bigger than it is. Everything has a bigger meaning than it did ten minutes ago. My anxiety amps up to a whole new level. Luke can probably feel me shake every time he touches me.

Miss Tasha pauses the music when we stop.

I don't give her a chance to tell us how much we suck. I don't know how to explain that this is different than all the other times I've freaked out. Luke's hands all over my body freak me out for an entirely different reason now.

"I need to take a break."

I can't shake the feeling even after I leave the studio and stand in the hallway. I pull deep breaths into my lungs. My skin is on fire, but it's cold to the touch. Goosebumps cover my arms and legs.

Luke steps through the doors. "Are you okay?"

He's genuinely concerned, but I need to be away from him right now. "I just need a minute. Please."

He doesn't say anything. The door clicks back into place behind him.

I lean my head against the wall and count my breaths. What the hell is wrong with me? If I'm not afraid he's going to drop me, then what am I afraid of?

But I already know what it is. Luke is becoming what Patrick used to be. Oh my God.

Calm down. Calm down. Calm down.

Miss Tasha purses her lips at me, but doesn't comment on my absence when I return to the studio. "What happened to you guys? We were making progress and it's like you took ten steps back in one day."

Because I think I might like my partner as more than a partner. She probably doesn't want to hear that, though.

"All right, let's go again," she says, clapping her hands.

It takes us a couple of hours to be able to run it all the way through from start to finish without mistakes. When she's satisfied we can do it without messing up, Miss Tasha puts the song on repeat and we dance it over and over to engrain it in our memories, only stopping to take water breaks.

When we finish for the umpteenth time, Miss Tasha presses a button on the stereo and the music stops.

"As far as technique goes, you guys are amazing. Thank you for stepping up and proving to me you can do this."

I smile, surprised to hear something good come out of her mouth for a change.

"But you both look so stressed when you dance. I can feel the chemistry, but it's like you're trying to cover it up. Don't do that. You have to have chemistry. And you two have way too much of it to even try to cover it up."

And there it is.

I know what she sees when she watches me because I do it on purpose. I've adopted the same mindset I usually reserve for barre exercises. I can't handle the feelings I have for Luke so I shut them off. Instead of listening to what I should be feeling, I focus on the muscle memory, how each move should feel, and shut out the world.

But I have no idea what's going through Luke's mind, why he's struggling. I glance up at him to get some sort of clue from his expression, but he's giving nothing away.

While I freak out constantly, he seems to have a handle on his emotions all the time. It's not fair. How am I supposed to know if he feels anything about me?

"I don't think this is going to work," she says, shaking her head. She paces the front of the room. Bad things happen when Miss Tasha paces. "We need something different, something you'll be able to pull off."

"This isn't hard. We can do this," Luke says. He glances over at me.

There was something in the look. A hint of something other than friendship—I couldn't have imagined it.

"You're not feeling it. You don't even look like you're having fun. You look like you're trying to hate each other. I'm changing your dance. You're going to pretend to be breaking up instead. It'll be less of a reach for you." Miss Tasha looks satisfied with herself and her solution.

I think it sounds like a terrible idea.

"That doesn't really fit with the dance," I say slowly, worried about where she's going with this.

"That won't be a problem. I have another dance in mind," Miss Tasha says.

"You've got to be kidding me. We spent weeks learning this one. I thought you wanted us to be ready for tryouts. How are we supposed to be ready if you change the choreography?" Luke's voice increases in volume and by the time he's done speaking, he's yelling at her. He runs his hands through his hair and walks to the other side of the room. He turns back when he can't walk any farther and stands beside me. His hands stay locked in his hair.

"You either want to get in front of the talent scouts or you don't. That choice is yours, but I can tell you right now, you won't make Fall Showcase with that dance. I'd rather watch paint dry."

———

The rest of the week is excruciating.

Tuesday is the same as Monday, but with different choreography. We spend the entire rehearsal learning a new dance. By the end of the day, I'm so tired that I start mixing up the steps. Miss Tasha gets annoyed and sends us back to our rooms.

Wednesday is only slightly better. Miss Tasha can't yell at us about the choreography anymore. Something clicked overnight and we're nailing the steps, but we still aren't playing the parts of heartbroken ex-lovers fresh from a break-up. I ask her if I look happy enough to be in love. She says no, obviously thinking I want to go back to the old dance. I tell her I can't fall out of love if I've never been in love. She doesn't like that very much and takes her frustration out on us, making us do stupid technique exercises for the rest of rehearsal.

Thursday, she tries to force us into our parts. She wants me to cry, to get into character. I tell her I can't cry on command. Luke looks entirely too amused about the whole thing until she turns on him too, telling him she's sure he's broken many hearts with all the girls he runs around with and that he should tap into that feeling. That pisses him off and he spends the rest of rehearsal dancing like he wants to punch someone in the face. It doesn't help the fake break-up sadness. And I kind of want to push him out the fifth-floor window by the end of rehearsal.

When I wake up Friday morning, I thank God that I get a break from Miss Tasha over the weekend. I walk as slowly as I can to the studio after saying goodbye to Adam and Brielle. Everyone is already there.

"Nice of you to join us," Miss Tasha says, looking over at me as I walk through the doors.

I smile brightly. "No problem." I don't want to play games today.

She rolls her eyes. "Okay, let's stretch so we can start."

Today is no exception to the monumentally shitty week of rehearsal. We make it halfway through the dance before she shuts the music off.

"What are you guys not getting about this? Let your emotions out. No one is going to want to watch you like this. Technique is not enough here. What do I need to do to get you to see that?"

"I'm trying. I really am."

No matter what I do, it's still not good enough. I know that. I don't need her constantly reminding me.

"Well, try harder. You got into this school because you're a good dancer, but all you're proving to me right now is that you're crumbling under the pressure."

"She's doing fine. You can't expect us to be perfect in a week," Luke says, taking a step between Miss Tasha and me.

I glance at him. He never fails to stick up for me when Miss Tasha's around, and I'm grateful for it. There's no way I would be able to put up with her on my own.

"I can and I do. Do you think a choreographer will put up with this? No. You'll get fired. I don't know what you guys need to do, but you need to figure out something because come Monday, I expect huge improvements." She grabs her bag and swings it onto her shoulder.

I groan, not sure what she expects to change in two days. The only thing that will be different is I'll be less angry with her after not seeing her face for the entire weekend.

She sighs, letting go of her bitchy mood for two seconds. "Maybe you should start by answering this: Why are you so afraid of letting go?" Then she leaves.

I glance at Luke. He's staring at the wall, completely ignoring me. I know what I'm afraid of, but it never occurred to me that he might be afraid of something, too.

THE HIT LIST UPDATE
October 17

I hope you are all enjoying your weekend. Here's yet another update for you. We've got some more girls crossed off this week and a new guy on top. The game is heating up. Make sure you continue to check in every week to find out which girl is able to claim the top spot on our list.

#11	28 points
#10	27 points
#2	25 points
#18	23 points
#1	22 points
#3	20 points
#5	18 points
#6	16 points
#14	15 points
#12	14 points
#17	13 points
#15	12 points
#13	12 points
#4	11 points
#9	10 points
#19	10 points
#16	8 points
#7	6 points
#8	----------

Sadie Bryant	34%
Rachel Barrons	29%
~~Samantha Jameson~~	13 points

NIKKI URANG

Brielle Watkins	24%
~~Rebecca Hemsworth~~	11 points
~~Noelle Sanstrohm~~	10 points
~~Courtney Turner~~	9 points
~~Jessie Freeman~~	8 points
~~Ashlynn Jenkins~~	7 points
Kate Williams	13%

I know this game has been picked up at other schools, which is fine, just remember that it started at The Conservatory and none of those other games are affiliated with this one in any way.

Until next time, happy hitting!

~ THE HIT MAN

12

Saturday morning is made for sleeping in, especially when my body hates me from a rough week of practice. Apparently Luke never got that memo. At exactly eight, he pounds on the door to my room.

"Sadie, wake up," he yells through the thin wood.

I pull my pillow over my head to block out the noise and try to go back to sleep.

"What's going on? Did someone die?" Brielle asks from her bed.

Groaning, I throw my pillow at the door, turn over, and pretend I'm deaf. Maybe he'll go away on his own.

"Go away. No one's home," Brielle yells.

Or maybe he'll go away now that he knows no one is here.

The pounding gets louder.

"You've got to be fucking kidding me." Brielle rips the covers off her body and stalks to the door. She throws it open. "What the fuck do you want? Do you have any idea what time it is?"

"Coffee?"

"I don't want your damn coffee. I want to go back to sleep. Go away." She slams the door in his face.

"Sadie, get out of bed or I'll come in there and drag you out. We need to practice."

"Do something about him," Brielle whines. She's already back under the covers with her eyes closed.

I push off my covers and get out of bed. I open the door, stifling a yawn. Luke is dressed in grey sweatpants and a white T-shirt. His dance bag is slung over his shoulder.

"I don't think you really understand the point of Saturday morning. It should be illegal to be up this early." My eyelids feel heavy and I let them close. I lean against the doorframe so I don't fall over.

"That's why I brought coffee," he says, waving a cup from the coffee shop down the street under my nose.

I open my eyes when I smell it and grab it out of his hand, taking a sip. "What do you want?"

He looks too good for eight on a Saturday morning. His hair is tousled in a put-together-messy kind of way, while I'm sure mine looks like a disaster. His eyes are bright, like he's been up for hours. The smell of his shampoo mixes with the coffee. I bet I would look better after a shower, too.

He smiles. "We need to practice."

So, no to that shower then.

My brain laughs at him, but I'm too tired for the sound to reach my mouth. "Not right now. Give me a couple hours. If you make me dance now, I can promise you I won't be able to be fake sad that we fake broke up. I'll be for real crabby as shit that you woke me up."

"Meet me in the studio in twenty minutes." He grabs the coffee out of my hand.

I answer him by pushing the door closed. He can keep his damn coffee. I'll get my own. Later. After a few more hours of sleep.

"I'm not kidding, Sadie," he yells.

I sigh, leaning my forehead against the door. He's not going to give up. "Yeah, fine, whatever. Twenty minutes," I yell back.

He laughs as he walks away from the door.

It takes me thirty minutes to get to the studio. Luke's warming up when I walk through the door, but he stops when he sees me.

"You're late."

"You're an ass. It's been a really long week and I'm exhausted." I know I sound whiny, but I don't care.

"You won't think I'm an ass when we make it into Fall Showcase."

I narrow my eyes at him. "No, I'm pretty sure I'll still think you're an ass." He's right, but I don't want to give him the satisfaction of knowing that.

He sighs. "Can we please get something done? Miss Tasha won't be here so rehearsal will be so much better."

I know that's true. Everything is better when Miss Tasha isn't around. "Fine."

I speed through a warm-up, hoping it will get me back in bed faster. Luke smiles at me and turns to the stereo to find the right song. I grab two folding chairs and place them in the middle of the room. The chairs are supposed to be a park bench and we'll have prop trees and bushes on the set, but this works for rehearsal. I take a seat on one of the chairs and cross my right leg over my left to get into my beginning pose. He walks off stage to prepare for the dance to start.

The first notes of the music start and I do my best to look like I'm waiting on a park bench for the love of my life. It's not a stretch to be attracted to Luke. He walks toward me and I launch myself off the chair, running full speed at him, jumping into his arms at the last possible second. His touch is warm against my leg and back. He holds me tight, tighter than he's held me in rehearsal before. I want to believe it's because he might like me as more than a partner, but really it's probably so he won't drop me.

He spins me around once and tries to disentangle my limbs from his body. I don't want to let go. He sets me back down on the ground and he keeps me at arm's length while I attempt to grab his hand. He pulls it away effortlessly every time.

This is supposed to be the part when he breaks up with me. But I can see him working hard to hide his emotions. Like maybe he doesn't want to let me go, either. But that's not part of the dance.

He stops dancing. "What's wrong?"

"I could ask you the same thing. You don't really look like you're about to break up with me."

He stops the music and crosses his arms over his chest. "Well, you don't really look like you're in love, so we're even."

I sigh and sit down in the chair. "This is useless. We're never going to make this work."

"Gee, thanks. Nice to know I'm so hard to love." The tone of his voice surprises me. He sounds like he actually believes that's what I meant by it.

"That's not what I meant. This isn't easy for me, Luke." It's surprisingly easy to care about him, but I'm not supposed to care as much as I do.

"And it's so easy for me?" He's borderline yelling at me.

I cross my arms over my chest. "This is insane. Now we're just pissed at each other. It's harder to pretend I love you when you act like this."

He bursts out laughing and runs his hands through his hair, looking up at the ceiling. "You're so frustrating."

I glare at him. Why is this funny? He won't think it's funny when our names aren't on the list for Fall Showcase. "Yeah, well, you're equally as frustrating, so clearly I learned from the best."

He looks at me with affection. I don't understand why he can't look at me that way when he dances. It should be the other way around.

I sit down on the bench and wait for him to press play. Instead, he pulls me off the bench. "What are you doing? This is where I start."

"We're not dancing anymore today. We're going out."

With tryouts less than a week away, we need all the practice we can get. We can't afford to go out anywhere, even if I smile just thinking about the idea. "Going out where? I'm not dressed to go out anywhere," I say, looking down at my spandex shorts and folded-under tank top.

He pushes me in the direction of the dorms. "Fine."

My heart picks up at the thought of spending another day with Luke. The last time had ended on a bad note, but there's no way I'm letting that happen this time. We're going to have a good day.

We pass a couple girls in the hallway. They whisper and stare at us as we pass.

"Looks like she won't be on the list for very long."

Luke stops walking and turns back toward them. "We're not having sex. And even if we were, it wouldn't be for that game and it wouldn't be any of your business."

The girl's mouth drops like he's offended her, but she recovers quickly. "That's not what I hear."

"If you spent half as much time studying as you do obsessing over this game, you probably wouldn't be failing History of Theater right now."

She glares at him, but doesn't say anything more. Luke walks back toward me, placing his hand on my lower back when he gets close enough. I choose to believe he said those things for me and not for him. He wouldn't have anything to gain by saying it.

"I'll meet you back here," he says when we reach my room.

"Okay."

I watch him walk partway down the hallway before I unlock my door.

The white board in front of me has a new message on it.

Went out with Adam. Be back later. But you'll probably still be rehearsing. Have fun!

Brielle

I smile at the board and walk into the room. It takes me longer than I expect to find my favorite jeans and a hot pink racer-back tank top. The pink looks great against my tan skin. In my rush this morning, I'd put my hair up in a ponytail, but now there's a crease from the ponytail holder and it looks weird when my hair is down. I run a brush through it, squirt some water onto it, and scrunch it with my fingers to give it some waves. When I'm done, I can barely see the crease.

I'm looking for my purse when someone knocks at the door. "Come in."

Luke opens the door and sits down on Brielle's bed. I find my purse shoved into my dance bag and pull it out. The smell of Luke's cologne spreads through the room.

"Ready?" he asks.

Butterflies dance in my stomach. "Where are we going?"

"It's a surprise."

The morning sun has already heated L.A. into the seventies, the breeze warm against my skin. Luke grabs my hand as we walk down the steps. I look up at him, but he watches the sidewalk in front of us. The touch is unexpected and I can't help my smile. It feels right.

People fill the lawn outside the school. Most are students looking for a little bit of sun before they have to spend another week busy with rehearsals. Adam leans against a tree, Brielle's head in his lap. Adam looks down at her and points in my direction. Brielle lifts her sunglasses and waves to me. I wave back.

Luke leads me to a truck parked at the curb and opens the passenger door.

I frown up at him. It makes me a little nervous that we aren't walking or taking a cab. "We're driving?"

"Trust me, you don't want to walk."

I get in and he shuts the door behind me. His truck is nice and it makes me wonder if it's his or if it belongs to his parents. It looks new.

He gets in, starts the engine, and plugs his iPod into the stereo system. "It's going to take us a little bit to get there."

I watch him, taking in his shorts and T-shirt, trying to get a hint of where we're headed. "You're still not going to tell me where we're going?"

"Nope."

We wind through the busy streets and pull out onto the freeway. It doesn't take us long to get out of the city and soon we're heading north, no longer surrounded by businesses and chaos, but rolling hills and trees. Every once in a while the coast shows through the landscape.

I glance over at Luke. He looks at ease, one hand on the steering wheel and the other on the ledge in front of the window. A breeze from the slightly open window blows his hair back. This is the most relaxed I've seen him since school started. He catches me watching and I stick my bottom lip out in a pout.

"You can stop looking at me like that. I'm not telling you where we're going."

I cross my arms over my chest and lean back farther in the seat. "I just assumed we were going somewhere in the city."

"You know what they say about assuming..."

I stare out the window, fascinated by the green hills and clear sky. I've never seen this part of California.

He plays with his iPod until he finds the song he wants. He punches play and sets it back on its holder.

The opening notes sound familiar, but I can't place it. It isn't until I hear the first chorus that I recognize it. The band sings about playing games and making the same mistakes while expecting things to be different in the end. I glance at him, wondering if he knew the song when we danced at the fundraiser together or if he had to track it down.

A smile plays at the corner of his mouth, but he doesn't look at me. Was this his plan all along? To take me back to that first night? To prove that we can have good times even with the bad swirling around us?

If it is, I think I'm okay with it. Honestly, it's better than being confused about how he feels all the time.

The song ends and I yawn, my exhaustion finally hitting me.

Luke looks over at me. "Sorry I woke you up so early, but I wanted to take you out here today."

"So you really had no intention of rehearsing at all?" I'm not upset by his ulterior motives. Rehearsal gets old after a while. No matter how much we need it, we need this, too. Whatever this is.

"No, I really did want to rehearse and I thought we'd get more in than we did. But oh well. We know the steps. That's not what we need to be practicing anyway."

"Are we going somewhere to rehearse?" I turn to look at him, hoping the answer is no.

"Not exactly." His hand slides against the steering wheel as we come out of a turn.

I narrow my eyes. His vague answers aren't any help. "How far are we going?"

"A little ways."

"How far is a little ways?" I ask, yawning again.

"A couple hours."

A twinge of fear settles in my stomach at being so far away from everything that's become familiar with a boy with whom I have a history of fighting.

I have no other way home. If he gets so pissed at me that he drives off, there's nothing I can do. He wouldn't do that, would he?

"What am I supposed to do for a couple hours?"

"Oh, I don't know. We could talk." He glances at me, a smile pulling at his mouth.

"What do you want to talk about?" I'm afraid this conversation will end in a fight like so many of our others. But I'm willing to take that chance.

"What was your favorite thing about New York?" He taps his thumb against the steering wheel to the beat of the music.

"I loved the chaos. There was always something going on all the time. I loved that I could get out of rehearsal at ten o'clock at night on a Tuesday and this amazing little Italian place right up the block would still be open. I loved seeing all the different people all the time." Talking about New York brings some sadness.

He smiles at the windshield. "Do you miss it?"

I'd be lying if I said I didn't. But I couldn't stay in that city anymore knowing I could run into Patrick at any moment. The city may be huge, but we had a knack for being in the same places at the same times. The dance world is a small one.

"Sometimes. But I chose to come here, so I can't really complain."

He shrugs. "It's okay to miss home. Even if you had to get away for a while."

I glance over at him, worried he's going to expand on his thought, but he doesn't. I change the subject before he thinks twice about it. "What about you? What do you love about L.A.?"

"I love everything about L.A. It's so laid back all the time. I love the beach and never really having a winter." He looks over at me. "Plus, all my favorite people are here."

My face heats up under his look. He doesn't notice because his eyes are back on the road.

"If you had to pick between either city, which would you choose?" He pulls his sunglasses out of the collar of his shirt and throws them up on the dashboard.

It's no contest. L.A. would win every time. But the reasons are changing. When I left New York to get away from my old life, I didn't anticipate creating a new life in L.A. that I would miss.

L.A. was a means to an end. A way to find a job and make a living as a dancer. But I have friends here. And I have Luke.

"L.A."

He smirks at me. "Interesting answer."

We spend the next couple of hours comparing the differences between L.A. and New York. I laugh at his impression of a New York accent, which sounds more like he's in an Italian mob, but mostly I just enjoy the side of Luke I rarely get to see. The side he reveals when he's outside of the studio and more carefree.

"We're almost there," Luke says.

We pull off the freeway into a town. Small shops line the street. The beach sits a few hundred feet behind the road and the shops. A long pier in the middle of the beach stretches out into the ocean.

Luke parks the truck. I stare around me in awe. Wherever we are, it's beautiful. The coast stretches through town and out onto the horizon. A couple swimmers bob in the water. A marina sits further back at the edge of the town. It's filled with sailboats. People walk around here and there, looking in shop windows, eating ice cream at the tables outside, fishing on the pier.

"Where are we?" I ask.

He smiles. "Avila Beach. Do you like it?"

It reminds me of the small towns in upstate New York I used to visit with my parents in the summer. I smile at the memory. My parents were both happy then. My dad was still alive and my mom wasn't bitter. "It's beautiful."

"I come up here sometimes when I need to get out of the city. It's usually really busy, but there's a huge music festival going on in the next town over so there shouldn't be too many people."

Luke gets out of the truck and opens the back door. He grabs a backpack and what looks like a blanket. "You coming?"

I grin at him and jump out of the truck. The air is cooler here and I can smell the salt on the breeze. A gust of wind whips my hair around my face and I sweep it up into a ponytail, using the hair tie around my wrist to fasten it.

We walk to the pier. Tables are set up along the edge. Some are occupied with people playing games or enjoying a cup of coffee. Luke spreads the blanket down at the end of the pier and sits down.

My stomach twists and turns against itself in nerves. Something about this whole thing feels off and it suddenly clicks why. "This feels a lot like a date, Luke."

He laughs. "Sit down. If I wanted to go on a date with you, I'd ask first."

Which means this isn't a date. Then what is it? I don't know what the point of this whole thing is. We don't need to get to know each other better at this point.

He pulls a couple of sandwiches out of the bag and hands me one.

"You thought of everything, didn't you?"

He nods, swallowing a bite of his sandwich. "I even brought a sweatshirt for you for when you get cold later."

I scoff at him. "What makes you think I'm going to get cold?"

"Because it gets cool when the sun goes down."

He must be planning to stay for a while if he's worried about the temperature after dark. I don't let myself dwell on it. This day is about relaxing and being away from the dance world for a while. I stare out at the crisp blue ocean and work hard to forget that tryouts are next week.

"I don't know how to be in a relationship." Luke looks out at the water, almost like he's talking to himself.

I stare at my hands, not sure whether I should respond. He's silent and it's awkward. We're not the kind of friends to divulge this kind of information to each other. We're barely the kind of friends who spend time with each other outside of school.

I play with a rock on the pier, tossing it between my hands. I don't know what to say, but I can't just not say anything. He's expecting some kind of answer after dropping that bombshell on me.

I knew he had commitment issues, but I'd always heard it from other people. Hearing it from him feels special somehow.

He continues, saving me from having to come up with something to say. "I don't know how to pretend to love you. I sleep around a lot because I can't do relationships." He leans back against his elbows on the pier.

My hand twitches when he mentions sleeping around and I find myself focusing more on how many girls he's slept with this year than on the important information he's giving me. I watch the horizon so I don't have to look at his face. The same sailboat drifts back and forth. For the first time today, I'm a little mad we're not back in the city. At least there are more distractions in L.A.

His vulnerability is back. I know it's to help me understand him better, to trust him better, but it has the opposite effect. It makes me want to dive off the end of the pier to get out of the awkward situation he's putting me in.

He tosses the corner of his sandwich into the ocean, still not looking at me. "My career will always come before a girl, and I feel like it's unfair to lead someone on like that. I don't know what it's like to be in love. Or to break-up. So it's kind of hard for me to act like I do."

I'm frozen, refusing to make eye contact, my arms wrapped around my knees, just trying to remember how to breathe.

In. Out. In. Out.

I resist the urge to tell him the truth about New York, the reason I'm so hesitant to trust anyone. I swallow my nerves and step off the edge of the cliff with him again.

"I thought I was in love once. Back in New York. But he did something that people in love don't do. And it took that for me to realize I probably wasn't in love with him. I was in love with the idea of being in love."

He watches me, but my eyes stay glued to the sailboat. "What happened?"

The sailboat gets blurry as tears form in my eyes. This is it. I have to make this leap. Just like Adam said, I have to choose to trust Luke.

"You've read the article, but I guess no one knows what really happened. We were dating, things were awesome. We had everything going for us. And then I got hurt when he dropped me."

He nods. "That was in the article."

I look out at the water again. I don't like that he's read the article. It paints me in a bad light. The injury had really bad timing and it became the sole focus. I've never wanted anyone to feel bad for me, especially not him. "What the article doesn't say is how that injury was right before our final show of the year—the show the New York Ballet Company's artistic director came to see. We were both supposed to be signed. And then I got hurt and I couldn't dance, so I didn't get a contract. But he did. And as soon as he was offered a spot, it was like I didn't exist anymore."

"You felt abandoned."

I glance over at him, nodding. His eyes burn into me in a way only someone who's felt the exact same thing can express. His mouth opens a little like he's going to say something else, but he doesn't. "It was like none of it mattered to him. He just wanted a step up in the world and he used me to get it. I never wanted to partner again after that. I won't be someone else's stepping-stone. That's why it's hard for me to trust you."

His hand finds mine at my side and we sit like that for a long time, silently staring out at the ocean while every thought fills my head. Thoughts of what it would be like if we were different, if we weren't afraid of our feelings, if I wasn't so scared all the time. We're crossing another line just by having this conversation. Pretty soon it's going to be hard to find our way back.

"Why do you do it? It's so hard for you to dance with me. You're doing better, but you still hold back. Why stay here and continue to put yourself through that every day?"

His thumb rubs against mine and I pull it out of his grasp to remove the sensation. I can't think when he does that.

"It's been my dream to do this since I was a little girl. This is what I love. I don't know who I am without dance."

Though I'm starting to get an idea. Every time he touches me, every time he lets me pull away, every time he celebrates my small victories, I'm starting to see the person I've become through the people I've met here, the person they're helping me to be.

A couple of kids run past us, giggling as they chase each other up and down the pier. The younger one stops to wave at us as she passes. I wave back. She takes off down the pier, her chaser in hot pursuit.

Luke stretches his legs out in front of him. His feet dangle over the edge of the pier. Earlier today he looked like a carefree guy enjoying a day off. Now the heaviness of the conversation weighs on his face. "Don't let dance define you. One day, you won't have it anymore, either from age or injury. And then you won't have anything left because you spent your life chasing something that has to end, eventually."

"What defines you?"

He looks over at me, a frown creasing his forehead. "I haven't decided yet."

198

He doesn't say anything else. I know he's right. Eventually, I'll be too old to dance. And if I'm lucky, another injury won't end my career early. If it does, it leaves me to find something else to focus on. Hopefully that never happens.

A shadow passes over the sun as the clouds begin to roll in. Luke sits calmly beside me, but he looks over at me when I shift my position to lean back against my hands. His eyes tell a different story than all the words he's spoken today. There's hope. Like maybe a relationship could work. He's the only one in his own way now, and I can't help him with that. Maybe he'll figure out a way before it's too late for him.

He stands up and holds out his hand to me. "Will you dance with me?"

The last thing I want to do is dance. I'm perfectly content sharing this space with him in silence. "Now? Can't we take a break from dancing? We dance all the time."

"Not on a pier in the middle of the ocean."

I raise an eyebrow at him and look around at the minimal space surrounding us at the edge of the pier. "We can't dance here."

I don't want to tell him the real reason I don't want to dance with him. I'm afraid I can't conceal my emotions right now. I don't want him to realize that I want exactly what he's already told me he can't give me.

"We'll be fine. We're not going to break out in choreography right here. Come on. Just dance with me. We won't fall in."

That's exactly what worries me. Falling. But I roll my eyes and grab his hand, letting him pull me up. "We don't even have any music. This isn't the movies. Music doesn't just start playing in the background."

He takes his phone out of his pocket and presses some things on the screen before tucking it into the pocket on his sweatshirt. Soft music from the phone speakers floats around us and I can't help laughing at him.

"This is weird," I say.

"This is fun," he says, pulling me close to him.

He leads me around in small circles, careful not to get too close to the edge. This is the most real we've been with each other since we met. And I can feel it in our dancing. Luke feels at ease, and I allow myself to relax in his arms.

"Truth or dare." He leans his head against mine on his shoulder.

"No. I'm not playing this again."

It ended badly the last time. I don't know why he thinks it will be any different this time.

"If you don't pick, I'm going to pick for you."

I lift my head off his shoulder and lean back to look at him, trying to decide if he's kidding. He's not. "Fine. Whatever. Dare."

He pauses for a beat before he answers. "I dare you to trust me."

All the blood rushes away from my head and I feel a little lightheaded. My hands shake and I clench them into fists so he doesn't notice. Maybe I heard him wrong.

"What are you afraid of?" His eyes sparkle with the challenge. A smile plays at the corner of his mouth.

There are too many things to name. I'm afraid of what I feel, what he feels, what will happen to us if we ever admit to each other how we feel.

I nod. "I do trust you. I wouldn't be here right now if I didn't."

His brow creases. "There's a 'but' in there somewhere."

If I don't tell him now, I probably never will. "I don't want to live the real-life version of our dance. And I don't want a repeat of New York."

His grip tightens around me. "I would never let that happen."

My heart soars at his words, but I won't allow myself to be happy. This isn't a relationship. This is the two of us, so far removed from what's normal, and grasping at anything that might work better than the two of us alone. "You can't promise that."

"I can't. But I can promise to try like hell not to hurt you." He kisses my temple and rests his chin on the top of my head.

I want to look at him, to ask him what he feels, but I already know. He feels exactly like I do. Scared shitless by the thought of caring about another person, but willing to try to make something work.

THE HIT LIST UPDATE
October 18

This isn't so much an update as it is a notice to let everyone know I'm officially shutting down the blog. Things have gotten way out of hand since it started. I wanted it to be big, but I wasn't really anticipating that it would be as big as it's gotten. I can't keep up with it and I don't have time for it. I hope all our Hitters had a great time and our audience playing along got some entertainment out of it.

Happy hitting!

~ THE HIT MAN

13

The cafeteria is packed. I grab an apple from the line, not feeling up to anything else. My stomach can't handle anything heavy on tryout day. Brielle grabs a granola bar from the line and hands a dollar to the girl behind the register.

We sit down at an empty table. Brielle doesn't talk as she eats her granola bar. It's fine with me. My mind is consumed with tryout stuff anyway. I take a bite of my apple and stare off into space.

There are so many things that could go wrong. Our chemistry could suck, Luke could drop me, we could forget the steps. Ugh. This is too much pressure.

A tray slams down on the table in front of me. "Good morning, ladies."

I smile up at Luke. "Morning."

Brielle rolls her eyes and stands up.

I grab her sleeve and pull her back down into the seat. "Get over it and sit down. You're fine."

"Fine." She points at Luke. "But I'm watching you, Morrison."

The table is silent as everyone chews their breakfast. Brielle looks content. Most of her attitude in front of Luke is all for show. She's already told me I should go for it with him if that's what I want.

"Did you guys hear about that blog? It was shut down last night." Luke pushes a chunk of waffle around his plate with his fork. He shoves it in his mouth when the waffle won't hold any more syrup.

"You're joking. It seemed so popular. Why would they shut it down?" Brielle shoves the last of her granola bar in her mouth.

"Maybe the faculty got involved." It's not like the blog was a secret. Anyone could find it with a Google search.

Luke shakes his head as he chews. "I don't think that's it. He said he was too busy."

"Well, that's probably true. Fall Showcase is right around the corner. Sex should probably take a backseat to your career." Brielle slides down in her chair and rests her head against the back to look up at the ceiling.

Luke points his fork at Brielle as he chews. "Unless sex is your career."

She rolls her eyes and turns sideways in her chair to look at me. "Why do you like him again?"

His eyes widen playfully. "You like me?"

"So, how about tryouts? Everybody ready?" I take a bite of my apple to avoid having to say anything else.

Luke watches me as he eats. The grin never leaves his face. "We're totally ready."

"I can't believe they're making us go to class today. That's like torture. I just want to get tryouts over with." Brielle balls up the wrapper from her granola bar.

"They'll be here before you know it." Luke leans back in his chair and stares at the table.

Brielle scoots her chair closer to the table. "Well, I think we're all going to make it."

"What if we don't?" Luke says it as a joke, but I can hear the seriousness behind his question. Even he isn't guaranteed a spot.

"You don't have a choice, Morrison. Sadie needs to be in that show." Brielle raises an eyebrow at Luke.

He looks across the table at me and shrugs. "I guess you have a point."

I cross my arms. "I feel so confident now. Thanks."

He reaches for my hand across the table. I don't pull it away. "We'll be fine. Promise."

The last time someone promised me something was Patrick. And he broke it. I have to believe Luke. I won't have anything left to believe in if I don't.

I can't focus in nutrition class. Tryouts are only a few hours away. It's dumb to even be here. No one will be paying attention.

"Has anyone seen Monica?" Miss Taylor looks worried.

No one answers her. A few students shrug their shoulders. A guy up front high-fives another guy.

"I heard she's a wreck. Like nervous breakdown material," Jessie says to Kate in front of me.

"Class doesn't start for two more minutes. Maybe she's late," Kate says.

I lean forward in my seat so I can hear more of their conversation.

Jessie waves off Kate's doubt. "I heard she slept with Brandon and then found out he used her to get points in The Hit List. Now she won't come out of her room. You can hear her crying when you walk by."

Kate's brow creases in worry. "That's terrible. Has anyone checked on her?"

"Who knows? She probably won't answer the door." Jessie smiles, flipping her hair over her shoulder. "I hooked up with a boy who told me he'll split the money with me if he wins."

Kate glances back at me, noticing me watching. "Can you believe this?" she asks, including me in the conversation.

"Don't you have a boyfriend?" I ask. It wasn't too long ago that Jessie and Rebecca fought in this very classroom.

Jessie shakes her head. "Not after he slept with some other girl. This was payback. It just happened to be sweeter than I was expecting."

Kate slides down lower in her chair. "You believed him? He probably just wanted sex."

"He's not like that." Jessie crosses her arms, looking defensive.

"They're all like that," Kate says.

"Don't you think it's kind of sketchy that he told you he's playing that game? Even if he does split the money with you, he still had sex with you for points." Does nothing about this situation strike her as abnormal?

"I've known him forever. He's a good guy." She raises an eyebrow, like that's all the proof we need that he'll pay her.

Because good guys totally sleep with girls for points in sex games. It's completely legit.

This conversation is pointless. The game doesn't even exist anymore. "You do know the blog got shut down, right? No one is even playing anymore."

Jessie laughs. "I guess you haven't seen the flyers then."

"What flyers?"

"There are flyers all over campus. Someone else is keeping track of points and stuff in the absence of the blog. They have an email account set up and they email out updates if you sign up with them." Jessie twirls her hair around her finger as she talks.

What the fuck? I thought we were done with this.

"Is that how they did it last year? Did you guys know anything about it?"

Jessie frowns. "No, I think they kept it pretty low key."

"Did you hook up with anyone last year that you think could have been playing?" I don't really expect an answer. I know it's weird that I'm even asking. I don't really know either of these girls.

"I hooked up with Luke Morrison." Jessie smiles like she's reliving the moment.

Kate rolls her eyes. "Everyone hooked up with Luke Morrison."

Jessie raises an eyebrow. "Did you?"

"No."

Kate and Jessie continue arguing, but I'm off in my own world. If the game is still going, that means people will still play. And that means I still have to put up with assholes hitting on me.

I'm still worth points. I can't trust any of the guys' motives for talking to me. Luke might be playing. Hell, he might even be running it. At least three girls on the list have some sort of history with Luke. How many other girls do too? That can't be a coincidence.

I can't think about this right now.

Every time I think about what's going on with the game, it leads to doubts about Luke. If I let myself get pulled down by this, I won't survive tryouts. Right now, I choose to believe Luke has no involvement and he's just a flirt. I focus on our time at the pier in Avila, on the moment everything changed, on the moment I chose to trust him.

———

It's a quarter to three when I enter the auditorium. Everyone is there, including Miss Catherine, and they all turn to look when the door slams behind me.

"Now that everyone has joined us, we can start. I want everyone in the first three rows. Move if you have to."

She walks to the front of the auditorium and sits at a table. Miss Tasha, Brandon, and the other teachers and assistants are seated already. Students shuffle between seats, most moving toward the front of the auditorium. I glance over the rows, but all the seats are taken. Seriously?

"Have a seat, Ms. Bryant. We're waiting," Miss Catherine says.

I narrow my eyes and open my mouth to ask her where exactly she would like me to sit, but Luke tugs on my hand hard and I fall into his lap.

"Don't even think about challenging her," he whispers in my ear as I try to sit up straight. He helps me as I perch at the edge of his knees. It takes every muscle in my body to keep from falling off.

"I'm sure I don't have to tell you that this is one of the most important auditions in your lives. Getting selected for Fall Showcase means a chance at dancing in front of some of the biggest talent scouts on the west coast. Most of you will walk away with a job." She scans the auditorium, giving us all a couple of seconds to let her words sink in.

Students stare at the front of the auditorium. Adam bounces his feet against the ground. It shakes the nearby seats. Brielle puts her hand on his knee to get him to stop. He starts fidgeting with his hand instead.

The girl sitting in front of us sighs and twirls her hair around her fingers. Nervous energy.

"Let's discuss some rules. There will be no talking during auditions. I'm going to read the order of dances. Keep track of your number. You may stretch in the aisles a couple dances before your turn," Miss Catherine says.

She reads through the list of fifteen pairs. Luke and I are tenth. I breathe a sigh of relief. It's too stressful to be one of the first ones up.

"Group One, you have ten minutes to warm up before we begin. Auditions will start promptly at three," she says.

Students break out into quiet chatter around me. Groups One and Two get up and move to the aisles to stretch. I want to go take one of their seats, but Luke's hand on my arm stops me.

"Relax," he says. "Why are you so tense? We're going to be fine."

"I know." I press my fingers against my temple, trying to ward off the headache that's forming.

It's been a long day already and I just want to finish tryouts so I can go back to my room. I can't help thinking about all the guys in this room who might be playing the new version of The Hit List. Probably a lot of them. Half of them have hit on me at some point. Nothing would stop them from joining the new game.

How many of the girls here have already lost something as a result of the game? I know I've seen several of them with guys, but that doesn't necessarily mean anything. Still, how many of them are carrying the weight of a broken heart or shattered pride around with them now?

Luke's hand runs up my leg. "What's wrong?" His face is etched with concern.

I can't think of a coherent response to his question with his hand on my leg. It takes all my energy to keep my body still right now. "Just a headache."

His hand finds my back and he starts rubbing in circles. I close my eyes against the sensation while I wait for tryouts to begin. The circles on my back become my focus. If he doesn't stop soon, I'm not going to be able to dance. I'll be lying on the floor. But I don't want him to stop. Every time he touches me, it means something. He doesn't do it just to do it. It's always to comfort me or make me feel better.

The music starts and Group One takes the stage. Technically, they're good, but they don't draw me in. I can't focus on their dancing as much as Luke's hands.

His hand moves to my neck, the pressure reducing minimally. It keeps moving up to the base of my skull. I lean back slightly so he can reach my head better. His fingers thread through my hair and he slowly massages my scalp. I don't notice that I've leaned all the way back until I feel his chest pressed against my back and shoulders.

It feels right to have him pressed against my back. I want to stay in this moment forever. Screw tryouts. Luke is better.

Luke's left hand drops and he laces his fingers through my left hand. His right hand massages slow circles on the crown of my head.

I glance to my right and meet Brielle's stare two rows in front of us. She smiles at me before turning back around to watch the stage. No other students even give us a sideways glance. They're either too nervous or too engrossed in the dancing to care what we're doing.

"Better?" he whispers, his breath on my ear.

"Much. Thank you." I can't move. I'm so perfectly relaxed, I don't think I'll ever move again.

"Good."

His lips brush against my cheek. It takes me by surprise, but they're gone before my mind works well enough to say anything. I won't allow myself to get tense after he's done such a wonderful job relaxing me.

The dances fly by and soon we're sitting in the aisle, stretching and waiting for our turn. It's too narrow to sit side by side so Luke sits directly across from me. I avoid eye contact, trying to focus on the dance instead of on all the feelings I'm having for him.

"Group Ten, you're up," Miss Catherine calls from the table at the front of the auditorium.

Luke gets up and offers me his hand, but I use the chair next to me to pull myself up instead. He frowns, but doesn't say anything. We climb up onto the stage and I glance over at Miss Tasha and Brandon, who sit next to each other. Miss Tasha watches us from her place at the table. Her eyes hold a warning and I know we'll hear an earful if we mess this up. Brandon looks bored by us already. I'm going to prove them wrong.

"Ready?" Miss Catherine asks.

I take my place on the bench in the center of the stage. Luke walks into the wings off stage. The guitar chords of our music fill the auditorium, echoing off the walls. Luke walks toward me and the look on his face is enough to tell me that he's let down his wall.

Everything comes together in that moment. All the touches, the closeness, the vulnerability. I would risk myself for Luke. I would break my rule of never getting close to anyone again. For him.

When I jump into his arms, electricity shoots through me, shocking my system. And when he pushes away from me, when we're so far apart that his fingers slip through mine and we're no longer connected, I feel the break and I want to be back in his arms again.

We dance with an intensity we've never had before. Every position, every lift, every feeling. I'm not acting anymore. Luke's eyes burn into mine. And instead of feeling the dance and waiting for the comfort of falling into the correct positions at each step, I find myself more focused on expressing myself. Through Luke.

The dance ends and applause erupts around us. Miss Tasha and Brandon are on their feet, along with half the students in the audience. My face heats against the unexpected attention. Luke grabs my hand and raises it over his head, ready to bow. I look over at him, smiling. His eyes are filled with affection and my smile falls. I gaze back at him, confused.

And suddenly it dawns on me. Despite my trust issues, I've fallen for Luke. I can't keep telling myself that it'll go away or that I'll stop wanting to kiss him. I don't want either of those things to happen. I have no idea what I've gotten myself into.

14

The line to Crave is long, but I wouldn't expect anything less on a Friday night. I'm not really sure what people crave when they come here, but if it's half-naked women and guys that think they're famous, then they're in the right place.

Crave is packed. Wall-to-wall bodies fill the dance floor. Electronic beats vibrate off the walls and bounce around in my chest. It jump-starts my heart and I can no longer distinguish between my pulse and the music.

"I need a drink," Brielle yells.

Grabbing my hand, she drags me behind her to the bar and screams an order at the bartender. Less than a minute later, she places a pink drink in my hand.

"What is this?" I yell.

"Lighten up, Sadie. We're celebrating," Adam says, bumping his shoulder against mine.

He's right. Tonight is about celebrating. All three of us made it into Fall Showcase.

"Does it matter? Try it. You'll like it," she yells back.

Here's to fake IDs and persistency. I take a sip of the pink liquid. It's fruity and bitter at the same time, but not horrible. I take a bigger swallow.

"Good girl," Brielle says.

The music changes and Brielle bounces beside me, her drink sloshing over the side of her glass. She doesn't seem to notice. "I love this song."

She grabs me again and pulls me onto the dance floor. I drain my glass and set it on a table as we make our way to the center of the club. Brielle raises one arm over her head and sways to the music. I feel a body close behind me and I turn around.

Adam hands me a glass with yellow liquid in it. "Wow, Brielle. You make sure you have a drink, but you don't worry about Sadie?"

Brielle pouts. "I got her one, too. Where's your drink?" she asks, looking at me.

"Gone," I yell back at her, taking a sip of the yellow drink. It tastes like pineapple and orange and is less bitter than the last one.

"Slow down," she says close to my ear. "You're going to make yourself sick."

I wave her off and take another sip. I've never been a huge drinker, mostly just at random parties back in New York, but I need it tonight. I've been thinking about Luke all week and I don't want to worry about my feelings for him tonight.

There's barely enough room to move. I look around to find an opening in the crowd, but there isn't one. The club must be at maximum capacity tonight.

My eyes meet Brandon's as he stands by the bar. He raises his glass in a silent cheer and smiles. I turn around. I don't want anything to do with him. He's not going to ruin my night.

I drain my second glass. Adam takes it from me and walks away. I dance with Brielle and watch Adam as he walks up to a boy that looks about our age. They dance together and I smile. The boy looks familiar, but he doesn't go to our school.

"That's Jake," Brielle says in my ear.

That's why he looks so familiar. His hair is shorter than it was last time I saw him at the fundraiser and he's wearing casual clothes instead of slacks and a button-up shirt. "So they must be on again?"

She shrugs and takes another drink. Her gaze drifts behind me. I frown and follow her eyes. A boy I don't recognize stands behind me.

"Hi," he says, smiling.

"Hi," I say, cautiously.

"Has anyone ever told you how pretty you are?" He takes a step closer to me and my heart beats a little faster.

I take a step closer to Brielle, wishing he would go away. "Thanks."

"Do you want to go out sometime?"

"I don't date people I don't know," I say. He needs to take the hint and leave me alone.

"Well, then I guess it's good that we go to the same school."

Seriously?

Brielle nods eagerly next to me. I refrain from rolling my eyes at her. She's too drunk to pick up the hints that I don't want this guy anywhere near me. And apparently, so is he.

I smile tightly. "I don't date."

"It's true. She doesn't. I, on the other hand, would *love* to date you," Brielle says. She pulls a rectangular piece of paper out of her dress. "Here's my number. Call me."

He smiles at her, tucks the paper into the pocket of his shirt, and walks away. I burst into laughter beside her.

"What?" She sounds offended.

"Did you just give him your card?" I've never seen anyone give out cards to potential dates.

She stares at me, confused. "So?"

"Why do you even have cards?"

She crosses her arms and glares at me. "I use them for casting calls."

"Did you think there was going to be an agent here tonight and you would wow him with your drunken dancing skills? That's classy."

She smiles at me. "You can never be too prepared." Her smile fades as she stares behind me. "Uh oh."

My smile falls. "What now?"

I turn to see what she's looking at. My eyes land on Luke as he enters through the arch at the front of the club. He walks forward and passes Brandon talking to some girl at the bar. Noelle follows closely behind Luke.

"Which one are you talking about?" I ask.

"All of them?" She bursts into giggles. "I'm sorry. This is so not funny." She manages to keep a straight face for three seconds before dissolving in laughter again.

I roll my eyes at her and grab her drink, finishing it for her.

I watch Noelle and Luke. They stand close to each other, her hand on his arm so she can balance on her tiptoes, closer to his ear. His hand moves to her lower back and pulls her closer to him. Smiling, he leans down and whispers something in her ear. She falls apart giggling.

A pang of jealousy spikes through my chest. I know we're not exclusive, but after what happened today and in Avila, I thought maybe something was happening. Or it is happening, and he's playing that game even though he says he's not.

Trust him. I should be able to do that by now. He kind of deserves some of my trust after everything we've been through and everything he's shared with me.

I turn back to Brielle. She dances with her eyes closed, not aware of anything that's happening. I join her, wanting to dance away the last of my stress. I'm not going to worry tonight.

A blue martini appears in my hand, and Luke stands in front of me. "Your hand looked empty," he says.

He's back to flirting with me. I don't know how long I can keep doing this. Going back and forth between partners, friends, and the possibility of more is exhausting.

I mouth thank you to him. He looks amazing in his dark jeans and white button-up shirt. His muscles pull at the fabric of his shirt in all the right places when he moves.

"How's your night been?" he asks.

"Good," I say, smiling up at him.

We're friends. Partners. We can't be anything more than that.

"To us. Congrats on Fall Showcase. Now we have to win." I raise my glass to him.

He clinks his glass against mine. "You know I didn't get there on my own, right?" He watches me as he takes a sip of his drink.

"Neither did I." It's true. And I never really thanked him for helping me get there.

"Luke! Oh my God, I'm so glad you're here. You have to dance with Sadie," Brielle says, hanging on Luke's neck.

"How much have you had to drink?" he asks, raising his eyebrows.

She frowns back at him. "None."

"Too much," I say at the same time.

He laughs. "Why don't we get you some water?" He puts his arm around Brielle's waist to lead her to the bar. "Are you going to be okay here for a couple minutes?"

I nod. He doesn't need to worry about me, but it's sweet that he does.

"I'll be right back," he says and walks toward the bar with Brielle.

I let myself get absorbed in the music again. Dancing like this is so different than at school. The Conservatory was my escape from classical ballet. Crave is my escape from The Conservatory.

An arm snakes around my waist and I spin around with a smile on my face. Now that Brielle has her water, Luke can spend the rest of the night dancing with me.

But it's not Luke. It's Brandon. My head spins at the movement and Brandon's blurry form flashes before me. I stumble backward into the table and he grabs my wrist to keep me from falling.

"Dance with me." He wraps an arm around my waist and pulls me flat against his chest.

I try to push his arms off me and move out of his grasp, but my hands are useless and he's a lot stronger than me.

His sick smile is the opposite of Luke's. His touch is rough. He grips my arm tighter the more I struggle. "It's just one dance. You owe me for all the shit I've put up with in your rehearsals."

"I don't owe you anything."

Where is Luke? He should be back by now.

Panic creeps into my chest and it feels like I'm on fire. He's holding me so tight, I can barely breathe. Tears prick my eyes. I need to calm down. I won't be able to get away from him if I freak out. He won't hurt me here. We're in a crowded club, for Christ's sake. If I can move him a little bit closer to security, maybe they'll notice something is wrong.

Calm down. Calm down. Calm down.

"Let go of her and back the fuck off, Brandon." Brielle comes up behind me.

She trips as she takes a step forward. Luke catches her around the waist before she lands on the ground and sets her on her feet again. She's holding her shoes in one hand and a glass of water in the other. I'm not sure how she managed to keep most of the water in the glass.

Brandon tightens his grip and I shut out everything else as it feels like something sharp stabs my lungs.

His grip is too tight. I can't breathe. My lungs burn in my chest. Stars light up in the corner of my vision. I'll pass out soon. Maybe then I'll be able to breathe.

Air.

"Let her go," Luke says. His voice holds a warning.

Brandon grins. "We were just having a little fun."

Brandon releases me and I stumble backward into Luke. I gulp for air and hold onto his hand to keep myself steady. His grip is the complete opposite of Brandon's. Luke's arm offers safety and comfort and

I'm glad he's here. I lean closer to him. He'll keep me safe.

"It's your lucky night, Luke. She's drunk enough to put out. That's a perfect *bonus* to end your night," Brandon says.

Luke's in front of me in a second, and he punches Brandon in the face. Brandon falls backward onto the floor of the club, blood dripping down his chin. People clear away from us like a huge ripple going through the crowd. Three bouncers appear out of nowhere.

What the fuck? Did that really just happen?

Brandon yells something from the ground, but the music and the people around us are too loud for me to hear what he says. Blood drips to the ground. Luke shakes his hand beside me. The blood from the ground has somehow managed to get onto Luke's sleeve.

Luke shoves me toward the door. "Let's go. Now."

My head spins. I stare down at my fingers threaded through Luke's and frown. I doubt this was what he had in mind when he said he would try for me. I turn to Brielle to ask her what I'm supposed to do now, but she's not here.

"What about Brielle? We can't just leave her here," I say.

We step outside and the cool air washes over my hot skin. Brielle, Adam, and Jake stand on the sidewalk.

"Oh, thank God," I say, hugging Brielle. "How did you get out here before us?"

"We took the side door," Jake says.

"We need to get out of here before the cops show up. At least two of us are far too drunk to pass for sober." Adam looks between Brielle and me.

I wave my hand at him. "I am not drunk."

"I'll get a cab," Jake says.

"We're walking," Luke says, looking at me. "The fresh air will do wonders for you right now and we need to talk."

"I don't think I want to talk to you right now. You just punched someone. You're angry." His face swims in and out of my vision. I look at the ground to try to get my bearings. His feet remain still as his body bobs and weaves in front of me.

Jake hails a cab. They pile into it, but Brielle rolls down the window to talk to me. "Call me if you're not coming home."

I frown at her and limp over to the window. My heels are killing me. I shouldn't have agreed to wear Brielle's shoes. "Where else would I be going?"

She shrugs. "I don't know." The cab pulls away from the curb and Adam drags Brielle back from the window.

Luke sighs and closes his eyes. "I'm not mad at you."

I squint at him. "Are you sure? You seem really mad."

He looks hot even though he frowns at me. He clenches his hands into fists. The fabric around his arms tightens. I stare between his hands and his biceps. What other muscle is he flexing right now that I can't see? I press my hand to his chest.

His heart beats like mine inside his chest. It stutters when I giggle. He sighs and pulls my hand away. "Come on."

I trip over my heels and fall to my knees. "Ow," I say, looking up at him.

He pulls me up off my knees and bends down to take my shoes off.

Gravel from the sidewalk pokes into the heels of my feet. "I can't walk without my shoes."

"That won't be a problem. Hold these." He hands me the shoes. He stands with his back to me and pulls my arms around his neck. "On the count of three, jump and wrap your legs around my waist. Okay?"

"Are you giving me a piggyback ride?" I haven't had a piggyback ride in forever.

He doesn't answer me. "One, two, three."

I jump and he grabs my legs. I giggle when his hand brushes my thigh.

"Stop wiggling or I'll drop you," he says.

"Sorry."

He walks in silence until we're a block away from the club. My arms are wrapped around his neck. My chin rests on my bicep close to his ear. I can smell his shampoo and I silently breathe in the scent.

"This would have been so much easier if you'd just stayed a dick." The alcohol swims around in my head and I feel dizzy. The motion of being carried doesn't help.

"What would have been easier?"

"Everything. Can I walk, please?"

He sets me down, helps me put on my shoes, and grabs my hand as we start to walk again. We shouldn't even be talking about this. It doesn't matter. It won't make him stay. Nothing will. Tomorrow we'll go back to being awkward around each other and hiding our feelings.

I trip over a crack in the sidewalk and Luke's grip on my hand tightens.

The corner of his mouth tips up. "I'm sorry I'm not a dick anymore. I'll work on that."

I turn to glare at him. "Just because you haven't left yet doesn't mean I trust you. I mean I do, but I don't."

He pulls me closer against his side. I snuggle into his body. This helps. It makes the moment last longer. Eventually I'll wake up and tonight will be over.

"What makes you think I'm going anywhere?"

"Because that's what people do. They leave." I grab his bicep to avoid falling on my ass.

He trails his thumb down my cheek. "Who else left?"

I can't breathe again. "Who didn't?" I rub my hand over my face. I don't want to be drunk anymore. I'd give anything to be back in control right now. Not being able to focus or shut the hell up is not working for me. "Can we not talk about this anymore?"

I take a step forward and stumble again.

He sighs and reaches out his arm to me. "Can I put my arm around your waist so you don't fall?"

I smile and move closer to him. "Sure, thanks."

His hand grips my hip and he holds me secure against his side. "I won't leave."

He's quiet when he says it and I look up at him. I want him to repeat it and confirm that I heard him right. But he doesn't. He looks straight ahead as we walk. The only confirmation I get is the circling of his thumb against my hip. Except instead of being comforting, it sets off every nerve ending in my side and it's all I can think about.

Is this how he treats every girl he takes out?

"Why did you come with Noelle tonight?"

He frowns. "What are you talking about?"

I roll my eyes. "Don't be dumb. I saw you walk in with her."

He bites his lip to keep a smile off his face. "You mean you saw her walk in behind me because she was behind me in line?"

Sure, that.

"Whatever."

"She stopped me by the bar because she wanted to say how well she thought we did in tryouts. She thinks you're amazing." Luke coughs a couple times.

He's laughing at me. Because I'm an idiot.

My emotions are fried. I feel stupid for thinking he came to the club with Noelle. He keeps trying to do the right thing and I can't even give him the benefit of the doubt.

We walk for another block in silence, Luke's protective arm around my waist. I like the excuse to stay close to him. His cologne washes over me. I might not wash this shirt for a month or so. He smells so good.

"You wanted points for me on that list, didn't you?" I haven't been able to think about much else the past few weeks and Brandon's comment about me being a bonus didn't go unnoticed.

He glances down at me and tightens his grip. "What list?"

"The Hit List. The one online that tells guys who to sleep with. Or I guess it's on a flyer now. Or by email. Something."

His voice is firmer when he speaks again. "Don't worry about it. No one's going to hurt you. I won't let them."

I smile despite the fact that he didn't deny my suspicions. I like protective Luke. I like the feeling of his arm around me. I like the way he pulls me into his side like he wants to protect me from the world. I like the way he's honest with me, even when it's hard for me. And I like these moments, even though they don't happen every day. These are the moments with Luke that I look forward to the most.

It's hard to like it when it feels like he's suffocating me, though. It's unbearably hot all of a sudden. I close my eyes and focus on the cool breeze on the back of my neck, but it doesn't take the nausea away.

"Are you okay?" He stares at me with worry etched into his face. He stops walking and pulls me in front of him so I'm facing him.

"Yeah, just a little dizzy." My eyes fall from his concerned eyes to his barely parted mouth. His arm is still around me, and I move closer to him. My hand runs up his arm and grips his bicep.

I want to kiss him. But I don't want to make the first move.

He stares at me for what feels like forever and I have no idea what's going through his mind. What if he thinks I'm just some clingy girl who gets dumped all the time? Maybe he said he wouldn't leave to shut up the drunk girl. What if he's still playing the game? What if he really did come with Noelle, but he's trying to lie his way out of it?

What if he really likes me and he isn't doing or thinking any of those things?

The ground spins below me as my thoughts spin within me. He's either getting closer to me or my depth perception is way off. I want to lean forward, close the distance between us. I can see in his eyes that he wants to do the same. His breath on my cheek is ragged. I know his heartbeat stutters just like mine is.

He pulls away before we connect and I silently scream. Why won't he just kiss me already? It's not like I've been fucking subtle.

"Truth or dare."

I stare at him, not sure he really just asked me that. Haven't we had enough truth for one night? "I don't want to play your—"

"I dare you to go out with me." He steps closer to me. So close I can feel the warmth of his breath.

I frown. "We go out all the time."

"We do. This would be different. More planned."

My cheeks redden and I can't meet his eyes. Maybe this is his way of making things different. "Are you asking me out on a real date?"

"Are you saying yes?"

"You don't date." I don't date either, but he really doesn't date. Ever. At all.

He shrugs. "I'm willing to make an exception for you."

He has no idea how happy it makes me to hear that. Luke doesn't do relationships. He's made that clear since day one. The alcohol might be making me a little happier than I really am. My head feels cloudy.

Maybe it's the alcohol that's giving me the feeling that I'm about to throw up in the bushes. My face falls. Nothing Luke can say will make this feeling go away.

He frowns. "I didn't mean to push you. I shouldn't have brought it up."

"It's not that. I think I'm going to be sick."

"We're only a block away. Then you can go to bed and sleep this off." He rubs my back. It's supposed to be comforting, but it increases the amount of fabric sticking to my skin from sweat.

"I don't think I'm going to make it that far." I stumble over the edge of the sidewalk and vomit into a bush.

Luke kneels beside me and pulls my hair back, holding it at the nape of my neck.

I try to sit down on the cement, but he pulls me back up.

"I'm so tired. Can't I just stay here?" The grass looks soft and warm, like the blanket on my bed, and I want to curl up on it.

"No. Come on. Let's get you to bed. I'm going to pick you up, okay?"

I nod and feel his arms behind my knees and back before he lifts me. I wrap my arms around his neck. My head rests against his shoulder, my nose brushes against his neck. His arms tighten around me. I'm as close to his chest as I can get.

"Luke?"

"Hmm?"

"I want to be your exception."

He doesn't say anything, but he's smiling when I look up at him.

THE HIT LIST UPDATE
October 26

Some fuck face thinks he can take over this game after I shut it down. Now that I have your attention, here's a message for you:

Back the fuck off.

This game is mine. You did not have permission to take things over. So this is me taking it back so I can run it with my rules. Hitters, please continue to submit all conquests using the email. Send me any hits you completed during my brief hiatus. I'll honor them. I'll have an update for you guys soon so we can have an accurate standings list.

Happy hitting!

~ THE (ONE AND ONLY) HIT MAN

15

The sun shines directly on my pillow, and my brain feels like it's trying to bash its way through my skull. My tongue sticks to the roof of my desert-dry mouth. This is a nightmare. Memories of Luke being sweet last night flood me. It wasn't typical. And now it's going to be so awkward in rehearsal. I pull the covers over my head in an attempt to shut it out. Things will escalate to a whole new level of awkwardness for us now.

Something to look forward to.

Luke asked me out. He asked me out after I'd told him about my issues with people leaving. But he'd been drinking, too. It wasn't tell-everything-you-never-wanted-anyone-else-to-know drunk, but he couldn't have been serious. He wouldn't magically change his mind about dating.

Would he?

Brielle rips the covers away from my face. Light shines in and I claw at my pillow. I hate light. I wish I could disappear completely into this bed.

The bed sinks next to me as she sits down. "Drink this," Brielle says.

I peek out from under my pillow and stare at the bottle she holds. She pushes the beer into my hand.

"I can't go to class drunk." That's the last thing I need right now.

"You can't go to class hung over, either. And it's one beer, not a case. You won't get drunk off one beer."

"How are you okay after last night?" I say. It isn't fair that I feel like shit and she looks perfectly fine.

"My tolerance is much higher than yours. Clearly." I glare at her and take the beer. Her eyes shift away from me. "You're awfully crabby this morning," she says.

"So kind of you to notice." I pinch the bridge of my nose. My head is pounding. "Do you ever regret saying something when you're drunk?"

She laughs. "You're not human if that doesn't happen at least once in your life."

I stare at her. I don't want to know how many times that's happened to her. "I told Luke some stuff I shouldn't have."

Her eyes widen. "Did you confess your undying love for him?"

I throw my pillow at her shoulder. "Not exactly."

She places two rust-colored pills in my hand. "Take these. You're going to need them when the beer wears off."

Ugh. This is why I don't drink. "He's going to think I'm dumb."

"No, he's not. He's not going to act any differently. Because for some reason, he seems to be less douchey when you're around."

Brielle walks to her dresser and digs through a drawer, flinging underwear, socks, and tank tops onto the floor.

"What are you looking for?" I ask.

"I can't find my favorite thong."

I stare at her back as she tosses more undergarments aside. "I didn't need to know that. Forget I asked."

"It was here a week ago. I wore it and now it's gone," she says.

The game. They have to have souvenirs. "Who'd you sleep with?"

She turns around and stares at me, a handful of underwear in her fist. "Excuse me?"

I raise an eyebrow. "You heard me."

She looks at the ceiling, deep in thought. I can see when she remembers because her mouth drops open and she gasps. "That bastard."

"I take it you know who has your underwear."

Her eyes widen and she gasps. "It was last week when I went to the club. I don't even remember taking them off. Sneaky little bitch."

"Please stop talking." I hold up my hand. I don't want to think about her having sex at a club.

My headache is worse—from the hangover or from Brielle, I don't know. I close my eyes and press my fingers against my eyelids.

"Oh, whatever, Sadie. There are so many worse things I could be talking about," Brielle says. "Let's go."

"Aren't you going to pick those up?" I ask, pointing to her discarded clothing littering the floor. I set my half-finished beer on the night stand.

"We're going to be late for class."

———

Luke stands in the hallway outside the studios when Brielle and I turn the corner on our way to class. My hands shake. What if everything that happened last night was just a mistake to him? Maybe he doesn't want me to be the exception to his rule.

If I don't talk to him now, I'll chicken out. I know I will.

"Luke," I yell. I wave to him when I have his attention.

He smiles and walks toward us.

Jessie passes him on the way and she tries to stop him with her hand on his chest. Luke gives her a tight smile and a nod, but he keeps walking. Her hand falls from his chest. She turns to watch him walk. When he's close enough, he snakes an arm around my waist and pulls me into his side. Jessie glares at me and continues down the hallway.

Brandon walks toward us on his way to the studio next door for the senior ballet class. I can see his black eye from halfway down the hall.

"Holy shit," I whisper. "That's worse than I remember."

Students turn to look at Brandon's face as he walks past them. He sneers at a couple of them. They don't ask questions.

Brielle follows my gaze. "Yikes. I wonder how long before he gets asked about that by the teachers."

She's barely done speaking when Miss Catherine comes up behind us, looking like she's on a mission.

"Brandon, can I see you in my office?"

Someone yells in the hallway.

I stare at the scene with my mouth open. Brandon catches my gaze and sneers before following Miss Catherine into her office.

This can't be good.

If he gets in trouble it'll be my fault. And then he'll be pissed at me.

Adam sits down between Brielle and me. "How's it going, ladies?"

I don't know what to say. Things could potentially be very bad depending on what happens with Brandon. I shrug.

Luke sits down beside me and smiles. "How are you feeling?" he asks.

I smile. "Fine." Better after I just watched him blow off Jessie in the hallway, but nervous as hell for what's to come.

He raises an eyebrow at me, but doesn't move from my side. "So I thought maybe we could grab dinner this weekend."

My lungs stop working. He obviously remembers last night and I can't use alcohol as an excuse anymore as the reason he asked me out. He actually wants to go out with me. "I'd like that."

Miss Catherine sweeps into the studio, her skirt flowing behind her.

"Shit," Luke breathes.

"Luke, I need to see you outside." Miss Catherine's voice is like ice. It's not the voice of an angry teacher. It's the voice of a pissed-off mother. I wouldn't want to get called out like that in the middle of class. Luke's in trouble.

The classroom erupts in chatter as soon as the door closes behind them.

"Does she know about the fight?"

"Shit," Brielle says beside me.

"It's not good if she does. They take that seriously," Adam says.

"How seriously?" They don't answer. "This is expulsion material, isn't it?" I ask, worried. If he gets expelled, my chance at doing well in Fall Showcase is gone. I'll get pulled from the line-up without a partner.

"Well," Brielle says. But she doesn't continue.

"Shit," I say.

The longer it takes for him to come back, the more I worry. I stare at the door. Miss Jasmine gives instructions, but I have no idea what she says. Any minute Luke is going to walk back through the door. Any minute.

I struggle through barre exercises, barely hearing what Miss Jasmine says. I'm too busy trying to piece together the events of the morning. Brandon doesn't seem to be in an ounce of trouble, but Luke's been gone for fifty-seven minutes.

Floor exercises are torture. What if Luke doesn't come back? The promise he made last night seems so far away in the light of day. He'll never be able to promise that he won't leave. Even if we stay at the same school, he'll get over me eventually and move on to some other girl.

"Sadie, are you all right?" Miss Jasmine asks.

Half the class turns to look at me. I look down at the floor. I don't like it when everyone stares at me.

"I'm fine," I manage.

Drills are too much. I'm so frazzled that I can barely stay still long enough to keep my balance. I stare at the clock as the seconds tick by, passing the time until I can get out of this room and find out what's going on. My eyes drift over to Brielle beside me. She looks just as nervous.

When class ends, I grab Brielle's arm and drag her out into the hallway. Brandon walks out of the classroom and glares at us before heading toward the studios. I glare at his back as he walks away.

"Did I get Luke expelled?" I ask Brielle quickly. This is my fault. It never would have happened if I hadn't been there. He can't lose this opportunity for Fall Showcase. I know how much it means to him. To us.

"You didn't do anything," Brielle says, sympathy in her eyes.

"That's not a no."

The last of the kids file out of the classroom. Brielle watches them drift down the hallway. "I'm not really sure. There's a zero tolerance policy for fighting here. His parents are the head of the department, but they also have to protect the school's reputation. Those two guys that were fighting over that girl last month got expelled," she says.

I run my hands through my hair. This whole situation is so fucked up. Why couldn't things be normal between Luke and me? Why did I have to fall for him? And why did I put his career in jeopardy? He's going to hate me.

Brielle wraps an arm around my shoulder and pulls me into her side in an awkward hug. "Come on. We're going to be late. Plus, you need to find Luke."

16

Luke sits outside our studio when I arrive. At least he hasn't been kicked out yet. That means there's still a chance to save him.

"Hey," I say.

He stands up when I reach him. "Hey."

"What did Miss Catherine say?"

He looks at the ground. "I'm suspended for a week. I'm not allowed in the studio during class times. I only hung around so I could tell you."

My mouth falls open. A week? How are we supposed to rehearse? He can't be suspended for a week. I've never gone that long without seeing him since we met. "She can't suspend you. This is because of me—I'm sorry."

"It's not your fault. I knew better than to punch him." He leans against the wall next to the studio door.

Yeah, except the only reason he punched Brandon was because of me. "You never would have done it if I hadn't been there."

For the first time, I understand that closing myself off to other people doesn't only protect me, it protects them, too. Without his feelings for me,

Luke wouldn't have felt the need to protect me from Brandon. And he wouldn't be suspended right now.

He reaches out to touch my arm, but I pull away. I don't deserve him. He needs to find another girl who doesn't have so many issues.

He sighs, running a hand through his hair. "Don't do this, Sadie. Not after we've worked so hard."

"I'm not doing anything." But I am. I'm slowly pulling away and I know it. It's probably for the best anyway.

"I can't do this right now." He scrunches his eyes closed and runs his hands through his hair. "I have to go. Mom will be pissed if she sees me still hanging around here." He walks away from me, heading toward the dorms.

Time apart is probably good for us anyway. I see him the most out of anyone, even Brielle. We might have taken a giant leap backward today, but it was for the best. A little distance will be good for us. We can focus on Fall Showcase and put everything else on the back burner for now.

———————

Miss Tasha's class is brutal.

It's more of a boot camp than a class since I'm the only one there. She drills me with technique exercises for an hour until she finally teaches me some new solo choreography. She's quick to criticize every flaw she can find. By the time three o'clock rolls around, I'm exhausted from all the work, irritated that she's in such a bad mood, and crabbier than shit that Luke isn't here to deflect some of her anger.

"You're distracted, Sadie. Focus," she yells as I lose my balance coming out of a fouetté pirouette.

I glare at her. My partner is beating up students and getting suspended. Of course I'm distracted.

I miss Luke. I didn't think I would, but he helps balance out rehearsal. I miss his jokes and the way he would fight back with Miss Tasha. And I miss the way he would stand up for me.

She turns the music off in the middle of my dance. "It's clear that we're both in a bad mood. You've worked hard today. Take a break. I'll see you tomorrow."

"Gladly," I say, grabbing my bag and storming out of the studio.

Brielle is sitting on her bed when I walk back into our room. "Miss Jess let us out early because we were doing so well. How was class? Did you find Luke?" she asks.

I fling my bag into the closet. It hits the wall with a loud thump. Flopping onto my bed, I bury my face in my pillow.

Rehearsal was a nightmare. It's hard to focus on anything when all I'm worried about is Luke and when he'll be back at rehearsal.

"That well, huh?"

I turn to face her. "Luke's suspended for a week."

"That's harsh," she says, frowning.

"I had practice by myself today. I think Luke's pissed at me for getting him suspended." And even though he doesn't know it, I'm pissed at him for an enormous amount of things. The list is never ending, really. The suspension for fighting, the delay on Fall Showcase practice when we really need it and the doubt that's slowly crept in over the course of the day about whether or not we can make something work when the odds are stacked against us.

"I'm sure he's not mad at you," she says.

"Tell that to him," I grumble.

"If anyone should be mad here, it's you. How are you supposed to be ready for Fall Showcase?" Brielle coats her fingernail in a layer of bright red nail polish. She blows on the nail when she's done. Like it will help it dry any faster.

"I can't get ready for Fall Showcase."

Without a partner, I can't rehearse my partner dance. Solos aren't allowed in Fall Showcase this year. So if Luke gets banned from performing, I'm screwed.

"You should probably go talk to him," Brielle says. "Tell him just how mad you are."

"You think?" The idea is tempting. After the three-hour rehearsal I had alone with Miss Tasha, it will feel good to get some anger off my chest.

"Totally. And then you should have angry make-up sex."

I gape at her. "I don't think so."

Brielle laughs. "Well, at least have an angry make-out session. Get all that sexual tension out there." She waves her hands around in front of her.

She can't be serious. Like I would ever do that.

"Well, it works for me," she says, shrugging.

I narrow my eyes at her. "I have no doubt."

Someone knocks on the door, but doesn't wait for us to answer. Adam walks through it and shuts it behind him. "Did you guys hear?"

"We already know Luke got suspended," Brielle says.

Adam's eyes widen, apparently forgetting his own news. "Luke got suspended?"

Brielle rolls her eyes. "This is old news. What happened?"

He pauses for a second, like he's thinking about what it was he actually came in here for. "There was a story on the news about The Hit List. Someone started a copycat game in Texas and some girl was sexually assaulted by a guy claiming he was participating in the game. The names of the girls up for points were announced publicly. The parents are pressing charges."

"Oh, my God," Brielle says.

I'm horrified. How could someone let this get so out of control? Now some poor girl in Texas is living with the ultimate betrayal. How many girls at The Conservatory have been hurt by this game already? And how many more will be hurt before it's all over? I've already seen a handful of girls here get hurt first hand.

Brielle leans back against the wall. "Is it really that crazy that this happened? I mean, it's a bunch of guys competing for girls."

"I thought it was supposed to be shut down, but now it's back. How is it even still running?" I'm furious that this happened. All because some boys wanted to have a little fun at some girls' expense.

"Yeah, but I'm sure they have no idea who started it even if they can guess who's been playing." Adam crosses his arms over his chest and leans against the wall.

"I think it's Luke." Brielle stares at the comforter on my bed.

It's not. It can't be. But hearing it from Brielle is somehow harder than hearing it from someone else. She's supposed to be my friend. She's supposed to stick behind the things that are important to me. "Why would you say that?"

Her eyes widen as she looks up at me. "What? Sorry. You have to admit, it's not like he's completely innocent here. I'm pretty sure he played the last two years."

I refuse to believe he's the one behind the blog. Despite everything—the flirting, the girls—I trust him enough to know he could never do this. He might not be proving he's stellar boyfriend material, but I already knew he wasn't. He still cares about what happens to people.

"It's not him."

She holds her hands up in surrender. "Okay. Whatever you say." Brielle sits down at her computer. She pulls up a search engine, looking for the story. "Whoever did it is messed up."

I don't believe I've changed her mind. Brielle is too hard-headed to ever give up that quickly on an idea. She probably just doesn't want to hear what else I have to say about it.

Whoever created the game here and the copycat in Texas is sick. I completely agree with her. But that person wasn't Luke.

Adam's cell phone rings and he fishes it out of his pocket. "Hello?"

He pauses, listening to the person on the other end of the line while we stare at him.

"I'll be right down." He pushes the screen on his phone and slips it back into his pocket. "I have to go. Jake is downstairs waiting. We'll talk more about this later." He walks out the door, waving at us as he goes.

"Have fun," Brielle says, shutting the door behind him.

I lie down on the bed and throw my arm over my eyes. It's too early to sleep, but that doesn't stop me from wanting to escape reality for a little while. It's too depressing here. My phone rings with a text message. I grab it off the nightstand. A picture. It downloads and I stare at it, not believing what I'm seeing.

It's Luke. With a girl. I recognize his clothes from Crave. He leans close to the blond. It's like déjà vu of all the times I've seen him with girls in the past.

He kissed her. The same night he told me he wanted me to be his exception. He's so full of shit. He didn't mean a damn word he said. From the looks of it, he's not as innocent as he claims about playing in The Hit List.

"Oh, my God."

"What?" Brielle jumps off her bed and sits down next to me, her hair tickling my arm as she leans in to see my phone. She squints at the picture. "Is that Noelle?"

"And Luke. That's the shirt he was wearing when we were at Crave the other night." I drop my phone and lie down on my bed.

The picture of Luke and Noelle kissing in the middle of Crave will be burned into my memory for eternity.

"Give me that." Brielle picks up my phone and punches some numbers. She holds the phone up to her ear. "It's a message saying the phone's been disconnected."

"Who does that?" Frustration burns in my chest. Whether Luke is involved with The Hit List is debatable, but the games he continues to play with my head are undeniable. Brandon, Noelle at Crave, The Hit List girls. It's too much. How can I trust him when there's always someone else? I've let myself fall for him, and it only hurts me. Over and over.

"You should go. To Luke's."

"I can't just go over there."

"Tell him why you're mad. Maybe he'll tell you why he's mad."

"I already know why he's mad."

"Just go talk to him," she says.

Brielle pushes me out into the hallway and shuts the door behind me. The deadbolt clicks into place. I pound on the door. You've got to be kidding me.

"Brielle! Come on. I don't have my keys. Let me back in."

"I'll let you in once you talk to Luke," she yells through the door.

"Seriously?" I yell back. She can't lock me out of my own room. Luke isn't going to tell me anything I don't already know. It's pointless to talk to him.

A couple of the theater students walk past in the hallway, watching me the whole time. "You could at least pretend like you're not staring," I snap.

I don't have time for these girls. I know I look crazy pounding on the door but I don't really care. They should mind their own business. I hit the door one last time with my open palm and stomp off to Luke's room.

I don't even know what I'm going to say to him. An explanation for the picture might be too much for me to handle. And what's the point of it anyway? I don't want to hear about what a good kisser Noelle is.

In the minute it takes me to walk to Luke's room, I only gain steam. Everything he's done keeps replaying in my mind. All the lies he's told me about flirting and whether or not he's playing the game.

I pound three times on the door. "Luke!" I yell. "Open the Goddamn door."

Nathan, Luke's roommate, answers the door. He's wearing sweatpants and nothing else. My eyes skim down his toned body as my breath hitches. His pants sit low on his hips, exposing his stomach and leaving little to the imagination. He crosses his arms over his chest and grins at me.

"Sadie, what a pleasant surprise. I knew you'd come around."

He doesn't look surprised. He looks at me like I'm a cupcake and at any minute he'll start licking off the frosting.

I smile up at Nathan, grab his arm and pull him out into the hallway. He smiles back. I don't like the way he smiles at me, but it's the only way I can get him in the position to do what I want. I push him out of my way, dart inside the door, and close and lock it behind me. If Brielle can do it, why can't I?

"What the fuck?" he yells from the hallway, pounding on the closed door.

"Asshole," I mumble.

Spinning around, I see Luke, eyes wide and headphones in hand, looking completely clueless as to what just happened. He's missing his shirt and it takes a second for my brain to unjumble. I was mad. I know I was. But seeing him without a shirt kills my anger.

"You have no right to be mad at me. I didn't do anything wrong." I take deep breaths, trying to calm down.

He stares at me. "Did you just lock Nathan out of the room?"

"Nathan's an ass." And so not the issue right now.

"That doesn't mean you can kick him out of his room."

"Why did you ask me out? Clearly being an exception to you doesn't mean the same to you as it does to me. And then I get this picture of you and Noelle kissing? What the hell, Luke? You keep telling me you're not playing that game, but it sure as hell looks like it. You flirt with anything in a skirt. You're with a different girl every time I turn around. You're going to have to get a lot better at convincing me because from where I sit, there's no other explanation other than The Hit List."

He sets his headphones down on his desk. "Back up. What picture?"

"I don't know. The one that someone texted me. It looked pretty unforgettable." I pull the picture up on my phone and wave it in front of his face. I'm annoyed that out of everything, he's focusing on the picture. He didn't even try to deny that he was playing the game.

"I'm sorry you saw that."

My mouth drops open. Seriously? That's all he has to say? "You're joking, right? That's all you're going to say?"

He glares at me and crosses his hands over his chest. "You're not going to listen to anything I tell you, so why does it matter?"

He might have a point, but that doesn't change the fact that I want to hear his explanation. Because it might make me feel better to hear from him that the picture isn't real or that it's not what it looks like.

"I need something more than that, Luke. Anything."

His tone turns angry. "How about this? I put myself out there for you. I asked you out. And now suddenly you're backing off because you're scared. What if something did happen in that picture? We weren't exclusive. Fuck, Sadie, we've never even been on a date."

I cling to the only thing I have. Because I am scared. I'm terrified. But I refuse to tell him that.

"What about Avila? You can tell yourself that it wasn't a date, but it was..."

How can he tell me Avila didn't mean anything?

"We can't do this anymore. I'm your partner and your friend. Nothing more than that." His voice is quieter.

"Then why did you ask me out? Friends don't ask friends out unless they're interested in becoming more."

He's shutting me out and my efforts to keep him with me are failing. I was scared when I shut him out earlier, but this alternative that he's creating is so much worse. I'd rather risk my heart than feel like he doesn't want me.

He stares at the floor. "It was a mistake."

"I don't believe you." I glare at him, daring him to lie to me again.

He runs his hands through his hair. "We can't be more than partners. I won't be the reason you give up on your dreams. Not like Patrick."

"Don't ever think you have that much power over me."

I focus on my breathing, calming myself and waiting for him to speak. But he's silent and when I open my eyes, he's pacing a couple feet away from me. And in that moment, I want him to hurt. I want him to feel everything he's made me feel. Because it's not fair. None of this is fair.

So I hit him where I know it'll hurt the most.

"I can't believe I ever trusted you. You've done nothing but string me along, making me care about you. But how can anyone ever really care about you? No one knows the real you. All you do is push people away. I feel sorry for you."

A sob breaks in my chest and the tears I've been trying to hold in fall freely down my cheeks.

"You're absolutely right." His face is completely blank.

I want to shove him, slap him, kiss him. Anything to get some kind of reaction. But all he does is stare back at me, his face void of any emotion. Even anger is better than what he's giving me. How can he feel nothing right now?

I step toward the door. I need to get away from the suffocating walls of this room. I open the door, but his words pull me back.

"I'm sorry, Sadie."

I don't look back at him. I don't want to see how not sorry his face looks.

I'm so done with Luke. He doesn't give a shit about me so why should I give a shit about him?

"Yeah, so am I."

THE HIT LIST UPDATE
October 28

I know you're here for an update, but I want to take the time to address what happened in Texas. The sexual assault against that girl would never have happened if the rules had been enforced. It's because of dumbasses like the one who took over during my hiatus and others who start up whole new games in completely different states that things like this happen.

So don't do it.

Please remember that all acts MUST be consensual between ALL PARTIES involved. Respect each other. This is not a game to determine how many girls you can force to have sex with you. IT IS 100% CONSENSUAL AT ALL TIMES.

Now that that's out of the way, here are this week's numbers:

#2	30 points
#10	29 points
#1	29 points
#18	28 points
#19	24 points
#17	22 points
#11	21 points
#6	21 points
#15	20 points
#3	20 points
#5	18 points

NIKKI URANG

#7	16 points
#16	16 points
#14	15 points
#12	14 points
#4	13 points
#9	12 points
#13	12 points
#8	------------

Sadie Bryant	89%
~~Brielle Watkins~~	14 points
~~Samantha Jameson~~	13 points
~~Rachel Barrons~~	12 points
~~Rebecca Hemsworth~~	11 points
~~Noelle Sanstrohm~~	10 points
~~Courtney Turner~~	9 points
~~Jessie Freeman~~	8 points
~~Ashlynn Jenkins~~	7 points
Kate Williams	11%

It's still anyone's game and our top girl is still up for grabs. Get on that. Happy hitting!

~ THE HIT MAN

17

Class is hard today. My hip limits my range of flexibility. The only good thing is that I'm not with Luke right now.

The general mood of the students has declined rapidly in the past few weeks. Or the general mood of the girls. A lot of them seem depressed or angry. There are more fights about petty things like barre space and water bottles. The ones who used to be friendly toward me and smile in greeting every day stopped a long time ago.

Miss Clara calls class a little early. "You guys did a great job today. See you tomorrow."

I sit down on the floor and pull off my shoes, shoving them into my bag. A senior I've never talked to walks up beside me.

"Sadie, right? I'm Mark."

"Hey." I stand and walk out into the hallway, in a hurry to get to my next class. But Mark follows me.

"I was wondering if maybe you'd want to get together and rehearse sometime. This is my last year here and I can probably give you a lot of tips that'll help you out over the next few years."

It'd be easier to take him seriously if he wasn't staring at my boobs the entire time he talks. I'm so over this game. It needs to disappear. "I'm going to have to pass. But thanks for the offer."

I reach for the door handle, but he opens the door for me, holding it until I walk through, and then jogs to catch up with me again.

"You really are a great dancer. Who have you studied with?"

At least he's not asking me to dinner, but I still don't want anything to do with him. I stop. I don't have time to chat because I'm going to be late for rehearsal.

He stands too close for comfort, and touches my elbow briefly before his hand drops to my butt. "You have a really nice body."

It seems like since news of the rape in Texas broke, the guys here have gotten worse in their advances. The lines are blurring. And that's not okay.

Brielle shoves him away from me. "Excuse you, what the fuck do you think you're doing? Did she ask you to touch her like that?"

Mark hits her arm away. "Nobody asked you, Brielle. What are you, her bodyguard or something?"

"No, I'm her friend. And even if she did agree to go out with you, I'd make sure she stood you up because you're a sexist pig." Brielle positions herself between him and me and shoos him away with a gesture of her hands. "Are you dense? Go away."

She watches him walk down the hallway before she turns to me. She tries to keep a straight face, but when I smile, she does, too.

"Seriously. The boys in this school need to learn to take a hint." She bumps her hip against mine and smiles.

"Agreed."

"I'll see you after rehearsal." She walks down the hallway toward another studio.

I walk toward my own studio, ready to start another hour of rehearsal. I pass a crumpled up piece of paper lying in the middle of the hall, no more than three feet away from a garbage can. The familiar handwriting makes me stop and pick it up.

Carefully, I unfold the delicate paper to reveal the writing. Luke's handwriting stares back at me with notes about our duet. He'd taken these one of the first days with Miss Tasha. We don't even rehearse this one any more.

Printing on the other side of the page catches my eye and I flip it over. I only have to see the first line to know what it is. The sickening words glare at me from the page.

Welcome to The Hit List: a game of sexual conquest.

The paper only confirms what he has yet to deny. He's been playing along since the very beginning, since the first day he met me. He's been trying to get points for me since then, and he hasn't stopped since our recent blowup.

I walk through the door to the studio, the paper still in my hand. I shove it into my bag and sit down to stretch before rehearsal starts.

Miss Tasha walks into the studio, Luke following close behind her.

"Since we've lost our assistant to a bar fight," Miss Tasha looks pointedly at Luke, "I expect perfection from you both. I don't have time to put up with your shit."

Rehearsal is long. We warm up and spend the next three hours running the different dances we've learned. Miss Tasha hasn't decided which one she'd rather see us do for Fall Showcase. But she's made sure to tell us that none of them are ready.

Every time Luke touches me, I flinch. I don't want him anywhere near me. He has his own issues getting close to me. It's like he's afraid to touch me. Probably because he can sense my anger and knows I want to trip him.

I'm grateful when it's over. I can't take the silence from Luke any longer. Miss Tasha is easier to put up with when Luke banters with her, but there hasn't been any of that today.

"Okay, guys. Thanks for your effort today. Let's see if we can do better tomorrow." Miss Tasha sounds like she's already made peace with the fact that we aren't going to do well at Fall Showcase.

She leaves and Luke sits down in front of his bag, packing up his stuff.

I pull the folded piece of paper out of my bag before I have too much time to think about it and drop it in front of him as I walk past.

"What's that?" he asks, picking it up.

I stop when I'm closer to the door than to him.

I shrug. "I don't know. You tell me."

It's now or never, Luke. Time to either seal my trust or break it forever.

His eyes narrow fractionally as he unfolds the page. "Where did you get this?"

"Does it really matter?" I roll my eyes at his confused expression. "I found it on the floor in the hallway on my way to the studio. Why does it have your writing on it?"

His eyes widen, finally understanding what I'm getting at. "I printed this a while ago to show to my mom. I guess I forgot about it. It must have fallen out of my bag."

I search his face for any sign that he's lying to me, but I come up empty. My heart flutters in relief. I know he's told me before that he wasn't involved, but confronting him with concrete evidence makes me feel better. He wouldn't lie about it right to my face when I'm holding proof, right?

I play with a string on my shorts. I didn't believe him then and I don't believe him now that he only sees me as a friend. Friends don't have the kind of chemistry we have when we don't hold back.

"Can I ask you something else?"

He sighs, leaning back on his hands. "Why not?"

"Why don't you want to be more than partners? You've been giving me mixed signals for two months."

His face hardens. "I have no desire to be in any relationship right now, Sadie. And I'm sorry you feel like I'm leading you on. I was just trying to make things easier for our partnership. To help you trust me a little more."

My heart breaks in my chest. All the tender moments I've shared with Luke have meant nothing to him. He used my emotions to strengthen our partnership. Betrayal invades my body.

"So, what? All those times you shared things, the places you took me that were special to you, the times you've almost kissed me, all that was just to make me trust you? So we could dance better together?" Unbelievable. He's such a dick.

"That's not what I meant," he says.

I can't believe what I'm hearing from him. "I'm trying to give you the benefit of the doubt here, I really am, but you're making it hard. You played with my feelings to get me to trust you."

He leans back against the wall. "Why are you so mad about this? You don't trust me. You never did."

"Because you told me once that you don't lead girls on. And that's exactly what you did to me." I shove his shoulder.

"And what do you think you're doing to me?" he asks.

"Seriously? You initiated all that shit. I just went along with it, thinking maybe I was something special to you."

He looks down at the floor. "You're just my partner."

I nod. "That's how it's going to be?"

He doesn't answer me. He doesn't even look at me.

Anger rages through me. "Fine. I'll see you later, *partner*."

I throw the door to the studio open, letting it bang against the wall. This is exactly why I never should have trusted Luke. He might not be physically leaving me, but he's closing himself off. That's probably worse.

THE HIT LIST UPDATE
November 2

I'm just going to dive right in here, since half of you don't read this shit anyway.

#18	38 points
#2	35 points
#10	34 points
#11	31 points
#1	29 points
#19	26 points
#17	25 points
#3	24 points
#6	21 points
#15	20 points
#14	18 points
#5	18 points
#7	16 points
#16	16 points
#9	15 points
#12	14 points
#4	13 points
#13	12 points
#8	----------

Sadie Bryant	15 points
~~Brielle Watkins~~	14 points
~~Samantha Jameson~~	13 points
~~Rachel Barrons~~	12 points
~~Rebecca Hemsworth~~	11 points
~~Noelle Sanstrohm~~	10 points
~~Courtney Turner~~	9 points

NIKKI URANG

~~Jessie Freeman~~   8 points
~~Ashlynn Jenkins~~   7 points
~~Kate Williams~~   6 points

Happy hitting!

~ THE HIT MAN

18

Luke stands in front of me at the barre. It's been twenty-four hours since we talked last. I would have been happier with any other spot, but there weren't any. I can't stand being anywhere near him. He does his part by ignoring me, which only makes me angrier.

In just under an hour, I'll have rehearsal with him again. I'd rather have all my teeth pulled without any Novocain. There have to be other options, other students who are just as unhappy with their partners. Maybe we could switch. Twelve days isn't a whole lot of time to learn a new dance, but I can do it.

I focus on my battements, not wanting to wait until afternoon practice to talk to Luke about changing partners. If we can get this out of the way, he can go talk to Miss Catherine right after rehearsal and I can have a new partner by lunch. The thought lifts my spirits a little.

"Luke," I whisper.

He either doesn't hear me or he ignores me.

"Luke," I say louder.

Nothing.

I glance at Miss Jasmine to make sure she isn't watching me before I deliberately miss a kick and scoot closer to him. On the next battement, I extend my leg and kick him right in his arm.

"Ow," he growls. But then he's silent.

So I do it again on the next battement.

He turns his head to the side. "What do you want?"

I continue with the exercise, my next kick sailing out past his arm into the empty space next to him. "You have to tell your mom you don't want to partner me anymore."

"No," he says.

"Why the hell not?"

It's much louder than I intend and Miss Jasmine looks up at me. "Is there something wrong, Sadie?"

"No," I mumble.

"Then you won't mind if we continue with the exercise." She narrows her eyes at me.

"Go ahead," I say, waving my hand in a gesture for her to continue.

Across from me, I see Brielle's mouth fall open. Miss Jasmine's face turns the slightest shade of pink in either frustration or embarrassment. I'll be in Miss Catherine's office again by the end of the day, but I don't care.

I can't believe Luke said no. Why wouldn't he want to switch partners? It's not like our rehearsals will be anywhere near pleasant from now on.

"Ballsy. I think I'm rubbing off on you," Brielle whispers across the barre.

I raise my leg for another kick and aim right for his elbow.

"Stop," Luke hisses.

"No," I counter.

He sighs and does his best to ignore me, but I can see the muscles in his back and shoulders tensing in frustration. I smile to myself, glad that I'm annoying him as much as he annoys me. The kicks aren't that hard, not even enough pressure to leave a mark, but for someone who's trying to concentrate, it's probably one of the worst things. I launch another kick into his arm.

"I swear to God, Sadie, if you don't stop that..."

"What? You'll be a dick to me again?"

Another kick.

"Knock it off. Right now."

"Or what?" I challenge.

Bad idea.

Luke whips around and grabs my upper arm, dragging me away from the barre and out of the room. I look back at the stunned faces as he shuts the door behind me. I'll definitely be back in Miss Catherine's office soon.

"What the hell is wrong with you?" he yells.

"What the hell is wrong with *you*? You're the one who's all over the place," I yell back.

He runs his hands through his hair. "I'm sorry I offended you, but it's not my fault I'm not attracted to you."

I stare at him with my mouth open, fuming. "I might believe you if you hadn't been trying to have sex with me since I set foot on campus."

He opens his mouth to say something, but is interrupted by Miss Catherine.

"You two, in my office. Now." She turns and stalks back to her office.

"Good job. If I get expelled, I will kill you." I glare at him and fight the urge to slap him. Getting kicked out of The Conservatory makes the last three months of my life an enormous waste of time.

"Watch it. They take threats seriously here." He moves to put his hand on my lower back.

"Don't touch me," I hiss.

His hand jerks back and a look of surprise and sadness crosses his face. I walk toward Miss Catherine's office and he trails behind me. Sitting down in the chair I use every time I'm here, I cross my arms. Luke takes the chair next to me.

"I don't know what's going on with you two, but you need to fix this now. Not only are you interrupting your own class, you're interrupting the entire school. Sadie, I could hear you yelling from my office."

My face heats up, wondering how much she heard. "Sorry."

"I really don't want to see either of you leave this school, but if you continue having these disruptions, you're not going to give me any other choice." She turns to me. "What's the issue?"

"I want a new partner."

This is it. This is my chance to fix everything that's gone wrong with Luke since I've been here. We weren't meant to dance together. We might have been able to pull it together for tryouts, but that's been the only time.

She sighs, running her hand over her mouth. "I can't assign new partners unless you have solid proof that you can't handle it."

I stare at her, wondering how yelling in the hallway isn't enough and what I need to do to cross her line.

Miss Catherine looks between us. "Is there any harassment going on? Has anyone been hurt? Those kinds of things."

I lean forward, putting my hands on her desk. "I can make that happen if that's what it takes."

Miss Catherine narrows her eyes at me. "Not funny, Miss Bryant."

I sigh, leaning back into my chair with a feeling of defeat. What am I supposed to tell her? He's helped me become a better dancer. I'm the one who let my heart get involved. I don't think that qualifies under her hurt category.

"You have to think of the bigger picture. If I break up you two, I have to break up another partnership so you both have someone else. That's not fair when there isn't a legitimate reason for it. I'm sorry you don't get along, but you'll have to stick it out until the end of the semester." She crosses her arms over her chest, leaning back in her chair.

"That's not an option. I need a new partner."

Luke shrugs. "Get over it. You're not getting one."

"No one asked you," I yell.

Miss Catherine holds up her hand. "Stop. Like it or not, this partnership got you into Fall Showcase. Your only other option is to forfeit your spot. You have twenty minutes left of class. Go talk, avoid each other, do something, but in twenty minutes you better be in that studio with Miss Tasha ready to rehearse. Try not to kill each other."

Storming out of Miss Catherine's office, I put as much distance as I can between myself and Luke. He doesn't try to stop me. I stop when I reach the coffee stand on the third floor. Sitting down next to the window overlooking the courtyard, I focus on forgetting about Luke and our partnership. Whether he likes it or not, we are not partners anymore.

A shadow falls across the table in front of me when someone walks up beside me.

"Go away, Luke. I have nothing to say to you."

"Good thing I'm not Luke then, huh?"

Brandon's voice makes the hair on my arms stand up, but I don't have the energy to fight with him. "What do you want?"

"You seemed pretty mad when you left Miss Catherine's office. I just wanted to make sure you were okay."

I keep my eyes glued to the road outside. "Why do you care?"

His chair scrapes across the tile and he sits down beside me. "He shouldn't treat you like he does. You deserve better."

To think that he could be referring to himself is laughable. He's not a decent person.

"Shouldn't you be in rehearsal or something?" Or somewhere else far away from me.

He shrugs. "I'm on a break."

He reaches out to grab my hand, but I pull away before he can touch me. "Let me know if you change your mind."

I sink back into the chair as he disappears into the stairwell.

Twelve days. I can make it through twelve days.

19

Miss Tasha looks especially chipper when we walk into the studio twenty minutes later. I'm angrier than I was before. The thought of spending the next three hours in practice with Luke makes me feel violent. He looks like he might be feeling the same way.

"We're going to work on a new piece today. The concept of this dance is about revenge and forgiveness. Luke, you cheated on Sadie and you're trying to earn her forgiveness. Sadie, you're hurt and angry that Luke cheated and you want revenge. In the end, you earn each other's forgiveness and love each other. Basically, it's boy loves girl, girl hates boy."

"I can handle that," I say, glaring at him. "Hating you is my specialty."

"I think you missed the part about forgiveness at the end," Luke says.

"I didn't miss it. I ignored it."

"Okay," Miss Tasha says. "Let's get warmed up and then we'll start."

I do my best to ignore Luke for the next half hour while I warm up. I catch him watching me in the mirror occasionally. I want to snap at him, but that will only make things worse. He's made it clear that he's not going to give up this partnership, no matter how bitchy I get.

"Ready?" Miss Tasha asks.

"Whatever," I say.

"Why don't we try one you guys are already comfortable with?"

She pushes play on the iPod stereo and the familiar strains of our duet for Fall Showcase blare in the room.

My body stiffens the second Luke touches me. And Miss Tasha sees it. She stops the music after ten grueling seconds.

"What's wrong, Sadie?" she asks.

"I can't dance with him." I can barely stand to be in the same room with him right now.

"Can't or won't?" he challenges.

I ignore his response. It's never been won't and he knows it. I've always tried, but at some point, I have to stop doing the same thing over and over and try something new.

Miss Tasha puts her hands on her hips and stares at me. "Try harder."

I nod at her. I need to just get through this and prove that everything we've been through doesn't have an effect on me. Easier said than done.

She plays the music again and I manage to loosen up enough to get through the dance. Every touch makes me cringe inwardly as I remember Luke's words, as I feel just how fake his emotions really are.

"That was better, but I can still feel the tension in this room. It's not the right kind of tension. Let's try a new lift that'll be in your next dance. Come stand over here, Sadie in front."

I do as I'm told, but make sure to leave a lot of space between us.

"Closer," Miss Tasha says, pushing us together.

I stumble backward into Luke's chest. I can feel his warm breath on my neck. His hands close on my hips to keep me from falling. I push them off when I've regained my balance. I can see the hurt expression briefly cross his face in the mirror, but I don't really care. It's not real anyway, just another part of his act.

"I'm just trying to help," he says.

"I don't need your help."

Miss Tasha seems to be ignoring the interaction. "Luke, you're going to lift her by the waist over your head. Sadie, you're going to kick your right leg up into a split as he lifts you to help with the momentum. Once you're completely upside down over his head, I want you to put your hands on his waist for balance. Stay in that position for five seconds then Luke, you can slowly help her over and Sadie, you'll land behind him on both feet. Understand?"

We nod at her in unison. A new lift is definitely something I don't want to try with him right now, but I don't really seem to have any other options at this point.

She smiles at us. "Good. Let's try this."

I take a deep breath as Luke's hands close around my hips again.

"Ready?" he asks.

I catch his gaze in the mirror and nod again.

He gives my hips a quick squeeze and I jump. My legs move effortlessly into a split and in a second, I'm above his head with my hands on his waist. I start counting in my head.

One.

It's not as bad as I thought it was going to be. I close my eyes and focus on the numbers. I can get through this. I can stay here for five seconds.

Two.

His fingers dig into my hips as he tries to hold me steady and keep both of us from toppling over. It reminds me of the lift that almost landed me on an operating table and ended my career. A shiver races through my body, radiating outward from his touch. Every muscle in my body tenses as I try to remain still. Any more movements and he'll drop me. Just like Patrick.

Three.

Tears prick my eyes at the memory of our last real conversation. His hurtful words. That he'd never meant to treat me like I was special, that he was only trying to get me to trust him. My body shakes and my hips turn slightly in his grip. Just like Patrick.

Calm down. Calm down. Calm down.

Four.

He loses control as soon as my hips turn. I feel myself falling, but everything's in slow motion. The way my hands are positioned on his waist gives me no ability to catch myself. Terror pools in my stomach at not being able to stop the movement. My back slides down Luke.

Five.

His hand closes briefly around my ankle as he tries to catch me and he twists his body to keep me safe, but it's not quick enough and my ankle slips right through his grip. I throw my arms out to catch myself, squeezing my eyes shut.

Another pair of hands grabs me, fingers closing around my arm and digging into my waist. I land on my right foot, my left foot losing grip on the floor and sliding underneath me. The hands lower me to the floor gently.

When I open my eyes, Miss Tasha stands in front of me, breathing heavy. She reaches out a hand to help me up.

I grab it and pull myself onto my feet. "Thanks."

"Are you okay?" Miss Tasha looks worried.

"Yeah."

No. I'm freaking the fuck out. That could've been really bad and it only proves that I can't do this with him. I glance over at Luke. I'm pissed at myself for losing control, but I'm more pissed at him for making me this way in the first place. I glare up at him.

"This is why I can't partner with you, okay? I don't trust you anymore." He's hurt me beyond what Patrick ever did. At least Patrick didn't try to hide the fact that he didn't want anything to do with me anymore. Luke lies straight to my face instead of talking about the issue.

Luke looks like I punched him in the face. "I'm sorry," he says, backing away from us.

Miss Tasha pats me on the shoulder as she walks past me. "Take a water break. Walk it off. We'll try again in ten minutes."

⊢——————⊣

Adam and Brielle sit on her bed when I open the door. Her laptop is open in front of her. They both stare at me.

"You look rough. What happened?" Brielle asks.

"Luke." And every other bad thing in my life that feels like popping up into my consciousness today.

She nods as if no further explanation is needed.

I stretch out on my bed, wishing I could just go to sleep. I don't have to think about all these confusing feelings when I'm sleeping.

"Okay, so what about Nathan or Brandon?" Adam asks.

"What are you talking about?" I turn toward them.

"The Hit List."

I stare at them. "About who's running it?"

Brielle glares at me. "Duh. They're not on the list, are they?"

It would make sense for either Nathan or Brandon to be behind it. They're both jerks who feel like they can do whatever they want to the girls in their life. It wouldn't surprise me to find out that either had forced something on a girl.

Brielle scrolls down further. "Ooh, what about...?"

I look up at her, waiting for her to finish, but she's staring at her computer like she broke something. "Who?"

She bites her lip. "Luke."

I frown. We've been over this before. "It's not Luke."

Even with everything he's put me through, I still don't believe it's him. He's had ample opportunity to try to have sex with me. And there wouldn't have been a point to him fighting with me if he were still trying to get me to sleep with him. He would have to know that he's ruined all chance of that ever happening.

He wouldn't do this. It would violate every ounce of trust I've ever placed in him, and he has proved that he wants that much, at least. Regardless of how other people seem to think he is, he's shown me that he isn't capable of such a terrible thing. He's worked so hard with me over the past few months to help me get used to dancing with him. Someone who has the brains to come up with a sex game doesn't strike me as a person who cares about other people's feelings.

One thing's for sure—if I knew that he'd created a game that has hurt so many people, there's no way our relationship could survive. There's no way that I would ever be able to let him touch me again.

They both stare at me.

"What?" I ask.

Brielle shrugs. "Nothing." She exchanges a glance with Adam before they go back to reading her computer screen.

As much as he infuriates me, I know Luke wouldn't do something like this. I sigh, regretting my behavior earlier today. It's my own fault for thinking he would move past the friend zone with me. I knew he wasn't the type. He told me so himself.

"So, confession. The Conversatory blog? I kind of know who started it originally, before it got taken over as The Hit List."

This can either be really good or really bad. "Who?" I ask.

He sighs. "It was Jake. He set it up, but there's a bunch of people that contribute to it. I doubt he has anything to do with it, but it's still a little sketchy."

Brielle gasps and a look of horror crosses her face. "You knew that this whole time and you didn't say anything? It's like I don't even know you."

"It doesn't mean he's behind it. It just means maybe it's not someone here. It could be anyone in the community that knows the students here."

"Or it could mean Jake is behind it. That little bitch." Brielle scrolls through the page on her computer.

Adam shrugs. "I just thought I'd let you guys know."

Shifting on the bed, I stare up at the ceiling. This opens up a world of possibilities for who could have started the game. People who aren't Luke.

Luke.

Why does he have to be so frustrating? I hate being angry at him all the time. I know he doesn't have anything to do with this game. Why is it so hard to let go and trust him?

I roll off the bed. I have to apologize. We can still set this right and dance together. Prove everyone wrong—those who think we can't, who think I'm less talented than Patrick, who think Luke's only a name because of his parents.

"Where are you going?" Brielle asks.

"For a walk."

I need to apologize. From his point of view, I've been the jealous girl with a crush for weeks. I'm sure he's had enough of me, but he's taken it in stride. He deserves a lot of credit for not freaking out at my crazy attitude. This is right.

I walk through the empty halls, trying to decide what I want to say. I don't want to fight with him anymore. We need to set everything aside so we can do well in Fall Showcase. As much as it'll hurt me, I need to let my wall down with him even though I know he won't return any of my feelings. If I ever want to prove to myself that a guy isn't going to screw up my dreams, I need to do this for me.

Luke answers the door right away and I breathe a sigh of relief when Nathan isn't in his room. I don't want to have this conversation with other people.

He stares at me and I have to look away so I can arrange my thoughts.

"Look, I'm sorry. You don't deserve to be forced to dance with a new partner this close to Fall Showcase."

"I understand why you wanted to work with someone else. This hasn't been easy."

I pick at my fingernail, unable to meet his eyes. It doesn't help that he isn't being a jerk. Nice Luke is more unsettling than when he's an ass. "I'm sure it hasn't been easy for you either."

He laughs. "What are we doing, Sadie?"

I glance up at him, a humorless smile on my face. I don't even know. I've been stumbling along since I got to The Conservatory. Dancing with Luke, falling for Luke, has thrown me for a loop and I've been struggling to stay above water for a long time. "I'm just trying to survive. What are you doing?"

He looks straight into my eyes. "I'm trying not to fall in love with you."

I don't know if I can say it back. I know he doesn't expect it, but he deserves it. All the hell I've put him through, all the struggles we've had, he deserves the real me. He deserves the truth on my terms.

"Truth or dare," I ask.

He doesn't move. "Truth."

"I hated you when I met you. I tried to go into it with no judgments after all the things Brielle said about you. But you were an obnoxious dick. Not because you were actually annoying. Because I needed to find a flaw in you."

He flinches at my words. It's harsh, but I need him to understand where I've been coming from the past few months. I need him to understand what it's been like, why it's so important that I trust him.

I know this isn't how the game works, but I don't care. He's been vulnerable with me so many times.

It's my turn.

"Truth or dare," I say again.

"Truth." His voice shakes.

"You're the only person who's cared enough to try to figure me out, and I am so grateful for that. Because of that, I can dance with you." I shake my head, a tear falling down my cheek. "But I can't dance with anyone else. Because I only trust you."

My wall has done an excellent job of keeping people out since Patrick left. And maybe that means that none of them were worth it. Maybe my heart had been waiting for Luke all along.

"Truth or dare."

"Truth."

I take a deep breath. This one will be the hardest. "I didn't come here expecting to fall for you. I wanted a fresh start, and I hated that you stood in my way of that. But I've realized something. You *are* my fresh start. If I hadn't come here, if I hadn't met you, I don't know if I would have trusted anyone ever again."

Luke and Patrick used to be similar people in my mind. But they're not. Patrick was cold and selfish, only caring about himself in the end. Despite all the times I've pushed Luke away, he's proven that he'll always be here for me, no matter what.

I brace myself for the last one. "Truth or dare."

His hands are gripped so tight, his knuckles turn white. "Truth."

Tears stream down my face. "I want you to kiss me. I want you to kiss me and tell me you don't feel anything. Because I know you do, and neither of us deserves that lie."

He's off the bed and standing in front of me before my brain can register the movement. His hands find my face and his thumbs wipe the tears away. He holds me there until I can't stand another second and I push up on my toes, closing the gap between us.

His lips are soft against mine and I can taste the salt from my tears as they fall. His hands slide off my face and find my waist, pulling me closer to him. My arms wrap around his neck and I thread one hand through his hair, holding him to me.

And I can feel it. Every single feeling he's ever denied. Every feeling I've told myself I didn't have. I can feel it in the kiss. The pain when we fight, the fear that we believe some of the things we've told each other, the hurt when we thought we were losing each other, the love that's been hidden until now.

I pull away, resting my forehead on his chest.

He rubs his hand up and down my back. "Truth or dare."

I take a deep breath, not sure if I'm ready to hear what he has to say. I don't think I'll be able to handle it if he says he still doesn't want a relationship.

"Truth."

His hand covers mine and he places it over his chest. "I love you."

THE HIT LIST UPDATE
November 2

I realize I just updated this today, but I have more to say. You all know how I feel about anonymity. It wouldn't be fair to only out the girls on our list. So here is the list of participating Hitters. Oh, I'm sorry, you thought you were safe collecting points? Bummer.

Nathan Roberts
Brandon Lancaster
Henry Davis
Jordan Young
Brent Finley
Aidan Moore
Paul Lopez
Mark Sullivan
John Hicks
Bryce Mitchell
Jack Hamilton
Dan Boyd
Max Tucker
Sam Chapman
Ryan Mason
Tyler Pierce
Noah Porter
Alex Shaw
Luke Morrison

The game is still on. Good luck to our Hitters now that their identities have been revealed. Happy hitting!

~ THE HIT MAN

20

I lay on Luke's bed, my head on his chest. He traces patterns on my arm with his fingertip.

I could lie here with him all day. Actually, that's most of what I've been doing for the past two days, ever since he told me he loved me. We go to class, meet up for rehearsal, and then just hang out. It's nice to finally have a happy streak with Luke. We deserve it.

"We should probably try to squeeze in some extra rehearsal since we've been slacking the last week," I say, shifting my head so I can look at him.

He shrugs. "We know the steps. We'll be fine."

I snuggle into his chest. He's probably right.

The door opens and Nathan walks in, throwing his bag on the bed. "Hey, love birds."

I sit up. "That's my cue to leave."

Luke walks me to the door. "I'll swing by later. We can go rehearse," he says, raising his eyebrows on the word "rehearse." "Do you have a studio reserved?"

I laugh at his suggestion. "I always have a studio reserved." I push him back into the room, but he grabs my arm, pulling me with him, and kisses me.

It's hard to believe that everything's changed so quickly. We were at each other's throats a few days ago. I'm glad I was able to be honest with him. I needed it for me and for our dancing.

I walk back to my dorm room, excited about the chance to dance with Luke for the first time since I've been here. I'm confident about Fall Showcase. We're going to do amazing, I can feel it. As long as we can keep being honest with each other.

Brielle sits at her desk when I walk through the doors. "Have you seen this new Hit List post?" Her voice sounds worried and a little angry.

I'm so sick of that stupid game. "No, why? Is someone new winning this week? Big deal."

"It doesn't say who's winning. It's the name of the guys who are playing."

"Seriously?" I lean on the back of her chair so I can read over the post.

Her hands fly to the computer screen. "I don't think you want to see this."

I pull them back. "I'm going to see it eventually."

"Okay." She chews on her lip.

I read through the post. A few names stand out at me. Brandon. Nathan. Several of the names are guys in some of my non-dance classes. A few I recognize from other departments. A few I expected to see aren't there. Like James. I remember when he asked me out a couple months ago. I guess he wasn't playing, after all.

My hand slips off the back of the chair when I read the last name on the list. Luke Morrison.

"Oh, my God."

"My thoughts exactly," she says.

All the times he's said he wasn't playing, that I had nothing to worry about, that he wouldn't let anyone hurt me. It was all a lie. He's been playing the entire time. This whole time I've been worried about every other guy on campus when he was the one I needed to worry about. He's the one who has the power to hurt me the most.

And he has hurt me. How are we supposed to recover from this? How are we supposed to dance at Fall Showcase when I know he's been using me for the last three months? He never wanted this to work. He just wanted to get some points in a fucking game.

"Oh, my God," I repeat. The walls start to close around me and I'm forced to sit on the floor so I don't pass out.

This cannot be happening. Not when things finally started going right. Not when I learned how to let go. Not after I'm happy. I deserve to be happy, dammit.

Brielle's computer dings again.

"Is that another post?" I ask.

"No, it's an email from Miss Catherine." She opens it into full screen so I can read it too.

The faculty has recently become aware of a blog game called The Hit List circulating around The Conservatory. Let this serve as a warning. Any future involvement will result in immediate expulsion. If you have any information about the person responsible for posting this game, please contact me immediately.

-Miss Catherine

"Wonderful." Brielle closes her email. "Took her long enough to get interested, but at least she's doing something."

"Yeah. Maybe it'll stop now."

She snorts. "I doubt that." She pulls her dance bag out of the closet. "I'm over this. I'm going to work out."

"Okay." I stare up at the ceiling, feeling like our small school has started to fall apart.

Any time a bunch of performing arts kids are grouped together there's bound to be drama, so I expected something. But I never thought I'd be part of a sex scandal. And I'd never thought the guy I finally fell for would turn out to be just like Patrick.

Someone knocks on the door. I don't feel like talking to anyone right now. It's probably Adam looking for Brielle anyway.

"Sadie, it's Luke. Please open the door."

Absolutely not. I don't ever want to see him again.

His voice is softer when he speaks again. "Please let me explain. Then you don't have to talk to me again. I'll leave you alone."

I roll my eyes and slide off the bed. Whatever he has to say can't possibly hurt me anymore than what I've read. I pull the door open.

Luke looks surprised when I open the door. His hair sticks up all over the place, like he's been running his hands through it nonstop.

"What do you want?" I cross my arms over my chest and lean against the doorframe to block his entrance. I might not have the strength to kick him out once he comes in. It's easier to keep him in the hallway.

"I just want to talk to you." He looks up and down the hallway. "But I'd rather not do it out here in the open."

I need to be strong. Just because I let him in doesn't mean I can't shove him out again. I'll give him a chance to explain. I'll dance with him at Fall Showcase because I don't have any other choice. And then I'll cut him out of my life.

I push the door open with my foot and walk farther into my room. He follows me and shuts the door behind us. I sit down on my bed. He stands as far away as possible, like he's afraid I'll lash out at him.

I'm sick of the silence. "What did you want to tell me?"

He crosses the room and pulls me up. His lips crash into mine before I have a chance to move away. His arm winds behind my back. I couldn't pull away from him even if I wanted to. And I don't want to.

The next words out of his mouth are going to ruin my life. I don't want to feel anything but hate for him, but I can't seem to hang onto the feeling. The second he touches me, I remember every single reason why I like him.

He's brought me so far since September. I wouldn't go back to that place if I had the chance. Back to the girl who couldn't trust anyone, who didn't have any friends, who couldn't dance with a partner. Not only am I a better dancer because of Luke, I'm a better person.

If our relationship has been a lie, does that mean my progress has been a lie? What if I go back to how I was before I met Luke? It will be like the last three months never even happened. The only difference will be my resolve to never let my wall down again.

I let my guard down. I convinced myself I could trust someone again. I put my heart out there only for it to get stomped on. And it got me nowhere.

Lesson fucking learned.

I lean back away from him. I can't do this anymore. I can't keep letting him in.

He scrubs his hand over his face. "You're going to hate me after I tell you this."

"You're not doing a lot for my confidence in you right now." I step away from him.

Being close to Luke increases my probability of forgiveness. I can't do that to myself this time. I need to put my heart first. I need to protect it from the harsh reality of life.

People always leave. And usually they take my heart with them.

"I don't know who is behind it now, but I started The Hit List. The piece of paper you found was part of what I printed when I was going to bring it to my mom. But then I decided to try to figure out who was behind it myself."

My heart collides with my lungs at his words. I don't know how to breathe. I don't know how to survive.

"What?" My voice comes out a whisper.

He can't be serious. He can't actually think I'm going to sit here and listen to this. I can't handle it.

"Two years ago, I came up with a game. I was here all the time and no one would have guessed it was me. I wasn't actually a student then. I was seventeen and dumb and I wish I could take it back, but I can't." He shifts closer to me. His eyes are glossy. Somehow that makes it hurt more.

"What?" I'm louder this time. My voice doesn't betray me with its sadness.

It was his fault. Everything that's happened this semester with this game, all the issues he's created within the school, it was all him.

"I'm sorry. I swear I wanted it to stop. I was a stupid kid when I started it and I've grown up a lot since then. I told everyone I wouldn't be doing it again. But someone took my game and my rules and put them online for everyone to get involved."

Like that somehow makes it better. Never mind the fact that if he hadn't created it in the first place, we wouldn't even be in this situation now.

"That doesn't explain why you were playing." Tears hover on the edge of my eyelids. I don't want to believe he has the power to do something so cruel. I wipe them away viciously. He doesn't deserve my tears.

He steps toward me again, but I hold my hand out to keep the distance between us. "I was trying to figure out who hijacked the game. All the girls this year were on it before. Except you. I thought if I got close to some of them, I might be able to figure out who was running it."

It sounds like someone trying to back their way out of a hole. He got caught and now he's trying to justify everything.

I back up against the wall and fold my arms over my chest. "That's a lame excuse."

"I know. But it's the truth." He steps back further away from me. "Sadie, I'm so sorry I didn't tell you, but you have to believe that everything that happened between us was real."

As real as what I had with Patrick.

I laugh bitterly. "You're joking, right? You have to be joking."

"Please," he pleads with me. Tears shine in his eyes.

I bet those tears have worked on girls before.

"Nothing between you and me has been real, Luke. You've been lying since day one. You can't build a relationship based on a lie."

"I wanted to protect you." His voice is barely above a whisper.

Something about it pisses me off. Maybe because it sounds like he's trying to come off like the victim when he's anything but.

"Did you ever think that maybe I didn't need that kind of protection?" I yell. "I don't need you, Luke. I was doing just fine on my own until you came and screwed everything up." I stare down at the floor so he doesn't see my lip tremble. The tears will spill over soon and I don't want him here to see it.

"I'm sorry."

I don't look up at him. "Please leave."

Silence engulfs the room. I can feel his eyes on me, but I don't lift my gaze from the floor. My resolve will crumble if I meet his eyes.

His footsteps are quiet as he heads toward the door. The latch of the door catching as it closes is even softer.

I'm alone.

I was wrong. People don't always leave. You can't lose something you never had.

21

The studio is quiet tonight. Saturday nights are the best time to venture out because everyone else with a life goes off campus for at least a few hours. I avoided all human contact today, with the exception of Brielle. I haven't felt like talking to anyone since yesterday. Since Luke crushed my heart.

If anything can help me right now, it'll be losing myself in the music.

The studio feels emptier than it should. It's been forever since I've been by myself in one. I plug my iPod in and turn on the music, feeling the beat in my chest.

The words move through me, the motion effortless. The music takes me to exactly the place I want to be, clearing my head of all thoughts.

But it doesn't last.

Luke worms his way into my mind. He started The Hit List, but he wanted to shut it down. He obviously didn't try hard enough. He could have gone to the faculty. His mom could have permanently shut it down. But he was more concerned with personal revenge.

Why would he think participating would actually protect anyone? He hasn't done anything to protect me. If anything, he's created the things I needed protecting from.

He's an excellent actor. Just like Patrick, he made me believe he was falling for me. I even believed him when he said he loved me. I guess he figured he'd finally be able to sleep with me if he said it.

Something about all of that doesn't make any sense though. If he really wanted to get points, he could have just gone after other girls. I saw him flirt a lot before I became his exception, but never after. What stopped him? I know the answer, I just don't want to accept it.

It's me. I'm his exception. I'm the reason he stopped flirting with other girls. I'm the reason he came clean about his involvement with The Hit List. I'm the reason he took a chance at a relationship, at love.

He's my exception. He's the one I put it all on the line for. He's the one who deserves the benefit of the doubt from me. He's the one I should fight to hold on to.

Not everyone in my life is going to be like Patrick. He hurt me and I've accepted that, but I haven't moved on. I hold everyone to that standard. Everyone is placed on some unattainable pedestal where I judge them for not being perfect. People have been leaving for so long, but maybe that's not it. Maybe I haven't given anyone a reason to stay.

I let them all walk out of my life. It was easier than completely letting my wall down. When I got hurt and Patrick left, I gave up on him. Even here, when he asked me how L.A. was, I didn't respond. And he never tried again. But of course he didn't. Why would he? I didn't give him any reason to.

Luke has stayed. Through everything I've put him through, he's always been there. I've said terrible things, lost my faith in him, doubted him, accused him of faking his feelings for me. If I were him, I would have left a long time ago.

But he didn't. Because he's a good guy. He might have flaws, but who doesn't? I can't fault him for being human. I've been so focused on finding reasons to push people away that all I see are his flaws. I didn't see the good he was trying to do. And yeah, maybe he could have done something different with The Hit List instead of pretending to play to try to figure out who was behind it, but his intentions were good. Everyone makes mistakes.

The music plays on around me, but I've stopped dancing. I stare at my reflection in the mirror, disgusted that I couldn't really give him the benefit of the doubt even after I told him I would.

I walk to the stereo, quickly unplugging my iPod, and shove everything in my bag. The air feels cool against my skin as I run through the hallways to his room.

I pound on the door harder than I need to. He answers quickly, a look of surprise on his face.

"Hey." I'm suddenly nervous.

"Hey." He leans against the doorframe, blocking the entrance to his room.

"Can I come in?" I'd rather not have this conversation in the hallway.

He stares at me for a few moments before pushing off the wall and opening the door wider.

I pace the floor while he sits down on his bed. He watches me, looking curious and nervous.

"I don't think you're the one behind The Hit List right now."

He frowns, his mouth opening and closing. "I wasn't expecting you to say that."

I shrug. "I believe you didn't want to be part of it anymore. I don't forgive you for everything you had to do with the game, but I'm willing to start trying to move past it."

He leans forward, resting his elbows on his knees. "You seem to be the only one. Miss Catherine put me on probation. She says a few students came forward and said I launched the game. Probation means no school functions." He glances up at me. "Which means no Fall Showcase."

"They can't do that. What kind of proof does she even have?" This can't be happening. Things were supposed to get better.

"People named me, so it doesn't matter."

I sit down next to him on the bed. "It matters to me."

He sighs. "Truth or dare."

"Truth," I say, watching him.

He grabs my hand, threading his fingers through mine. He doesn't look up at me, instead focusing his gaze on our hands. "When I met you, you weren't anything like I expected. I'd read that article about you and I thought you were just some hotshot ballerina coming to L.A. to prove yourself. I wanted to get closer to you because I thought I could shake your confidence. I even went so far as to throw out the suggestion of us partnering together to my mom. I wanted to keep an eye on you because I didn't want you to be better than me."

I grip his hand tighter. I'm worried about what else he has to say.

"I never expected for you to be how you are. And I never expected to fall in love with you. You are better than me, but it's not just at dancing. You're a better person than me. You make me want to be a better person."

This must be what a real relationship feels like. Working through issues instead of running from them. I worry it'll slip through my fingers like sand if I'm not careful.

I've never been good at relationships, especially the real ones, but maybe ours will be my exception. And while I can't just go back to the way we were before he told me, I'm willing to work toward it.

We're worth it. He's worth it.

THE HIT LIST UPDATE
November 12

This will be the last update post. Here are the final numbers. Funny how, when you out all the players, no one can score.

Brandon Lancaster	35 points
Nathan Roberts	35 points
Paul Lopez	34 points
Jack Hamilton	31 points
Ryan Mason	29 points
Mark Sullivan	26 points
Brent Finley	25 points
Bryce Mitchell	24 points
Henry Davis	21 points
Sam Chapman	20 points
John Hicks	18 points
Max Tucker	18 points
Aidan Moore	16 points
Noah Porter	16 points
Dan Boyd	15 points
Jordan Young	14 points
Alex Shaw	13 points
Tyler Pierce	12 points
Luke Morrison	----------
Sadie Bryant	15 points
~~Brielle Watkins~~	14 points
~~Samantha Jameson~~	13 points
~~Rachel Barrons~~	12 points
~~Rebecca Hemsworth~~	11 points
~~Noelle Sanstrohm~~	10 points

~~Courtney Turner~~   9 points
~~Jessie Freeman~~   8 points
~~Ashlynn Jenkins~~   7 points
~~Kate Williams~~   6 points

~ THE HIT MAN

22

Sleep hates me.

It's almost five-thirty in the morning. My alarm will go off in fifteen minutes. I groan and turn to face the wall, annoyed that this has happened every morning for the past four days.

I stare at the wall, knowing I won't be able to go back to sleep.

Luke hasn't been dancing with me for over a week. He's not even technically allowed to be in the studios since he's on probation. Miss Catherine only has the words from students, nothing concrete, but he remains on probation through the rest of the semester. It's bullshit.

It's still hard for me to wrap my head around Luke creating The Hit List. Just because I've decided I can put it behind me to get through Fall Showcase, doesn't mean I forgive him. He might have been a horny teenager when he started it, but it was still an awful thing to create. It scares me that he was ever the type of person that could dream up the idea.

Once the semester is over, we might need to take a break. Things have happened way too fast since we were thrown together as partners. Maybe I'll spend some time at home in New York. If I still have a home to go back to.

Harsh beeping comes from my alarm clock and I slam my hand against the snooze button to shut it off. Brielle turns in her bed, but she doesn't get up. I slip out of bed, throw on some workout clothes, and grab my bag.

The walk to the studio is quiet. Most of the school is still asleep or has just gotten out of bed. The eerie night-mode lighting casts shadows down the hallway.

The studios are empty. I haven't reserved time today, but I don't care. No one is here, anyway. I enter the one I'm most familiar with, leaving the lights off. A light shines right in front of the door and it's enough to brighten the room so I don't run into anything. I don't want to see myself in the mirror, see the haunted look in my eyes. I just want to dance and forget the world.

I plug my iPod into the stereo. Scrolling through my songs, I find the song Luke and I first danced to at the fundraiser and put it on repeat. Music blares through the speakers, but I don't turn it down. The walls are mostly sound proof and the dorms are on the other side of campus.

My body is stiff at first, but the music relaxes me and it doesn't take me long to fall into my old groove. The music consumes me and my heart soars as I let go.

It's been such a long time since I danced for me. Such a long time since I've enjoyed it this much. Before I found out about Luke and the game, dancing with him was as close as I'd come to feeling like my old self. To feeling like I belonged in the studio again.

My body falls into the rhythm of a solo I haven't done in two years. The moves are still cemented in my memory. I'd spent weeks trying to perfect it. Miss Leah, my teacher back in New York, wanted it to be perfect. She wanted to challenge me. It was the hardest technique in a routine I'd ever done. On top of the technique, I'd had to tell a story of a girl who'd fallen in love, something I had never experienced.

I practiced in front of Patrick for weeks, trying to nail the part. I had no problem with the technique. It was flawless, as always. But I didn't have the heart, mostly because I had no idea what to feel.

I'd broken down crying one day. I couldn't fake it, and everyone would see right through me. He told me I didn't have to be in love with someone to be able to play the part. That I was already so much in love with dance, all I had to do was let it show through my dancing. I'd been so focused on loving a person that I'd forgotten about my love for dance.

I let myself forget about the concept, forget about focusing on my acting. And I danced. After the competition, he'd hugged me tight and said it was the best dance I'd ever done because I wasn't acting. I was simply being me.

I smile as tears slide down my cheeks. I don't know when I stopped dancing, but I stand facing the mirror now. I reach up and trace the lines on my cheeks from my tears.

A noise near the door catches my attention and my eyes flick to the entrance of the studio. A figure leans against the doorframe. It's dark and I can't see his features, but I can tell from his posture that it's Luke. He walks into the studio, but stops several feet away from me.

"Hi," he says.

"What are you doing here?" I'm surprised to see him. He's not supposed to be in the studio.

"I wanted to see how you were doing."

I stare at him, not speaking for a few seconds. It's been such a struggle for me since he was placed on probation. I don't know what to feel. I want to be able to forgive him for everything, but it's hard to just forget. Even if he didn't run it this year, is it okay that he was involved at all?

"I don't know how to answer that question."

"I'm really sorry, Sadie. I never meant for you to get hurt in all of this."

But I did get hurt. I'm still hurt. "It's fine."

"Do you believe that I'm not behind that game this year?" His face betrays his calm voice. He's scared to hear my answer.

"Yes." And I do.

He slips his arm around my waist and I step into him. We move seamlessly. He pulls me into a lift and it's easy to let him. He spins me and pulls me back to his chest. His left hand finds my right as his arm wraps tight around me. I rest my head against his chest as he softly sings the lyrics to me.

This is what it's supposed to be like. This is how we should feel. This is what we should've been like since the beginning. But we're here now and that's all that matters.

The words get quieter until they're gone, and I look up at him.

He squeezes my hand. "I have to go."

I nod at him because I'm afraid that if I open my mouth, I'll tell him we're okay. I'll tell him how much it doesn't matter to me that he played the game.

But it does matter. I refuse to let him off the hook so easy.

His hand runs down my arm and tingles follow in its wake. "Don't forget why you're here."

His hand still grips mine. When I'm far enough away that I can't hold on any longer, I let my fingers slip through his.

Never in my life have I felt so alone. Luke isn't allowed to dance with me. Even Miss Tasha left after teaching me the solo she wanted me to perform at Fall Showcase, but it's not the dance I want to do. Miss Catherine had made an exception for me to dance a solo because of everything that's happened, but it doesn't hold the appeal it used to. I don't feel whole without Luke on the stage with me.

Every day for the past four days, I've sat on this floor. I don't have a solo ready for tomorrow. I push a button on the remote, letting the music wash over me.

I've replayed this song over and over since day one, hoping something will come to me other than tears. But the only thing that comes to me is the feeling of my body wrapped around Luke's as he tries to pry me off.

It starts over for the twenty-third time this morning and I pull myself off the floor. I have to do this. I can use these emotions. Pour them into a solo that will captivate everyone and land me a job from the scouts at Fall Showcase.

If I can stay off the floor long enough to put something together, that is.

I try to focus on the counts instead of the words and it's a little easier. I pull myself into a triple pirouette, but I'm shaky and I step out of a sloppy double before I fall. I lean against the barre, frustrated with myself, frustrated with the world.

When I came to L.A., I wanted to find myself. Now I'll just be satisfied if I can get out in one piece.

23

I stare at myself in the mirror. At the caked-on concealer that covers my face, the dark and heavy eye shadow that makes my eyes pop, the fake eyelashes that touch my eyebrows when I look up, the ruby red lipstick so I don't look dead under the lights.

I hate it. It makes me look like a doll.

"Sadie, you've got fifteen minutes till you're up. Put your costume on," Miss Tasha yells across the room.

I unzip the garment bag and stare at the tiny fabric patches on my costume that will barely cover the essentials. I was supposed to wear this costume with Luke.

Brielle walks up behind me and puts her hand on the small of my back. "Calm down. Take a deep breath."

I take a deep breath and count to ten in my head.

"You're going to do fabulous. You just need to start believing that yourself." She gives me a quick hug and runs back to her station to finish getting ready.

My costume is pretty. The top is equivalent to a bra. A strip of satin fabric runs down the middle of my stomach to connect to my super short skirt that barely falls past the built-in underwear. It's a gorgeous midnight blue that brings out the blue in my eyes. The whole thing is dotted with sequins.

Miss Tasha walks up behind me as I stare at myself in the mirror. "You look beautiful, Sadie. That costume is amazing."

"Thanks," I breathe. My body shakes from nerves. Under any other circumstances, I would love this feeling. The anxiety of performing.

But not today. Today I'm stepping in front of an audience, in front of some of the most important people in the talent industry, and I'm dancing something that isn't me anymore, that I don't connect with.

"I'm sorry you can't do this with Luke." I hear what she's really trying to say: "Don't screw this up and make me look like a fool in front of all these important scouts."

Miss Tasha leads me out into the wings next to the stage. I watch Adam and Courtney on stage and a spike of jealousy rips through me. If only I'd been able to partner Adam. I would still have a partner right now.

But then I wouldn't have Luke.

They finish and applause erupts in the auditorium. I take a deep breath. One more dance, less than two minutes, separates me from that stage. The music starts and Rachel and James take the stage from the other side of the auditorium.

I don't even notice I'm no longer alone in the wings.

"Hey," the familiar voice says.

My heart jumps in my chest and I turn around to look at him. "Luke, what are you doing here?"

"Miss Catherine took me off probation. Turns out Adam emailed her with proof he knew who ran The Conservatory blog before the game started. She said she doesn't have any real proof, and she can't punish me for something she isn't confident I did."

I'm grateful to Adam for doing what he did, but I don't understand why he would. Maybe he felt bad for knowing that Jake created the blog even if he had no idea who was behind The Hit List. Maybe he's seen how much not dancing with Luke has affected me.

He grabs my hand and leads me onto the stage as soon as Rachel and James exit. I can hear the whispers of confusion from my place on the bench. Luke's name isn't in the program.

The music starts and I count out my cue in my head. When it's time, I launch myself into his arms. It might be the amount of time that's passed since we last practiced this number or my body coming alive again under his touch, but it feels like he holds me a little tighter, less willing to let my fingers drift though his than he should be.

And when we finally separate, I can sense his every movement around me, as my body counts down the seconds when he'll touch me again. My emotions bleed into the dance and I'm no longer acting. I feel every word of the music, every tiny movement of my body that conveys even the smallest pain.

I feel everything.

When we get near the end, I can't help the feeling that comes over me—the need to be so close to him again. I know what we've rehearsed, but it's not the ending I want. It's not the ending I deserve.

He's supposed to let go of my hand, let me drift off stage, dejected and hurt. But he must see the change in my eyes because he doesn't let go. Instead he pulls me back, his hands finding my thighs and wrapping them around his waist. My hands lock behind his head. I refuse to let go.

My forehead rests against his, my lips close to his. And when the lights go out around us, signaling the end of our dance, I press my lips to his, needing him more than anything else in the world in that moment. He walks us into the wings, never breaking contact with my lips, and I know how much he needs this, too. My legs drop from around his waist, but I can't break away from him yet. Not before I'm convinced his feelings for me are still real.

As soon as I feel his tears against my cheeks, I know.

He pulls away first, leaning his forehead on mine. "Hi," he says, smiling.

I match his expression. "Hi."

The lights come on around us and Miss Catherine walks onto the stage. Luke wraps his arm around my waist and rests his head on mine. I'm afraid to move.

"Thank you all for coming to the Los Angeles Conservatory for the Arts Fall Showcase. Let's hear it again for our performers." She claps into the microphone.

Applause roars through the space. It's deafening.

"The next performance will be the last of the evening." Miss Catherine walks off the opposite side of the stage.

I want to stay and watch Brielle dance, but Luke pulls me through the wings and into the hallways behind the stage.

"Why did you come back?" I pull hard on my hand to remove it from his grasp.

He runs a hand through his hair. "I was almost out of here. I packed up my dorm room, I bought a plane ticket to Miami, and I told my mom I was taking a leave and I'd be back next semester. Maybe."

"What made you stay?" I can guess, but I want to hear him say it. I chew on my lip to keep it from trembling.

"I made a promise to you once that I would never leave. And I realized there's a reason you are the way you are. No one has ever proven to you that they won't do what you expect."

He's right. Every single person in my life has eventually done exactly what I expect them to do.

Leave.

But he didn't. And that's worth something to me that he'll never understand.

"I can't just forget about everything that's happened." I stare up at him.

He sighs. "I know. I wouldn't expect you to."

We've been through a lot of shit since we met. Trust issues, dishonesty, fights, deliberate hatefulness. It's a lot to overcome. But we've also been through happiness, finding comfort, truth, and trust. And that's too powerful for me to throw away.

Luke isn't perfect, but he's never claimed to be. From the first day I met him, he's been honest about who he is.

I fell for him anyway. Despite what happened with Patrick, despite telling myself I couldn't, despite his flaws. It was inevitable. He got under my skin and made me care for him.

"I can't just forget, but I want to start over."

He looks relieved. "If that's what you want to do, we can start over."

"It sounds stupid, but it's what I want. I want honesty and trust right from the beginning."

"Anything," he says.

24

The bass from the party downstairs thumps through the hallway as I walk to my dorm. I want to change into something fancier than the sweatpants I wore to Fall Showcase even though Luke told me I was beautiful in them. I think he's just worried I won't come back.

Fall Showcase was better than I ever could have imagined. My life is falling back into place. For once, everything I want and need is in one place. Even through all the struggles, moving to L.A. is the best decision I've ever made.

L.A. is home.

My phone buzzes with a new email. I unlock the screen, but accidentally hit the message button. The text from Patrick fills my screen.

How's L.A.?

This is the first time I haven't wanted to answer him back with how much I hate it here. I type out a reply.

Better than New York. It's where I belong.

I'm done with this. It's time to let go of the past. A new message pops up on my screen. **"Are you sure you want to delete this contact?"**

"Yes," I whisper, pressing down on the screen.

Goodbye, Patrick.

I push through the door with a smile on my face. Brielle isn't there, but her computer lights up the room. She must have forgotten to shut it down. I reach to shut the screen, but the open webpage catches my attention.

It's The Hit List. Again. She has a weird obsession with this game.

The game looks different here. I lean down to angle myself to the screen better. It's in edit mode. A new post has been started, but so far it's empty.

Brielle is posting something to The Hit List. But there's only one reason she would do that.

Oh, my God.

I sink down into the chair, no longer able to hold up my body weight. It was bad enough to think Luke was behind the blog, but Brielle? How could she do this?

The door opens behind me. "I wasn't sure you would come up here before the party."

I shove back in the chair to look at her. "What is wrong with you? Why would you do this? You knew I had trust issues, and you put me in a fucking sex game?"

She's timid and scared. I'm not used to seeing Brielle like this. "I didn't actually know that when I did it. I just figured everyone already knew who you were so you would make it interesting."

"That's not really the point. You can't go around wrecking people's lives like this. Think of all the girls you screwed over. People got expelled. Luke almost missed out on Fall Showcase because of you." I pace next to my bed. I'm afraid of what I'll do with this negative energy if I stop moving.

"Maybe he should have thought of that before he put me on that fucking list last year," she yells.

I glance up her. "What do you mean?"

"He put me on The Hit List last year. I thought he liked me, but he just wanted to use me. So I decided I would get him back for it. It wasn't hard to make people think it was him."

She's hurt. She just wants to make someone else hurt, too.

"How could you just sit back and watch me fall for him? You didn't feel the least bit guilty about that?"

What kind of friend does that? This entire semester has been about revenge for her and somehow she's managed to hide it from everyone. I've lived with her for three months and I had no idea.

A spark of the old Brielle returns to her face and she laughs. "It's not like I didn't warn you. I took you out of the game and you had a fucking panic attack because your name got crossed off the list. I even shut down the damn blog, but *that* didn't work either."

"Who else knew about this?" She can't be doing this by herself.

"Do you think I'm dumb enough to tell someone else about this? God, even Adam doesn't know."

The Brielle I thought I knew wouldn't be able to do this. She might have a vindictive streak, but she would never intentionally hurt this many people to get back at one.

"I feel like I don't know you."

Tears flood her eyes. They reflect the overhead light. "I'm sorry. Everything got completely out of hand. It was just supposed to be a game. I wanted to make him lose something. The Conservatory was the only thing he cared about before you and I wanted to take that away from him. I never wanted to hurt you or anyone else."

I believe her. I know what it's like to feel unwanted. We're not that different. She made a stupid mistake. Just like Luke.

"I'm sorry you felt like this was the only way."

She chews on her lip. "Are you going to tell Miss Catherine? I don't blame you if you do."

I sigh. I wish this whole thing would just go away. Luke's probation is over. Miss Catherine isn't on the manhunt for the person behind the blog anymore. What good would even come from turning Brielle in? She'd get expelled. It won't erase the past. It won't make anyone feel better.

"No. But I don't think I can talk to you for a while."

She moves to give me space to walk past her on my way to the door. I need to get out of this room and away from her. She speaks again as I pull the door open.

"Sadie?"

I turn back to look at her. A tear runs down her cheek.

"I'm sorry. I would take it back if I could."

I don't look at her as I let the door shut behind me.

———

The after party in the lobby is in full swing with students and teachers from every department.

There are even some talent scouts offering jobs. Miss Catherine walks by me and waves.

I don't feel much like partying. The only reason I'm here is because I promised Luke I would come back.

The entire first floor of the building is decorated. Streamers hang from the chandelier and a banquet table is set up at the opening to the lobby. A stage is set up at the other end and the music students are performing. It reminds me of the fundraiser at the beginning of the year.

I spot Adam by one of the tables and make my way over to him. I lean into him so he can hear me above the music. "Thank you for emailing Miss Catherine."

He sighs. "I couldn't let you suffer through Fall Showcase without having a partner after how hard you've worked all semester."

I wrap my arms around his neck in a hug. "Thank you."

He hugs me back. "I'm starving. Let's go grab some food."

As if on cue, my stomach growls. "Okay."

We walk to the tables loaded with food. Adam starts piling things on a plate.

The music stops and someone taps the microphone at the front of the room. I turn around to see what's going on. Miss Catherine stands on the stage, microphone in hand.

"Can I have your attention?" She waits for some of the noise to die down before she continues. "This semester, the dance department offered up a special prize in addition to spots performing in Fall Showcase. One lucky dancer would get to spend a semester in London, studying with some of the most influential teachers in the world."

There are some "ooh's" and "ahh's" from the crowd. I roll my eyes at the dramatics of it all.

Brielle enters the lobby from the hallway by the dorms. Even from here, I can tell her eyes are red and puffy.

Miss Catherine continues on the stage. "The teachers and I met after Fall Showcase to discuss who we thought had the best year as a whole. The dancer we chose has made tremendous strides, overcoming a lot in the process."

The crowd is silent as it waits for the winner to be announced.

"I'm pleased to announce that Brielle Watkins was picked as our winner. Brielle made a lot of improvements this year. She deserves this."

Her eyes widen and her gaze meets mine. Adam leaves my side and collides against Brielle in a hug.

She climbs the stairs and waves at the crowd. Miss Catherine gives her an awkward hug.

Brielle leans toward the microphone. "Thank you for the opportunity, Miss Catherine."

She steps off the stage to applause. I join in. No one else knows what I do. Right now I look like the jealous roommate.

Adam rushes up to her again. "Congrats. You're going to love London."

I head back toward the food so they can chat. I've said all I need to say to her. I hope she can find some peace in London away from the chaos of The Conservatory and L.A.

"Sadie Bryant?"

I turn to see a man in a suit standing behind me. "Yes?"

"My name is Emmett Brower. I'm a talent scout at Premiere Talent Agency in L.A. I'd like to talk with you and Luke about a couple of jobs. Give me a call and we'll set up a meeting." He hands me his card.

I smile, unable to form coherent thoughts. "Thanks. We will."

He walks away and my mouth drops open. My goal for the last month had been to make it through Fall Showcase in one piece. I'd been so wrapped up in it that I didn't expect to get any kind of job.

"Excuse me, can you pass me a napkin?"

I grab a napkin and turn to the person behind me. I smile when I see who it is. "Here you go."

"Thanks. I'm Luke Morrison. I'm a sophomore in the dance department."

I shake the hand he offers me. "Sadie Bryant, freshman, in dance, too."

"I saw you tonight. You were beautiful. I'm wondering if you'd like to go out to dinner sometime. I'm not really good at it. I don't date a lot. But I want to try with you." He runs a hand through his hair.

When I asked him to start over, I didn't expect it to be like this. But I'm glad it is. It's almost perfect.

I shrug. "I don't know. Most of the people I know lie or leave. It's hard for me to trust anyone."

The smile drops from his face. "I'll make it worth it. You won't regret it."

It's cute that he's taking this so seriously.

"Okay. I'll take a chance on you. I trust that you won't hurt me."

It's relieving to say. I've wanted to forgive him, but something stood in the way. Now that we've started over, we can start fresh. I came to L.A. wanting a fresh start—maybe that's him. My fresh start, my chance at the life I deserve, full of happiness and laughter.

He holds out his hand. "Dance with me?"

I take his hand, letting him lead me out into the small section of tile set aside for dancing.

Familiar guitar chords sound through the microphone. It takes four counts for me to place the song as the one we first learned together, the dance we couldn't nail because we couldn't fake love. I glance up at Luke in time to see him wave to the singer.

We sway to the music. His arms are wrapped tightly around me, like he's afraid to let go. I hold him close, never wanting the moment to end.

I don't know what's going to happen when the song ends or when we stop dancing. I don't even know if the fragile relationship we have will survive the break between semesters. But there is one thing I'm certain about at this point in my life.

I won't give up.

Luke leans down, kissing my shoulder. Goosebumps trail down my arm at the soft touch.

"I know I don't deserve it, but let me be your exception."

I press a kiss to his lips, burning the memory and his words into my mind forever. His request is sweet, but it's pointless for him to ask.

He's always been my exception.

ACKNOWLEDGEMENTS

Writing this book has been a journey and there are so many people who have helped along the way.

The biggest thanks to my readers, for taking a chance on my debut novel. I appreciate it more than you will ever know. I hope Sadie and Luke inspire you to go after your dreams, no matter how big.

To Josh, for being the supportive husband even when I was crazy on deadlines. We've been through a lot in the last year and a half and you've never failed to be there for me no matter what. I love you.

Thank you to my mom, for putting me in ballet class to improve my balance. I don't think it worked, but all that experience fueled this book so that's something, right? Your unwavering support and love over the years has made me the person I am now. There's nothing I can say to thank you for that.

Huge thanks to my agent, the wonderful Nicole Resciniti, who has supported me through this process. I appreciate everything you've done for me already and look forward to where we go from here. To my agency siblings at The Seymour Agency, for your wisdom and guidance. To Danielle and the rest of the team at Spencer Hill Contemporary, for your endless support and enthusiasm. I am so grateful to you.

To Kate Brauning, for reading this book multiple times and still loving it, putting up with my insecurities, and for keeping me grounded during this process. You are invaluable, bestie! To Lizzy

Charles, for coffee outings, Google Chat dates, and just being you. Your optimism is infectious. To Dahlia, Brandi, Amanda, and Delia, for reading early versions of this book, giving excellent feedback to make my writing better, and falling in love with my characters. To my peeps at MNYA, for being there to listen and share in this journey with me. To Heather and Sarah, for getting me out of the house and away from my computer. You guys have no idea how much you've helped this process. Love you! And to Tiffany, for being an amazing photographer and all around awesome person.

And finally, to everyone else who has supported me throughout my life. I appreciate you. This book is for every single one of you.

damsel distressed

kelsey macke

Hot girls get the fairy tales. No one cares about the stepsisters' story.

When Imogen's new stepsister, Ella Cinder, moves in down the hall, Imogen begins losing grip on the pieces she's been trying to hold together. Now, Imogen must resign herself to be crushed under the ever-increasing weight of her pain, or finally accept the starring role in her own life story.

And maybe even find herself a happily ever after.

The Fine Art of Pretending

"Compulsively readable… Rachel Harris is a master at creating sizzling but sweet romances." — Paula Stokes, author of *The Art of Lainey*

Rachel Harris

According to the guys at Fairfield Academy, there are two types of girls: the kind you hook up with, and the kind you're friends with. Seventeen-year-old Alyssa Reed is the second type. And she hates it. With just one year left to change her rank, she devises a plan to become the first type by homecoming, and she sets her sights on the perfect date—Justin Carter, Fairfield Academy's biggest hottie and most notorious player.

ABOUT THE AUTHOR

Nikki Urang grew up loving books, so it's no surprise she started writing them. When she's not writing, she works as a chemical dependency counselor to help people overcome their struggles with opiate addiction. While she doesn't dance anymore, she enjoys all things related to it, especially ballet. She lives in Minnesota with her husband and two stubborn cats.